weddings
& wishes

Berry Lake

friendship

CUPCAKE
POSSE

romance · cupcakes

BOOK FOUR

Weddings & Wishes
Berry Lake Cupcake Posse
Book Four

Copyright © 2023 by Melissa McClone

Cover and Photography by Cover Me Darling
Cupcake from SAS Cupcakes

ISBN: 978-1-944777791 (paperback)

Published by:

Cardinal Press, LLC
July 2023

🧁 get a free read 🧁

To receive a free story,
join Melissa's newsletter.
Visit subscribepage.com/w9w0y1 to sign up.

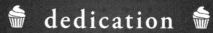

dedication

IFor those who've found the courage to do the hard thing.

Thanks for picking up Weddings & Wishes. I'm so happy to be back in Berry Lake with these five women and their friends and family. I love these characters and the town so much!

The Berry Lake Cupcake Posse series is a women's fiction friendship saga and will be best enjoyed if the books are read in order. Can you read this one before the first three? Of course, but please understand the stories are not standalones, and you may be a little lost. There are also cliffhangers in each, so I wanted to let you know about that, too!

Happy Reading!

In case you forgot how Kittens & Kisses ended…

HOW MUCH FARTHER *to the top?*

The question looped through Nell's head until she might scream. Okay, the lactic acid buildup in her muscles made her want to yell, but swallowing her frustration was easier than being a total wimp. Gage and Welles waited above the rock face for her to climb the pitch. She should concentrate on the path up the route, but instead she kept thinking about being out of shape.

Stop.

Her mind might be spinning out of control, but that didn't need to stop. She physically needed to stop what she was doing. Her gut had been telling her to stop before they had even started to climb. The gray stone seemed ominous, and something in the air felt…wrong. But the feeling was strong. She only wished she could put the sensations into words. If so, she might have saved them all the trouble of coming out today.

Okay, that was silly.

Nothing bad had happened. Today, minus the feelings, had been… Well, as much fun as climbing could be.

Her mind was probably on edge, overreacting to Missy being stuck in jail for a crime she didn't commit. The hearing on Thursday had almost seemed like a farce to Nell, and her friend was paying the price for shoddy investigative work and circumstantial evidence. The powers that be seemed to want a suspect—any suspect—whether or not that person had done anything or not. Nell's guilt intensified for being there with the guys and not with Missy.

Sure, Missy wasn't facing this on her own. All of them were trying to help her as best as they could. Doing so kept Bria's mind off the unresolved issues with Dalton. Juliet didn't have as much free time with hosting parties for Charlene, but at least the divorce from Ezra was underway. Selena's life was moving along as smoothly as ever. Even though she was in Seattle, she was making sure Missy had the legal team and resources she needed.

Unlike her friends, Nell had nothing serious happening in her life. That was why she was rock climbing with two handsome men on Halloween day, even though she still had to carve her pumpkin and buy another bag of candy for the trick-or-treaters.

Yeah, climbing today hadn't been Nell's brightest idea.

The Posse was supposed to stick together. Yet she wasn't with them at the county jail for visiting hours. That must be why she couldn't shake off the feeling that she shouldn't be on the climb.

But she'd had her reasons for not canceling. Gage had taken her to dinner and a movie earlier in the week. They'd also eaten dinner with Mom last night. Nell couldn't remember the last time Mom had seemed so pleased with her. Of course it was only because she thought Nell was seriously dating him. So not the case, but he'd been a good sport about Mom's questions, making it appear as if they were a couple and not just hanging out.

To be honest, Nell hadn't wanted to cancel their climb today. Not because she felt like she owed Gage. But the outing with him and Welles had been planned and on her calendar for the past week, and both Gage and Welles wanted her to go, so she felt obligated. And no one would blame her. She shouldn't feel so guilty for being there and not with her friends.

Nell would visit Missy as much as possible next week. The county jail didn't have that many visitor hours, but Nell would take time off from work if need be. That would make up for not being there today with Bria and Juliet.

Nell wiped her face with the back of her forearm. Even though it was autumn, the sun heated her skin. Was this how a lizard felt?

Her hand wrapped around an outcropping of stone. The rock dug into her fingers, and she gripped it tighter so she wouldn't fall. Her climbing skills were improving because she hadn't gone second this time. The guys had climbed before her, and Gage belayed her from above. He kept the rope tight, which she appreciated. His send-off with a kiss had provided extra encouragement.

Nell found a nook and shoved her foot into the crevice between two boulders. Crack! A loose rock under her foot gave way.

Her heart lodged in her throat. A shard sliced into her shin. She gulped in a breath and then took another through her nose, trying to calm herself. Her leg didn't hurt much, which meant the cut was nothing serious, but she wouldn't check the damage.

She knew better than to look down—fear of heights. The first-aid kits she and Welles had brought would come in handy.

Nell found a sturdier foothold, pushed herself up, and continued making progress upward, one move at a time, one limb at a time. Arm-arm-foot-foot-repeat. It sounded easier in practice. Neither Gage nor Welles yelled encouragement, so she had to be doing okay or was too low to hear them.

Please don't be the latter.

Sweat dampened her hairline. Add in her helmet, and she was giving Medusa a run for her money for the worst bad hair day.

She didn't care.

Gage had seen her like this and worse, yet he still wanted to go out with her. Welles didn't seem to care about her looking disheveled. His constant flirting didn't have an off button.

Good.

One shouldn't have to worry about personal grooming when doing outdoor activities anyway. She would die on that hill.

Get out of there.

The words struck hard and fast. Nell didn't understand where the sense of doom came from, but all she could do was keep going. She licked her lips, tasting salt from her sweaty skin. There might have been some dirt in there, too. No problem. She could do this.

Mind over matter—or in this case, gravity.

She reached up for the next hold. The hard rock cut into her fingertips—one more to add to the dozens of others. Having pretty hands wasn't a prerequisite for nurses.

Her left foot found another hold, and she pushed herself up. Stood.

When all she wanted was to sit.

Oh, and not die up here.

That was a distinct possibility, and she tried hard not to think about it.

Gage had called the climb easy for her abilities. Welles had warned the section she was on now was the most challenging part.

Nell hoped it didn't get more difficult. She took a breather. Talk about tough.

Not tougher than me, she hoped.

"You're doing great, babe!" Gage yelled down. "You're almost there."

She'd also learned not to look up, so she waved, uncertain whether they would see her.

Tell them it's time to go.

That feeling of unease reappeared.

She was more worn out than she'd realized. But the sooner they got to the top, the sooner they could come down. The descent always went faster.

Her legs shook—they'd only trembled on the lower pitches of rock.

As if sensing her struggle, Gage tightened the belay rope. She got a short lift, just enough to reach a hold.

Maybe he was mellowing out and forgetting his *no pain, no gain* motto.

He'd made her earn every inch in the past, but she would happily take the help.

"You've got this!" Welles shouted. He was always her cheerleader, which was why she enjoyed it when he joined them on these weekend outings. If he hadn't been there, she might have anchored to a clip below and watched Gage do this alone.

He probably would have.

Even climbing without a rope on a sheer rock wall wouldn't faze him.

Unlike her, the guy had nerves of steel.

Or maybe a death wish.

Each time she tried to decide which, he kissed her, wiping the question from her mind.

Where was she?

Oh, right. The climb.

Nell reached for a handhold, but she couldn't quite touch it. She tried again.

Nope.

It was too far away.

"Angle the shoulder of the arm you're reaching with toward the rock!" Gage yelled.

Why? This is futile.

"Try it, Nell," Welles called out.

Nell blew out a breath, put her left shoulder toward the rock, and reached up with her right arm.

Wait. She reached higher. An inch or two more. All she needed.

Nell gripped the hold. "Got it."

Gage was skilled, but Welles was a stronger climber. She slowed them down. They should go without her the next time.

Welles and Gage cheered.

Okay, this part doesn't suck.

The guys' handsome smiles might have motivated her, but fear kept Nell from glancing up at them. Instead, she stared at the rock in front of her. As Nell climbed, she pretended to be encased in a bubble that started at her fingertips and ended at her toes. That way, if she fell, she didn't have far to go.

A total delusion, but hey, whatever worked.

"Keep going, babe!" Gage shouted.

Something in her stomach fluttered.

Guess I like the endearment more than I realize.

She climbed, working her way up the rock. Shaking limbs and straining muscles slowed her ascent, but she had to be almost there.

Please let me be close.

She reached up, found her footing, and pushed herself up. Two sets of dirt-covered climbing shoes came into view.

Relief flooded her.

I made it.

Using her hands for support, she hoisted herself onto the ledge—a move made easier by whoever helped her up. She glanced at Gage, who was gathering the rope as if preparing for the next pitch. Welles must have his hands on her, but more climbing?

Please, no.

Nell needed to rest. A nap sounded perfect.

Hands touched her shoulders. "Clip in."

She clipped onto the climbing bolt.

Better safe than sorry.

As tired as she was, slipping would be easy to do.

Welles glanced at the climbing bolt before lifting his hands. "You're getting better at this, Nurse Nell."

"Self-preservation instincts help, Paramedic Welles."

Welles aimed a charming grin her way.

He was, however, less flirty than usual. Had he finally given up on asking her out? That would make her shifts at the ER more boring, but it was for the best, given Gage.

Nell undid the figure-eight knot on the rope to hand it off to whoever would climb next. She'd learned to belay but preferred to do it on the ground, not halfway up a mountain.

"Let's keep going," Gage said.

Welles handed her a water bottle. "Let's take a break. Have a snack."

Give Nell time to recover was unspoken but implied.

If only she could ask Missy to make Welles a dozen of his favorite cupcakes, but Nell would just have to be sugary sweet to him instead. Soon, Missy would be out of jail and the baking would commence. Nell would put in a cupcake request then.

No one believed Missy was the arsonist except Reggie Lemond, and his so-called evidence had to be a big stretch. Nell had no idea why Sheriff Dooley was going along with this farce.

"I don't want to wait." Gage was fully cloaked in his weekend warrior persona. The only thing missing was a cape. "We've had a break."

"I haven't," she reminded him. "I need a minute."

Or ten. Twenty would be better. Calling it a day would be best.

Gage handed the rope out to Welles. "Belay me."

Welles kept his arms at his sides. "We've got plenty of daylight left. What's the rush?"

Gage shrugged. "Don't like standing around."

"Why not?" Welles motioned toward the horizon. "It's gorgeous up here. Why not enjoy the view and a snack?"

Welles understood the importance of snacks and rest. At least for her. Nell liked that about him.

"We'll eat at the summit." Gage shoved the rope into Welles's hand. "This next part won't be as hard for Nell. Lots of bigger rocks to hold on to."

Something flitted across her skin. She slapped her arm, but nothing was there.

Welles leaned back and studied the route. "A couple of those rocks look sketchy to me."

Gage rolled his eyes and tied in, still clipped to a bolt. "You sound like a dad. I researched the route. It's well traveled and tested."

Welles shot her an *I-tried* glance.

He had. She smiled at him. "Belay him, Welles."

Nell wanted to get out of there. She kept getting weird vibes. Ones that didn't seem related to her guilt for not being with the Posse. She would ask Selena about them.

It wasn't Gage. The guy had two speeds, fast and faster—when they were doing something physical. He was different when they weren't outside. But something about this place left her feeling unsettled.

"I'm ready to get to the top."

So we can go home.

She wouldn't move from the couch. Well, except to answer her door and pass out candy to any trick-or-treaters who showed up. Though, if she didn't get that extra bag, she might run out.

A smile spread across Gage's gorgeous face. "Now that's my Nell."

His Nell?

That was new, but she had no complaints. Especially when he happily played the dedicated boyfriend in front of her mom, but...

She shook the thought from her head.

Climb first, think later.

As Welles prepared to belay, Nell grabbed her water bottle from her pack and drank.

"On belay?" Gage asked.

Welles held the rope. "Belay on."

"Slack," Gage called, and Welles let out the rope. Gage moved closer to the rock. "Up rope."

Welles stood with his legs apart and his hands on the rope threaded through his belay device. He was strong and solid, especially with his tight shirt showing off his muscles. He called himself a paramedic, but he had to pass all the firefighter training first.

Why was she staring at Welles?

Nell focused on the water bottle's logo. Not as interesting, but safer.

"You'll enjoy this pitch," Gage said.

She assumed he was talking to her and glanced up.

Gage stared at the hold above him. "Climbing."

"Climb on," Welles said.

The physical part of climbing didn't appeal to Nell much, but the partnership aspect of the sport did. The forced intimacy and trust of your safety in someone else's hand brought her and Gage closer. Welles, too.

Gage headed up the next pitch of the climb, what Nell hoped would be the last part. If Gage stuck to his usual MO, it would be—a glance around the summit, a snack, and a photo. Then they would rappel down. Not her favorite part, but if she closed her eyes, she could almost believe she was on a carnival ride.

"Gage was over at your place again." Welles kept his eyes on Gage. "Are you two getting more serious?"

"We're doing more things that don't require nerves of steel and a helmet."

Welles laughed. "Good for Gage, trying something new."

"Trying is a fitting word. I consider walking from a restaurant to the movie theater an extreme sport, but he's not complaining too much. We even had dinner with my mom."

"Meeting the family already?"

"He met her before our first date. The same day as the cupcake shop fire."

"Oh, right. I remember that."

"Slack!" Gage yelled.

Welles let out some rope. "Gage is a nice guy. An adrenaline junkie, but…"

"We're nothing alike."

"Opposites." Welles peered up. Squinted. "Stay on the route, Gage. You're way off to the right."

Gage laughed. "Yes, Dad."

"As long as you're happy." Welles's expression grew more serious. "*Are* you happy, Nurse Nell?"

Nell nodded. "I am, Paramedic Welles."

"Good." He glanced up. "I just never imagined you with someone like him. But you're happy, so—"

"What would make me happier is a bag of peanut M&Ms."

Welles laughed. "Front pocket of my backpack."

"I love you."

"If I'd known candy was all it would take for you to admit that, I would've locked you down years ago."

She laughed and reached for his pack.

"Off belay," Gage called.

Welles took the rope out of his device. "Belay off."

Nell removed a familiar yellow package. "He climbed that fast."

"It's the easiest pitch on the climb. But be sure not to go off route like he did. You don't want—"

Something popped from above.

Nell froze.

Welles's face paled.

Dust fell.

"Rock! Rock! Rock!" Gage screamed.

Huh? The popping turned into cracking.

"Nell!" Panic edged Welles's voice, sharp like broken glass. He grabbed her, and as if time had slowed, he pushed her against the rock.

Her helmet hit something, and the jolt shot to her toes.

He covered her with his body. His arms tightened around her. "I've got you."

A roar filled her ears.

Something hit Nell, and pain ripped through her. She cried out.

Dirt coated her mouth, filled her nostrils…

Welles gasped.

She wanted to ask how he was, but she couldn't see or move. A weight pressed against her. She couldn't breathe…

🧁 chapter one 🧁

WHY WAS THIS happening? Missy Hanford sat on the hard bed in the county jail cell. The arrest on Wednesday had been bad enough, but at least then she'd been in Berry Lake. On Thursday, they'd transferred her to the county jail an hour's drive from her hometown, where she'd made her initial appearance at the county courthouse. The memory brought a chill. She rubbed her arms, wanting to forget about standing in front of that judge.

Her attorney, Elias Carpenter, seemed confident there wouldn't be enough probable cause to justify her arrest. The judge, however, agreed with the DA, and there she was, stuck in jail, to await a bail hearing on Monday at the county courthouse.

This place…

She shivered.

Missy missed her cats, Mario and Peach, and her foster animals, Mama cat and the kittens. She also missed Jenny, Dare, Briley, her friends, and Sam. Sweet, supportive Sam, who'd stepped up in so many unexpected ways that both thrilled and worried her. But she was grateful for him. If only he were with her now...

The walls seemed to be closing in, amplifying the loneliness settling deep in her soul. But she had a feeling she looked as disheveled and distraught as she felt in the bright-orange jumpsuit. It was Halloween, but this wasn't the costume she ever thought she'd be wearing today. And this was the last place she'd expected to be.

Elias said he would do everything possible to get bail set on Monday. He was hopeful with her not having a record and being a Gold Star widow they wouldn't keep her in jail until the trial date as they'd planned to do with Brian Landon, who'd been the first person arrested for the crime. Only he'd been innocent, too. Neither of them should've been arrested. Mr. Landon wasn't an arsonist, and neither was she.

Yet Sheriff Dooley had acted like she was a ruthless criminal. She didn't understand. Missy had always treated him with kindness and respect over the years. Whenever he and Elise had a disagreement, Missy would drop cupcakes off at his office. And whenever he'd come by to see her late boss, Missy would give him whatever cupcake he'd wanted from the display case. She didn't understand how he could turn on her like that, making a big show of arresting her at the Carpenter law office as if he were starring in a crime drama or reality TV show.

Tears stung her eyes. She struggled not to curl into the fetal position and cry. Instead, she wrapped her arms around herself.

Missy didn't get it. All she'd ever done was try to be nice to everybody. Sure, some thought she was the crazy cat lady who stayed home and the grieving widow who never dated, but she worked hard, volunteered at Sabine's animal rescue, and tried to give back however she could. Yet nothing she'd done mattered.

Most everyone in Berry Lake seemed to believe she was guilty of setting the cupcake shop on fire, even though she'd nearly died inside the burning bakery. She glanced at the shoes they'd given her when she arrived. She'd had to ask for a size larger because of her injuries. The correct size hurt too much to wear because her feet still hadn't fully healed from the burns. No one at the prison cared though. Based on how much her feet ached now, her recovery had gone backward since her arrest, and if she remained in jail, it would continue to do so.

What did I do to deserve this?

Despite being a part of this community her entire life, only a few people were willing to stand by her. Was there something in the water or were people in a small town so easily swayed by false accusations and she'd just never been on the receiving end of it before? It made no sense.

A part of her kept thinking this had to be a bad dream, but she'd barely slept. This was real—her reality—and she wanted that to change. She wanted to be free.

Freedom.

Was this the freedom Rob had been willing to fight and die for in a distant country? Missy wouldn't take her freedom for granted again. She would cherish her second chance at love with Sam.

Warmth flowed through her. Somehow, she'd lucked out and found two good men to love, who loved her back. She took solace in that, but would she and Sam ever get to be together the way they wanted? With the way things were going for Missy, she was scared to know the answer.

Heavy steps echoed in the aisle between cells. Since she'd arrived, her sense of hearing seemed more attuned with the slamming doors and the screaming and crying from other inmates.

The current sound shouldn't have been ominous, but she kept thinking something else bad was going to happen, even if the approaching footsteps only suggested a prison guard making the rounds.

As a shadow loomed across the entrance to her cell, she straightened.

"You have visitors." The prison guard was gruff and taller than the one who had been there last night. He unlocked the door and opened it. "Come on. I don't have all day."

Standing, Missy wiped her palms against the orange jumpsuit. Sam had said her friends would be coming to visit today, but she'd lost track of the days. She couldn't wait to see Bria, Juliet, and Nell. If only Selena could be there, too, but she was at her house in Seattle.

At least this guard hadn't made any remarks or called her a stupid arsonist nickname. That had happened to her when she first arrived, but after that, others had been friendlier to her. Maybe Sam had gotten the word out to the guards about them being together now—a couple. For all she knew, some sort of secret law enforcement network could exist. Except...

Her heart seized, and she stumbled. Sam was no longer LE. He was levelheaded, but he'd quit his job as a sheriff's deputy because of her arrest, saying it was the right move for them both. She hoped he didn't come to regret doing that.

The guard grabbed hold of her. "You okay?"

No, but he probably knew that. Not trusting her voice, she nodded.

He slapped handcuffs around her wrists as if she were a dangerous criminal who would attempt to escape the first chance she got. Her feet made running impossible. Besides, dressed like this and with no money, she wouldn't stand a chance out there on her own.

He tilted his head. "Then let's go."

She walked next to him, quickening her steps to keep up with his long strides, even though pain sliced through her feet.

Missy glanced around the hallway. Both the floor and walls were made of concrete. The air stank, a mix of sweat and industrial cleaners, but worse was the stench of desperation in the air. Her stomach turned.

A door slammed.

She flinched.

Doors always closed, never opened. Missy hated that. So many constant reminders of where she was. Not that the metal cuffs around her wrists would let her forget. At least she didn't have to wear them inside the cell.

"Your two visitors are waiting," the guard said, his voice deep and sharp.

Missy stopped. "Two?"

"Is there a problem?"

She continued walking. "I thought there would be three."

"Landon and Jones are here."

Bria and Juliet. That meant Nell must've had to work. Life as an ER nurse could be unpredictable if someone called out or took a vacation. Missy had become friends with the three women along with Selena Tremblay when she was fifteen and took a job at Elise Landon's Berry Lake Cupcake Shop. That seemed like two lifetimes ago, especially now that Elise had died.

Missy had been the one to stay in their small hometown while the others moved away. Nell came back first, brokenhearted. Then Juliet returned with her husband—make that soon-to-be ex-husband, Ezra—and she wasn't the same vivacious woman they'd all known. But when Bria arrived to help her aunt fight cancer, things had gotten better.

The closeness of the Berry Lake Cupcake Posse, Elise Landon's name for the five young women who worked for her that fateful summer, had never really gone away. It had just been on hiatus while the five of them were apart from each other.

Since they reunited at Elise's funeral in September, everything had been…better. They'd laughed, cried, and shared secrets. None of them were the same, but that didn't matter. Their friendship was stronger than ever. Only now…

Missy wasn't sure if she could weather this storm.

I didn't do it.

Her close friends and family believed her. Sam, her beloved Sam, and his family did, too. But would a jury?

She tensed, unsure what would happen if the DA didn't drop the charges the way he had against Bria's dad, Brian.

The guard ushered her into the room, but she was too preoccupied with her thoughts to notice. Something rustled, and she saw Bria and Juliet stand. Bria's eyes were wide as if surprised, and Juliet trembled. Just seeing them brought tears to Missy's eyes. She wanted to run and hug them, wrap herself in their protective cocoon, but the guard held on to her, so she couldn't.

"Sit in the empty chair," he said firmly.

Sam had told her to do exactly what she was told, so she sat.

"Missy!" Juliet's voice rang out like a beacon of light, but anxiety was etched in lines on her forehead and around her mouth.

Still Missy didn't miss the concern on her friend's beautiful face, despite her dealing with a divorce, and that made her love Juliet even more.

"Hey." Missy swallowed around the lump of emotion in her dry throat. She attempted a smile, but she had a feeling she might be frowning. "Thanks for coming."

Concern filled Bria's warm eyes. "I'm so sorry this is happening to you."

"Thank you." Missy's voice sounded raw. She blinked, trying to hold back the tears threatening to spill over. "I'm so glad you could come."

"We'll be here as much as we can, but you won't be here that long." Juliet's voice was princess perfect and must have been the same one she'd used when she worked at that theme park. "We believe in you, and we'll do everything we can to help you get through this."

Missy tried to put on a brave face. "I appreciate that. Did Nell have to work?"

Bria wiped her eyes. "No, she's out with Gage and Welles on a hike."

"Climb," Juliet corrected. "She'll be here on the next visiting day. She was sorry to miss this first one, but she'd told them yes before…"

Before Missy's life had fallen apart. She nearly laughed. That wasn't something she'd expected to do in jail. "Please tell Nell it's fine. She doesn't have to come. I'll be—"

"Stop," Bria interrupted. "Don't you dare say you're fine. None of this is okay. We're here for you."

Juliet nodded. "We've got your back, always."

"Cupcake Posse forever," Missy said, wishing her voice was stronger.

"Cupcake Posse forever," Bria and Juliet said in unison.

Missy's heart swelled with gratitude at her friends' unwavering support. She had something to tell them, something unexpected, but she hoped they would be happy with her news despite the challenges ahead. "There's something I need to tell you. Sam and I… We've fallen in love. I didn't expect it to happen—"

"But it did," Juliet finished, a warm smile on her face. "And now you're together."

Missy nodded. "Odd timing."

"It's wonderful. And I'm so happy for you." Bria reached across the table and patted Missy's forearm. "We knew the two of you had something special, even if you weren't ready to admit it."

"Things with Ezra didn't work out, but I still believe love is the most powerful force there is." Juliet's smile grew. "This is exactly what you need and when you need it."

"It is." Missy had no doubt about that. The man had stolen her heart, and she didn't care. "Sam's been like a rock for me and so supportive. It's almost as if Rob sent him to me."

Bria squeezed her arm. "Maybe Rob did."

That wouldn't surprise Missy, given her dream in the hospital and other things that had happened since then. "Everything is a mess though. Reggie Lemond, that fire investigator guy, thinks I set the fire, and the sheriff told Sam that he couldn't see me. Guilty until proven innocent in my case, so Sam quit. Because of me."

Bria's eyes widened. "Really? Usually news like that would have spread through Berry Lake like wildfire."

"That's true, and Charlene never mentioned it at work. She's usually at the hub of all rumors, but it's wonderful." Juliet leaned forward. "Sam must really love you."

Missy's insides warmed again. Thinking about him always made that happen. Even when the world seemed determined to tear them apart, Sam chose her. His belief in her gave Missy hope that maybe, just maybe, they could find a way out of this terrible situation. "Sam said it was the easiest decision he ever had to make, but he couldn't stand by and watch me be blamed for something I didn't do. He wants to try to prove my innocence."

"Sam's a good guy," Juliet said softly. "He'll fight for you."

"Absolutely." Bria's eyes gleamed. "We'll be fighting for you, too."

"Thank you." Tears pricked Missy's eyes. "You have no idea how much that means to me."

Juliet reached across the table and squeezed Missy's hand. "We're in this together, remember?"

"Always," Bria added with a smile.

A flicker of hope grew inside Missy. If she had both these women's love and support, she might have a fighting chance of proving her innocence and reclaiming her freedom—her life. "Thanks. I don't know what I'd do without you."

"That's what friends are for," Bria said. "You'd do the same for us."

"Without question," Juliet agreed. "And as soon as we get back to Berry Lake, we'll talk to Sam. Help him uncover the truth."

"Thank you." Missy needed to change the subject or she'd ugly cry. "Enough about me. How are you and Dalton, Bria? I saw you together at Elias's office…"

Bria shrugged. "I don't know what's going on with him. We didn't discuss our situation. He only wanted to share what he'd heard from Ian because it seemed off. And I haven't heard from him since."

A different uniformed guard approached the table. He glanced at the women. "Bria Landon?"

Bria stood. "That's me."

"Can you come with me please?" he asked.

"Of course." Bria smiled at Missy. "Be right back."

"Sure." Except Missy had no idea what was going on.

As Bria walked away, Juliet looked confused, too. "Maybe she left her headlights on."

"Maybe." Missy didn't think they would take someone out of a visit for that, but everything she knew was from crime podcasts and procedural TV shows. Real-life stuff was new to her. She focused on Juliet. "So anything new with you?"

"No. I'm still worried about Lulu. She hates being limited with her activities."

"It won't be forever, and this is better than her needing surgery for the disc narrowing."

"Spoken like a true animal rescuer."

If she hadn't gone to get the kittens that had been dumped, she might not have met Sam. "Sabine rubs off on me."

"I don't doubt that. She has a superpower when it comes to animals and getting people to take care of them."

Bria returned, only her face was pale.

Juliet pulled out her chair. "Sit. You look like you're going to pass out."

It appeared whatever the guard wanted with Bria had been for something serious. She was the most practical of them all. The only time Missy had seen her look like this was when Elise had died. "What's wrong?"

"I just spoke with Sabine. She tried my cell phone, but those aren't allowed in here, so she called the jail. It's Nell—" Bria's voice cracked. "There was a rockslide. She was injured. So was Welles."

"No." Missy covered her face. Welles had saved her life during the fire. And Nell…"How bad?"

"I don't know." Bria crossed her arms over her chest. "Sabine thought we'd want to know. Max is on the way to the hospital. She'll be there soon."

Sabine was married to Max, which made her Nell's stepmother.

"Does Charlene know?" Juliet asked, her face pale now.

Bria nodded. "Charlene is the one who called Max."

Missy trembled. She tried to imagine how Nell's and Welles's families must be feeling. "You need to go to the hospital. Let me know how they are."

"Visiting hours—"

"Do this for me." Missy would go crazy not being there. At least Bria and Juliet could try to get word to her or Sam. No phone calls were allowed for inmates, unfortunately. "Please."

Bria shook her head. "We don't want to leave you."

"There isn't much visiting time left," Juliet added.

"Nell was there for me when I was in the hospital after the fire. Trust me, she needs you. Nothing will happen to me here." That much Missy could say with certainty. "Please go."

Bria and Juliet exchanged glances.

"We'll try to get word to you on their condition," Bria said finally.

Juliet nodded. "And we'll be back as soon as we can."

Bria lowered her arms. "I promise."

"Thank you." As Missy's friends stood and hurried out of the visiting room with a sense of urgency, she wondered if Bria had told her everything. Not that it mattered, Missy couldn't even help herself right now. She was useless to everyone else.

She pushed to her feet. At least she would get out of the handcuffs when she returned to her cell. She turned to the guard.

He glanced at the clock and then at her. "You had a lot more time. Why did you tell them to leave?"

"They have to go somewhere else." Missy's heart ached. She prayed Nell and Welles would be okay, but where was Gage in all of this? "I'm ready to go back to my cell."

🧁 chapter two 🧁

O N THE WAY from her car to the hospital's entrance, Bria's heart pounded. With each step on the parking lot's asphalt, she labored to breathe.

Nell. Sweet Nell had been injured. Welles, too.

No mention of Gage, but Bria hoped he was okay since he was with the other two. But her concern rested with her friends. If only Nell had come with her and Juliet to the jail instead…

Juliet ran two steps ahead. She huffed. "Nell's going to be okay. She has to be okay."

"Right." *Anything else…* "It feels like we were just here with Missy."

"It's hard to believe that was only seven weeks ago." Juliet didn't slow, but she glanced over her shoulder. "Did you ever think something like this could happen to Nell?"

Bria shook her head. "We mentioned she might get hurt if she kept doing stuff with Gage, but I never imagined something like this."

13

"Me neither."

As they approached the entrance, the glass doors automatically opened. Juliet glanced her way. "But I guess that's how life is. Full of surprises, some good and some bad."

It sure had been that way since Bria returned to live in Berry Lake.

She and Juliet burst into the hospital. The smell of anxiety and disinfectant hung in the air, fueling her worry for Nell, Welles, and Gage.

"Sometimes it takes a tragedy to make us realize what we truly value in life," Juliet added.

"Maybe this and what's happening with Missy will bring everyone closer together." Bria wanted to find a silver lining. She only hoped she succeeded.

Juliet scanned the emergency room waiting area. "I don't see Charlene."

"If she's not here, we can ask at the front desk." Bria flexed her fingers, trying to keep them from balling into fists. She glimpsed something out of the corner of her eye and turned.

Charlene Culpepper waved. She wore an orange shirt and black pants, no doubt in honor of Halloween, and clutched a crumpled tissue.

Bria released the breath she'd been holding. "There she is."

She made a beeline to Charlene who sat in the far row of chairs between Nell's dad, Max, and Sabine. All three appeared distraught. Worry deepened the lines on Max's face. Sabine focused on the other two, as she always did with humans and animals in need. But Nell's mother's normally immaculate makeup was smeared and her eyes red rimmed. Charlene's vulnerability sent a shiver down Bria's spine.

She stopped in front of the three of them. "We got here as soon as we could."

"Thanks for calling us, Sabine," Juliet said a beat later. "Any news?"

Charlene shook her head, her usually styled hair falling across her face. "As soon as Nell arrived, an entire team was attending to her. No one's told us much since we got here."

"They're taking X-rays and a CT scan," Sabine said to fill them in.

Max nodded. "They haven't told us more than that, but Nell's one of them. The staff is the best in the area and will take care of her."

"We're glad you're here." Charlene dropped the tissue onto her lap and reached out to hold Bria's and Juliet's hands.

Bria squeezed, wishing she could do more to support the woman who'd been Aunt Elise's best friend. Even when cancer had ravaged her aunt's body, Charlene had remained strong. Now, the woman trembled.

"Is there anything we can do?" Bria asked.

"I'm just relieved you're both here," Charlene whispered, forcing a weak smile. "That's what Nell would want."

Two people, however, were missing. Nell's younger sisters. "Where are—"

"Evie and JoJo will be here soon," Sabine answered. "The girls were in Seattle for Halloween, so they have a bit of a drive ahead of them."

"Has anyone contacted Selena?" Juliet asked.

Sabine nodded. "I left her a message."

Charlene's head jerked to Sabine. "Logan is getting home from a road trip tonight. Selena needs to be there with him."

"Selena will do whatever she needs to do." Bria had no doubt about that. "She'll be in Berry Lake when she can."

"Or she might not need to come because Nell will be fine." Juliet's cheerful tone sounded forced, but at least she was trying to see the bright side.

Bria crossed her fingers. If only she could cross her toes, too. They'd almost lost Missy in the cupcake shop fire. Bria didn't want to lose Nell…

Her heart seized.

No. She wouldn't think about the worst-case scenarios. She couldn't.

"I pray that's the case." Charlene sniffled. She let go of their hands. "But Nell and Welles were unconscious. That's never a good sign."

Missy had been unconscious, but she was fine now. Well, not fine being in jail, but she was no longer in a coma in a hospital bed.

This wasn't the time to ask for details, but Bria wished she knew more. That reminded her… "What about Gage?"

Charlene stiffened. "We heard Gage caused the rockslide. Welles… He shielded our Nell. He saved her life."

"Brave man." Max's voice cracked. He rubbed his eyes. "Not sure how we'll ever repay him. I hope we get the chance."

"Oh, you'll get your chance." Sabine reached across Charlene's lap to touch Max's thigh. "Welles Riggs is tough. They don't make 'em like that any longer. He's got way too much life in him to call it quits now."

Welles's heroic actions brought a faint glimmer of hope to Bria's heart. If anyone could survive, it was Welles Riggs, the fearless firefighter who had been in love with Nell since he'd been in elementary school. He would do anything to protect people, even at the risk of his own life. He'd saved Missy the night of the fire at the risk of his safety.

As Max covered Sabine's hand with his, he leaned forward. His mouth curved upward slightly—not much, but the smile was directed at his wife; as was the love in his gaze.

Love remains, even when tragedy strikes. The kind of love that would see two people through whatever life brought them. The same kind of love Dad had for Molly, both when they were younger…and now.

Bria glanced around the waiting room. A few faces were familiar, but the one she wanted to see wasn't there. She swallowed a sigh and focused her attention on the three parents sitting there. "Sabine's right. We'll help you think of something to do for him. We're here for you. Whatever you need."

"Whatever happens," Juliet said. "We're family. We'll get through this together."

Charlene, Max, and Sabine nodded. "Sit. We might be here for a while."

Juliet took a seat across from the others, and Bria sat next to her. For a major holiday, the waiting room wasn't that crowded. Though it was still light outside, so most people hadn't headed out to trick-or-treat or party yet.

"I meant what I said," Juliet whispered to Bria. "We're family. The Cupcake Posse and all the people you four love."

Four. Juliet hadn't included herself in that, and Bria understood why. Juliet had lost Ezra because of his cheating and her grandmother, who'd taken Ezra's side.

Bria leaned into Juliet. "I don't know what I'd do without you."

"Same."

Bria had Dad. The only other person she had in her life was Dalton. Only now…

He'd been so kind and caring after Missy's arrest, holding Bria and comforting her as Sheriff Dooley had dragged Missy out of Elias's law office. Dalton had driven her home, made her eat, and then tucked her into bed. Those didn't seem like the actions of a man who didn't care. A part of Bria believed things had returned to normal, that she wouldn't be forced to choose between Dalton and Dad.

Only nothing had changed. After Dalton had left her bedroom on Wednesday night, he hadn't contacted her again. Before leaving to visit Missy, she'd texted him "Happy Halloween" with a couple emojis, but she'd had no texts or missed calls from him. Was he ghosting her?

It could be his idea of a Halloween joke or maybe he didn't plan on contacting her again?

"At least one of us doesn't have anything going wrong," Juliet joked.

"Selena," they said in unison.

"Thank goodness," Juliet admitted. "It gives me hope I'll come out of the divorce in a better spot."

"You're already there." Bria was proud of the changes in Juliet after leaving her verbally abusive husband. Those kinds of scars, however, took time to fade. "But Selena and Logan Tremblay are the definition of relationship goals."

Juliet nodded. "I'd like that someday."

"Me, too." Only Bria already thought she'd found that again when she reunited with Dalton. She blew out a breath.

Buddy Riggs stormed into the waiting room, his face red with anger. His eyes locked onto Charlene, and he pointed a finger at her accusingly. "Your precious daughter's boyfriend is the reason my boy is lying in a hospital bed!"

Bria understood him being upset over Welles being injured, but this wasn't the time for blame or accusations. They were all hurting and scared. "Mr. Riggs—"

"I'll handle this, Bria." Charlene's voice wavered slightly. "Lower your voice, Buddy. There are sick and injured people waiting to be seen, and they don't need any additional drama. We've all heard rumors about what happened."

"Of course you defend that city slicker!" Buddy's hands shook. "Say what you want, but it's that guy's reckless behavior that caused the rockslide! The paramedics said—"

"Not now, Buddy." Charlene shook her head.

Buddy sucked in a breath. "Not now. Our kids might die. All because of some X-Games wannabe."

Bria's heart ached for all the parents, but this had to stop. Buddy was upsetting everyone. She rose from her chair. "Nothing will change what happened, Mr. Riggs. We're all worried. Let's just stop pointing fingers and wait to see how everyone is doing."

"Stay out of this, Bria," Buddy growled, fear in his eyes. "My son puts his life on the line each day at work. What happened today was uncalled for. Avoidable. No one will change my mind about that."

"Please, Buddy." Charlene's voice cracked. Her words hung heavy between them, as if there were an undercurrent of tension between her and Buddy, one that went beyond the rockfall. "Let's focus on our children right now. They need us now more than ever. Welles, Nell, *and* Gage."

Tension filled the waiting room, but Bria appreciated Charlene saying that, even as she struggled to hold herself together.

"Did I hear my name?"

Everyone turned toward the male voice. Cami Marks, an RN who worked with Nell, pushed Gage's wheelchair. The guy was attractive, but his usually tan face was starkly pale and his hair stuck up every which way. A bandage covered a quarter of his forehead.

"Hey," he said, slumped in the wheelchair. His bandaged hands rested on top of the blanket that covered him. The adrenaline junkie seemed to have become a different person. No trace of his usual carefree spirit remained. "Any word on Nell and Welles? No one will tell me anything."

Bria exchanged an uneasy glance with Juliet.

Cami parked the wheelchair next to Juliet's chair and locked the wheel. "I told you. HIPAA."

"I need to know." Gage's tone was a mix of hurt and defensiveness.

Charlene remained silent. She stared at Gage's bandaged hands.

"Your hands…" Bria said finally. No matter what had happened on the climb, he had to be hurting, both physically and emotionally.

Gage stared at the tile floor. "Yeah, I tried… I tried my best to dig them out before I ran to find cell coverage so I could call for help." He swallowed hard. "I didn't think—" His shoulders hunched. "I'm so sorry."

Juliet placed a comforting hand on his shoulder. "We know you'd never intentionally hurt Nell or Welles."

He nodded and raised his hands. "I did all I could."

Even though Bria had her doubts about Gage being right for Nell, her friend wouldn't want her to be cruel and blame him. And the guy didn't seem mean, just self-absorbed. "I'm sure you did."

Buddy crossed his arms over his chest and pressed his lips together. His expression made it clear he didn't believe a word of what Gage had said.

Tears gleamed in Gage's eyes, and his injured hands trembled. "I never meant for this to happen."

The silence stretched between him and the others. Bria was known as the practical one of their friend group, but she was at a loss about what to do or say. If anything, what he'd said made him sound guiltier. She just hated to see everyone, including Gage, hurting so much.

"Welles and Nell were below you on the climb." The accusation in Buddy's voice cut sharply. Several people in the waiting room glanced his way. "You caused the rockfall!"

Pain filled Gage's expression. He blinked. Opened his mouth, but no words came out. He pressed his lips together in a thin line.

"Enough!" Charlene looked at Gage. "We're all scared. You were there. We weren't. We just want to know what happened. Not knowing…"

"It was an accident." Gage's voice cracked. "I swear. I reached the top, and a rock let loose."

"Thank you," Charlene said sincerely. "Sometimes blaming is easier than facing the truth because sometimes accidents just happen. Especially outdoors and climbing. You know that, Buddy. It's why you have clients sign waivers."

Buddy said nothing but crossed his arms over his chest. His tense face suggested he was about to erupt. Bria needed to diffuse the situation.

"Let's focus on what's important right now. Nell and Welles. Everything else can wait." Bria glanced between Buddy and Gage. "They need us to be strong for them. Not fighting each other."

Max nodded. "Couldn't have said it better myself, Bria."

Buddy remained quiet, but he nodded, too.

The door from the treatment area opened, and a doctor in scrubs came out. Bria hadn't met her, but she'd seen her around Berry Lake.

"Thanks for waiting so patiently." The doctor offered a sympathetic smile. "This must be a trying time for all of you."

"Please." Charlene shifted her weight between her feet. "How is my daughter?"

The doctor took a deep breath. "Nell sustained a few injuries. We're concerned by some internal bleeding in her abdomen—"

"What?" Charlene nearly toppled over. Max and Sabine held her up. "Is there anything you can do?"

"We're prepping Nell for surgery now," the doctor explained. "She's stable and, thanks to Welles, came out of this much better than we expected. We're acting quickly to minimize any long-term consequences."

Relief washed over Bria. The doctor sounded hopeful. She glanced at Gage, who blinked rapidly.

"What about my boy? Welles Riggs?" Buddy asked, his voice strained as if he were trying to be civil but struggling to contain his anxiety. "I'm his dad."

"Welles's condition is stable," the doctor replied. "He has a concussion and a few broken bones. One requires surgery, but we expect him to make a full recovery."

Buddy Riggs let out a shuddering breath, the lines on his face appeared less deep. "Praise be."

"Though someone will have their hands full during his recovery." Humor sounded in the doctor's voice. "Let's just say he's a difficult man to keep down. He's concerned about Nell."

Welles hadn't enjoyed his recovery after being injured in the cupcake shop fire or being on probation for disobeying orders to rescue Missy from the burning bakery, but Bria had no doubt Buddy would be able to handle his son.

"Can we see them?" Charlene asked, her voice barely audible.

"Family members can visit briefly before we take them into surgery," the doctor said. "But I must ask that you keep it quiet—we don't want to add any additional stress."

"Of course," Charlene agreed. "Thank you, Doctor. Max?"

Sabine touched her husband's shoulder. "Tell Nell we're praying for her and Welles."

"I will." Max kissed her and then looked at Bria and Juliet. "Please watch out for Sabine while I'm with Nell."

"We will," Juliet said.

"Come on, Buddy," Max said. "Let's go see our kids."

Charlene's and Buddy's eyes met briefly, and the look lingered longer than Bria thought it would. That was odd. The three followed the doctor into the treatment area.

Sabine plopped into a chair. "Well, surgery sucks, but those prognoses are better than I expected."

Bria rubbed her arms to get rid of another chill. "I just want them to be out of surgery and into recovery."

Only then would she breathe easier.

Gage sucked in a breath. His eyes gleamed with tears. He wiped his face with his upper arm. "I can't believe this happened. Nell was doing so well on the climb. I was so proud of her. I didn't think… I didn't mean for anyone to get hurt."

Bria went over and sat next to him. She didn't like the outings Gage took her friend on, but Nell wouldn't want her to ignore him. "We all know you didn't want this to happen. Accidents happen."

"How will I ever make this up to them?" Gage choked. "Will they forgive me?"

"Nell and Welles don't hold grudges." But sometimes forgiveness wasn't enough. She'd forgiven Dalton, yet now she found herself in a similar position as when they'd dated in high school. Only this time was a thousand times worse. "All you can do is apologize and see."

Gage sighed. "I hope you're right, but I'm not the patient type."

"You might need to be now." She wasn't sure what she wanted Nell to do about Gage. If anything, today proved what Missy had been saying all along—Nell should be dating Welles. Now that Nell had gotten hurt because of Gage, Bria didn't want her friend to go out with him ever again.

chapter three

THE SKY AND the house were dark by the time they drove home. Juliet fought a bone-weary tiredness. It wasn't just physical either. Her emotions had run the gamut from seeing Missy looking so scared and vulnerable yet trying to appear strong earlier to sitting in the hospital waiting room for hours.

Charlene had finally told Juliet and Bria to go home when the surgery had been delayed and Nell couldn't see them tonight. Juliet hated leaving, but it made sense for them to go. She and Bria would need to be there to support the family who couldn't stay at the hospital 24/7. They needed to sleep at some point.

Sitting in the passenger seat, Juliet undid her seat belt. "I'm so tired I don't want to move. But I'm dying for food and a shower."

She'd wanted to shower ever since leaving the jail. Being at the hospital had only intensified the need to get clean. She knew she wasn't as grimy as she felt, but both places had left an icky feeling in her gut.

Bria removed the key from the ignition. "Same. I plan on taking a long soak in the tub later, so grab a shower while I heat up leftovers. We'll feel better after we eat."

They'd grabbed something to eat in the hospital cafeteria, but Juliet hadn't finished her meal. She'd had too much on her mind. "Thanks. I'm hungry."

"If only we had…"

"Cupcakes," they said at the same time.

With Missy in jail, she couldn't bake. She considered baking therapy, but she'd also been trying new recipes to prepare for when they reopened the Berry Lake Cupcake Shop again. All they needed was the cottage food permit from the state to do that. Though now, they also needed Missy.

Bria turned toward her. "Do you want me to grab Lulu from next door?"

Juliet shook her head. "When I texted to say we'd be home soon, Roman offered to keep Lulu overnight since he's off tomorrow. He said Katie loves having her there."

"I'm sure Lulu's being spoiled rotten over there." Bria slid out of the car. "Katie's such a sweet kid."

Juliet got out and shut her door. "She is. And Roman will make sure Lulu doesn't overdo it."

A click sounded. Bria must have locked the doors with her key fob.

Bria came around the front of the car. "Having a vet for a next-door neighbor has its perks."

Nodding, Juliet glanced at the house next door. Roman wasn't Lulu's veterinarian, but he'd been there when she'd brought Lulu into the clinic for an emergency visit. Dr. Goya, one of his colleagues, had diagnosed the senior dog with disc space narrowing.

Since then, Lulu had been confined to help her heal, but she'd slowly been gaining a little more freedom.

"Did you tell him what was going on, or is the rumor mill working again?"

That made Juliet laugh. "I told him, but he already knew."

Bria yawned and rubbed her eyes. "It wouldn't be Berry Lake without all the gossip making the rounds."

They headed to the front door. Someone moved on the porch. Juliet grabbed Bria's arm to stop her. "Who's there?"

"It's me, Juliet." Ezra Monroe used the flashlight on his phone to show his face. The shadows made him look much older than fifty-five. He'd always taken such care to look younger, but the years had caught up with him since she'd seen him last. "I heard about Nell and that you were at the hospital. I thought you might be hungry. I brought dinner."

He held up a bag as if to prove what he'd said.

Not once during their thirteen-year marriage had he ever brought her food, not even when she was sick. He'd demanded she cook for him when she'd had the flu.

"Thank you, Ezra. That's very kind of you." Bria offered a tight-lipped smile and then headed to the front door. "We've been at the hospital, and Juliet hasn't eaten much today."

"I'm sure you haven't, either," he said. "There's plenty for all of us."

All. Juliet nearly scoffed. Of course he would want to join them. But a ready-to-eat dinner beat microwaved leftovers. "Thank you."

The words came out tight, but she didn't care. Ezra wasn't there out of the goodness of his heart. He wanted something, but she would eat his food after all the meals she'd made for him, if not for her sake then for Bria's.

His gaze flickered to Bria. "Nice to see you again."

Bria offered a tight smile. "You, too, Ezra."

Ezra moved out of the way for Bria to unlock the front door.

As soon as she opened it, she flicked on the porch light. "I'm going to look for Butterscotch. He's not on the couch, so I'm guessing he's in Aunt Elise's old room."

That was the room Selena used when she was in town.

"I'll get dinner ready." Juliet noticed the bag Ezra held. "Is that from Lago Bacca?"

He nodded, handing it over. "Lasagna and garlic bread. Your favorite."

Juliet didn't think he'd noticed what she ordered. She took the bag and entered the house, heading straight to the kitchen. "Thanks."

Ezra followed her inside and closed the door. "How's Nell doing?"

Juliet didn't know why he was asking. He hadn't wanted her to have any friends, and she hadn't until Elise died and she reconnected with the Cupcake Posse. "She's having surgery right now."

Ezra's brow furrowed. "I'm sorry to hear that."

She didn't buy his concerned tone or look. Something about this entire visit felt off. "The doctor said her prognosis is good. We'll go back to the hospital in the morning."

Juliet removed the containers. The delicious aromas made her mouth water. She remembered the first time they'd ordered from the place. It was right after they'd moved to her hometown to live closer to her grandmother. She'd hoped the move would strengthen their marriage, turning it into what she'd dreamed her life would be when she'd said "I do" at just twenty-two. Little did she know, the move would be the end of it.

"Tell Nell I'm thinking of her."

It was all Juliet could do to keep her jaw from dropping. He acted as if he cared, but Ezra Monroe wasn't a white knight. Oh, once upon a time, he'd been a charming, older man who'd swept her off her feet. Her heart squeezed at the memory of how he used to buy her jewelry and flowers during the early years of their marriage. He'd loved showing her off to his friends and colleagues. But as she got closer to thirty, he changed. The jeers and taunts and criticisms quadrupled, making her doubt herself until she was nothing but a shell of a woman. He'd never been her prince. He'd just been able to hide what a lying, controlling jerk he was. He didn't care about anyone but himself, so she remained quiet.

"There's enough for leftovers," he added as if wanting to fill the silence.

"That will come in handy this week."

"Anything I can do, just let me know."

Strange, how he kept talking. Their house used to be quiet all the time. He rarely talked to her, only demanded what he needed her to do: cook, clean, do the laundry, shop. She'd been his wife in name only. She'd been more like his housekeeper and cook. Once his affair with Remy Dwyer had taken off, he didn't even want to have sex with Juliet. For that, she was grateful. He only cared about his satisfaction, never hers.

But the past was behind her. All she could do was move forward beyond their marriage, his lies and affair, and her tears.

Juliet pulled down plates from the cabinet and set the table quickly. Ezra leaned against the doorway, never taking his gaze off her.

He was playing some sort of game. She just didn't know what. Juliet carried silverware and napkins to the table.

"You look beautiful, as always," he said finally.

Liar. She'd been gone all day and was exhausted. Beautiful was far from how she looked. But she was too tired to fight, so she ignored him.

"I've heard you're hosting wonderful parties with Events by Charlene and making quite the name for yourself," he continued. "I shouldn't be surprised. You always threw the best dinner parties for me. A couple of my clients still mention that duck dish you made for them."

Juliet bristled, irritation flaring hot and swift. So that was his game. Flatter her, play the hero with a grand gesture, casually mention he was keeping tabs on her, and remind her of the good old days. As if he had any right.

She grabbed a spatula from a drawer and wielded it like a weapon. "Why are you really here, Ezra?"

He ran a hand through his salt-and-pepper hair. That was his natural color, but he'd colored his hair in the past to keep the gray from showing. "I told you the last time I was here. I miss you, Jules. I've made mistakes, but we had something special. I want another chance to make things right and get back to where we once were."

Juliet stared at him, momentarily stunned into silence. Was he delusional? After everything, he thought she'd forgive and forget his infidelity and verbal abuse?

A bitter laugh escaped her lips. "You want another chance? Now? After you treated me like a maid for years, cheated on me with a woman young enough to be your daughter, and turned my own grandmother against me after I filed for divorce?"

Ezra's expression shifted into one of regret. "I never should have let things get that far with Remy. It was a mid-life crisis. I know it's no excuse—"

"You should have bought a sports car or a boat." Juliet bit the inside of her cheek, impatience simmering beneath her skin.

"Every day, I regret treating you the way I did. And your grandmother…" Ezra's jaw tightened. "I was wrong. So wrong. I see that now." His eyes met hers, dark and earnest. "I love you, Juliet. I always have, and I always will. I'm asking you to find it in your heart to forgive me. To give me…us…another chance."

Her heart twisted. She'd loved him so much and would have done anything for him. Who was she kidding? She'd given up her dream of having children because he didn't want any until Remy pretended to be pregnant. Juliet never thought love could die so quickly, but he'd killed whatever she'd felt for him. Even if she could find it in her heart to love him again, she didn't trust him. His actions had shattered her trust into a million pieces. That wasn't something she could move on from.

She opened her mouth, a tumble of conflicting emotions swirling inside her, but no sound emerged.

Did she miss the lifestyle he'd offered her? Yes and no. She used to never have to worry about money. That wasn't her reality now. Forget about buying new clothes, shoes, and the top makeup brands. If not for Bria offering a room at the house, Juliet wouldn't have had anywhere to live. But she hated him for destroying the hopeful young woman she'd once been. Their twenty-year age gap had done her no favors. Ezra had taken advantage of her naivety and used it to his advantage without her even realizing it until her friends made her see what had happened.

How could she possibly forgive him after all that? They were too far gone. The damage was done.

She drew in a shaky breath, steeling her resolve. There was only one thing left to say—the same thing she'd told him the night Remy had rear-ended Juliet's car. "No."

Ezra's face fell, his eyes dimming in disappointment. "No? After everything we've been through together? Thirteen years of marriage, one of dating, and you can't give me another chance?"

His presence grated on her nerves. The fact that he'd shown up unannounced and expected to be welcomed with open arms galled her beyond belief. As if a single act of kindness could undo years of callous indifference and emotional abuse. Not to mention his affair.

"You had your chance," Juliet said softly. "And you blew it. We can't go back to the way things were, Ezra. Too much has happened. Too much pain, too much hurt." She shook her head. "I loved you with all my heart. I spent every waking hour waiting on you, trying to please you, loving you, and you betrayed me. You tore me apart piece by piece. I can't risk putting myself through that again."

"I'm sorry." His eyes, dark and brooding, bored into her, silently willing her to change her mind. "For everything. If I could take it all back, I would. You have to believe me."

She didn't believe him. She deserved better.

"I'm sorry, too." Juliet's voice sounded stronger than she felt. "But it's over. We're over. It's time for you to accept that and move on."

Ezra swallowed hard, his Adam's apple bobbing in his throat. "I meant what I said earlier. I want us to try again. We can work through this—all of it. I'll do whatever it takes. I've done so much for you. I deserve the opportunity to prove myself to you."

"No." Selena had told Juliet that no was a complete sentence. She sure hoped so in this case.

Ezra's face crumpled. "You've changed."

She raised her chin. "I had to because of what you did to me."

"I am sorry. I hope someday you believe me." His eyes pinned her, and she resisted the urge to squirm. He straightened, glancing at the three place settings at the table. "Enjoy the dinner. I'm going home."

A million and one words sat on the tip of her tongue, but the less Juliet said the better. She just wanted him to leave. The man had nerve, coming there and trying to sway her, especially when she was under so much stress with one friend in jail and another in the hospital.

Typical Ezra.

Three months ago, she wouldn't have seen that. Now, it was all too clear. Juliet couldn't wait to tell Selena.

Without another word, Ezra turned on his heel and left. He didn't even glance her way. Of course not. He hadn't gotten his way, so he needed to storm off like a toddler about to throw a tantrum. The front door slammed shut behind him, and the walls vibrated.

Juliet released a shuddering breath, feeling as though a weight had lifted from her shoulders. It was over. Really, truly over. A bittersweet relief filled her. She had no regrets. The man she'd fallen in love with and married had only been a figment of her imagination. Nothing like the reality of who he truly was.

With her cell phone in hand, Bria entered the kitchen. "I was just around the corner ready to call nine-one-one if he decided to pull something. You okay?"

Juliet took a deep, steadying breath and let it out slowly. "Yes. It's over. Ezra just needed to hear me say that again."

"You did the right thing." Bria reached over and squeezed her hand. "I'm proud of you."

Juliet felt her eyes prick with tears. She squeezed Bria's hand back, grateful for her unwavering support. "Thanks."

Bria squeezed Juliet tighter. "I know this is hard for you. You loved him once."

"I think I loved the idea of him."

"Still, letting go of that idea—of the life you thought you'd have together—is one of the hardest things you'll ever do."

Juliet nodded, a lump forming in her throat. "I know. It's just—even after everything he did, I can't forget everything we shared. I don't love him, but I don't want anything bad to happen to him, either."

"That's because you're a good person, Juliet," Bria said gently. "But Ezra hasn't been good for you in a long time. You deserve so much better. Someone who will love and respect you the way you deserve to be loved."

A watery laugh escaped Juliet's lips. "Look at you, giving advice. Selena would be impressed."

"Hey, I might not always follow my own advice, but it's still good," Bria teased. She gave Juliet another squeeze. "Seriously though. You're strong, you're kind, you're talented, and you're smart. Any man would be lucky to have you when you're ready."

Warmth flooded Juliet's chest. "You're my friend. You have to say that."

"I say it because it's true." Bria pulled back to meet Juliet's gaze, her eyes solemn. "Don't you ever doubt how special you are. Okay?"

Juliet blinked back tears and managed a smile. "I hear you. And...thank you. For being here for me, and for believing in me even when I can't."

"That's what friends do," Bria said simply. "Now, let's eat that lasagna or it'll get cold."

Gratitude swelled in Juliet's chest, chasing away the last lingering shadows of doubt and heartache. She had lost a comfortable lifestyle and a wealthy husband, but she still had what mattered most: friendship, love, and a place to call home. "We should. There's garlic bread, too."

"Oh, you should have opened with that," Bria teased.

They sat at the table, filled their plates, and ate.

Bria wiped her mouth. "This hits the spot."

"It does." Juliet reached for another piece of bread. "I wish everyone was here with us."

"I can't stop thinking about Nell and Missy," Bria said softly.

"Me, too." Juliet stared at the lasagna on her plate. "I'm just glad we all found each other again. Without the Posse, I might still be with..."

"You wouldn't have stayed. I know you wouldn't have."

Juliet wasn't as convinced, but her heart swelled with gratitude for her friend. "I guess it doesn't matter. I'm out now. And all of us will be back together again soon."

"We will be," Bria said firmly. "Now let's finish eating so you can shower and I can take a bath. We need to get some sleep. I have a feeling tomorrow will be a long day."

chapter four

THE QUIET OF the house pressed in on Selena like a weighted blanket, only tonight she wasn't as comfortable with the silence. She hated the loneliness surrounding her, which was what drove her to leave Seattle and visit Berry Lake whenever Logan was away for games. Their dream house in Seattle was beautiful but too large for just the two of them. When she was there on her own, their home felt more like a mausoleum.

She eyed the bottle of pinot noir and decided on a bottle of water instead. Drinking alone wouldn't solve anything. What the house needed was a pet—a dog or a cat. She'd settle for a fish, but Logan wouldn't allow it. He'd said no kids, no pets, and no plants when they were dating. He'd stuck by that even after they married. It had taken years, but she'd finally convinced him to get a plant. Now, succulents lined the sill, an explosion of pinks and greens in ceramic pots.

She smiled sadly, running a fingertip over a plump jade plant leaf. "Looking good, Harvey."

Yes, she'd named each of her plants. They were the closest things to children she had, but she picked names that were inside jokes to her and hadn't shared the names with Logan. She didn't think he would find them cute because of the trauma from his childhood and teenage years, which she understood. But the names didn't hurt anyone and made her happy.

With her water bottle in hand, she padded her way to the living room, where she curled up on the sofa, clutching a throw blanket around her shoulders. Her gaze flicked to the time on her phone sitting on the coffee table—nearly midnight.

Not unexpected.

She took a sip of water, hoping his flight didn't arrive too late.

Tonight's game had gone into a five-minute overtime period and then a shootout determined the winner. It wasn't the Volcanoes, but that had delayed their flight home. She loved that Logan was living his dream as an all-star player. He was one of the oldest in the league now and still a starting defense player, but being apart was getting old.

Her gaze drifted to the framed photos adorning their living room walls. Each captured a moment in time of their relationship. In some, they stood side-by-side, their love strong enough to conquer anything life threw at them from trades to new teams to her business taking off like a rocket. Others were of Logan in his uniform and some of her as Selena T, personal development coach extraordinaire. So much had changed since they'd met in their mid-twenties. He'd been a star then, and she had been a life coach for a little over a year. Now, they were both celebrities.

As Logan's accolades grew, the retirement date they'd mutually decided upon kept getting pushed off. She hadn't minded the first time and accepted the second. The third time had frustrated her, but now she wondered if he wanted to set a record for most games or career starts or if it was something else. She loved hockey, but she didn't like the game much these days.

She enjoyed watching him play and had tonight, but…

"We can't go on like this forever."

Selena rolled her eyes. *Great. Now I'm talking to myself.*

She had everything she'd once dreamed about, but she was lonely. Tonight was no different than the times before, but it felt worse for some reason.

As Selena sank into the cushions, worry gnawed at her. Not just for Logan's late return, but for Nell lying in a hospital bed after her accident. The last Selena heard, Nell was in surgery, which was scary enough, but imagining rocks tumbling down on her and Welles brought a shiver.

Please let the surgery go well.

That was when it hit her. She shouldn't complain about being lonely when Missy was stuck in jail and Nell was injured in the hospital. At least Selena could text Logan after the game. He'd called her as soon as he could, telling her to go to Berry Lake, but she wanted to spend time with him before he had to leave on the next road trip. Nell was surrounded by her family. Bria and Juliet were there, too. Selena would find out more information in the morning and figure out when they needed her.

It would be so much easier if she and Logan already lived in her hometown. Her eyes drifted shut, and she allowed herself to imagine a life after his retirement from the sport that consumed him—and by default her, too. No more nights waiting for him to return from away games, living out of a suitcase half the year. They could keep this house for whenever they wanted to come to Seattle, but they'd spend most of the time at their new home on Berry Lake.

Until that happened at the end of this season, she would make do the way she had—with her work and her friends and home stands.

The door from the garage opened.

Selena bolted upright, excited to see him. Her pulse quickened. That feeling she got from Logan had only grown stronger over the years.

He rounded the corner. He left his bag and came toward her. She couldn't help but feel a pang of sympathy for him. Road trips took a toll on him physically and emotionally. This one was no different.

Dark circles were under his eyes. His designer suit looked worse for the wear from the flight. His slumped shoulders might have had something to do with that, but he looked like he'd been traveling for days, not just a few hours tonight. His tie had been shoved into his jacket pocket and his dress shirt unbuttoned. Still, he was the most gorgeous man she'd ever seen, and home with her. That was all that mattered.

She hurried to him, enveloping him in her arms. His familiar scent—cedar and sweat—surrounded her. "Sorry about the game tonight, but I'm so glad you're home."

"Hey, gorgeous." As Logan hugged her tightly, he pressed a kiss to the top of her head. "All I wanted was to get home to you."

The slow cadence of his words showed his tiredness. Though he seemed more worn out than he had after the last road trip. If anything, this was more proof this would be his final season. But until he stopped playing, she knew how to take care of him.

"And here you are." She rose onto her tiptoes and kissed him on the lips. He tasted like coffee, which told her how tired he must be. "Welcome home. Missed you."

"Missed you more, babe." He kissed her again.

As they stood there in each other's arms, their lips moving over each other's, Selena imagined the future awaiting them—a future filled with love, laughter, and the simple pleasures of life. *Soon...*

Selena reluctantly released Logan from her embrace, her gaze roaming over his weary features. More lines fanned out from his eyes, but the new crinkles only added to his attractiveness.

Her fingers curled into his shirt. "Are you hungry? Need something to drink?"

His gaze met hers. "All I need is right here."

He always said the right things, but lately she felt as if she made the most sacrifices. Marriage wasn't a *quid pro quo* relationship. She told her clients compromise was key and sometimes one person had to give more, but it balanced out. Selena wanted that balance to return. Maybe that wouldn't make her feel so out of alignment. Because she did, and that made her uncomfortable. At the end of the season, things would get better.

She smiled at him. "Love you."

"Love you more." Logan's expression softened. He cupped her face in his hands. "I couldn't stop thinking about you while I was away."

"You texted and called more than you usually do."

"That's because I'm so lucky to have you. You've been so patient." His gaze darkened. "After this season, I'm done."

"Really?"

He half laughed. "I've said that before, but I'm serious this time. I'm tired and hurting. I played well, but I'm no longer at my peak. I control the narrative if I go out now."

Joy and relief flooded Selena. She wiggled her toes. "You do."

"Ted will be here this week."

She forced herself not to sigh. Ted Vanderbeck was Logan's agent, and Selena didn't like him. Never had. Ted didn't care much for her, either, so they avoided each other as much as possible. The guy looked clean cut, but he was shady at best and sketchy at worst.

Despite what Logan believed, Ted didn't have his best interests at heart. Ted only cared about Ted and didn't want to lose his cash cow—aka Logan Tremblay—to retirement. He'd kept Logan playing past their agreed-upon retirement date, and she hoped Ted didn't continue pushing him to play.

"Are you going to tell him about retiring?"

Logan nodded. "I wouldn't be surprised if he's figured it out himself. He wants to discuss future opportunities."

"Endorsements?"

"I can't think of anything else it would be."

Knowing Ted, it could be anything. "Just watch your back."

Logan tucked a strand of hair behind her ear. "Ted wouldn't screw me over. He's like a father to me."

"Except you pay him."

Logan laughed. "He only wants the best for me."

Not true, but Logan never believed her. Still, she would try again. "Which is to earn him as much money as possible."

"Ted has strong opinions, but you'll see he's on our side."

Hearing him say *our* helped Selena's muscles to relax. She searched his face and found nothing but truth in his eyes. Her fears and worries melted away, replaced by a surge of love for the man before her.

She leaned into him. Oh, she didn't agree about Ted, but nothing she'd said over the years had prompted Logan to find a new agent. That wouldn't change now. So she merely nodded. Time would tell, but she had serious doubts about Ted supporting Logan's retirement. For Logan's sake, she hoped he was right.

"Do you want to invite him to dinner?" Selena asked. Ted wasn't one of her favorite people. If anything, he was on her "don't like" list next to Penelope Jones, Ezra Monroe, The Dwyer family, and Sal DeMarco. But she was an adult and could pretend with the best of them if Logan wanted Ted to come over. "We can do something here or go out."

"That would be great." Logan yawned.

"We can figure it out when you're not so tired."

"I'm ready for bed." He winked at her, and then his arms snaked around her waist. "But I'm not ready for sleep yet. I didn't score during the game. I'm due."

A laugh bubbled in Selena's chest. That was what she got for marrying a hockey player. Not that she was ready for sleep, either. She grinned wryly. "Oh, is that right?"

He swept her off her feet and carried her like a princess. He'd done the same when they first entered this house. She traced a heart on his chest. His heart beat steadily beneath her hand, a soothing rhythm as strong as the man himself.

"You're my world." Logan's breath was warm against her cheek. "Always have been, always will be."

Selena T told her listeners and clients to follow their hearts. That was what she'd always done, and it had led her to this wonderful life with this amazing man. At this moment, the future was theirs for the taking, yet something was still there in her gut. A twinge or a shadow, and she wanted that to disappear.

"Smile, babe." He kissed her forehead. "It's all going to work out as we planned."

His words eased the niggling feeling, and she snuggled closer. The future she'd dreamed about was within their grasp. Even though the season was still in the early stages, she could count it in months, not years. No more lonely nights and bittersweet hellos and goodbyes. Just her and the husband she loved, together at their lake house in Berry Lake.

It couldn't happen soon enough.

🧁 chapter five 🧁

WHERE AM I? Nell's eyelids felt heavy. A pain in her abdomen throbbed, pulling her from the fog clouding her brain. She inhaled and recognized the smell. She was at work, but why couldn't she remember driving there, clocking in, or…anything? As she blinked away the blurriness, familiar faces swam into focus.

What are my family and friends doing here? Nell tried to remember but couldn't. Her hand lay on linen, and something covered her. What was going on?

She tried to ask the question, but her throat was so dry and hurting that no words would come. An icy chill shot along her spine. What had happened?

"Hey, sleepyhead," Bria said softly, her eyes filled with concern. "It's about time you woke up."

"For sure," Juliet chimed in. Worry etched her face, but the rest of her looked beautiful as always. "Everyone's been waiting for you to open your pretty eyes."

Mom, Dad, Evie, and JoJo formed a tight circle. Their smiles appeared forced, and Nell could see the anxiety in their expressions.

"Wh-what happened?" Nell forced out. She sounded nothing like herself. "Wh-where—"

"Easy, honey." Charlene brushed hair off Nell's face. "You've been through a lot. You're at the hospital, recovering from surgery."

"You got banged up from the rockfall and had some bleeding in your abdomen, but the surgeon said it'll heal just fine," Dad added, attempting to reassure her. "You're going to be okay, baby."

The news of the rockfall shocked Nell. Maybe she was in denial or in shock and she would remember later, but she hoped the surgery had been successful. She knew the dangers of internal bleeding. Yes, a part of her felt detached from everything that had happened. She didn't understand why.

Pain meds, perhaps?

"I've been praying so hard." Evie's eyes glistened with unshed tears. "We've been so worried."

"Thank you," Nell whispered, touched by their genuine concern.

JoJo motioned around the room. "Look at all the stuff people have sent you."

Nell raised her head slightly. Colorful bouquets filled every flat surface in the room. So many flowers. She didn't understand. "Sent me?"

Mom nodded. The corners of her mouth curved upward. "Everyone loves you, Nell. The whole town has been praying for you and Welles."

Nell's chest tightened. She forced a breath, but her eyes still stung. Welles. *Oh, no...*

"Don't cry, sis. Welles is going to pull through, too." JoJo handed Nell a tissue. "You're both going to be okay. That's all that matters."

"Your family and the Posse are here for you," Juliet added.

Bria nodded. "Not to mention all your coworkers and friends here at the hospital."

As Nell dabbed at her eyes, her gratitude over the bonds of friendship and family grew. She was hurting and disoriented, used to being the caregiver, not the one on the receiving end of care.

Nell sniffled. "I'm so glad you're all here."

Bria touched Nell's hand lightly. "You mean the world to us, Nell. There's nowhere else we'd rather be."

"Absolutely," Juliet agreed, her voice wavering slightly. "We'll do whatever it takes to help you through this."

Nell still wasn't sure the extent of her injuries, but she wasn't facing her recovery alone. Her heart swelled with love for her family and friends. "Thank you."

But she realized something else. Two of the Posse were missing. Selena was in Seattle with Logan. Nell remembered that much. But Missy...

If Nell had gone to visit Missy at the jail instead of being so selfish , would she and Welles have been injured? Nell wasn't sure she wanted to know the answer. But she had to ask... "How's Missy?"

"Don't worry about anything except your recovery." Mom's words shot out of her mouth, but not before a glance passed between Juliet and Bria.

"Listen to your mother," Dad said. "Your friends and Elias will make sure Missy has everything she needs."

That wasn't good enough for Nell. "Is Missy still in jail?"

Another glance passed between her friends. What was going on?

"She has a bail hearing later today," Juliet said softly.

Wait. What? Nell sucked in a breath. "You should be there."

"We will be," Bria said calmly. "But we wanted to be here with you, too."

"You've been here and seen me. Now go. Please." Nell didn't want to be rude, but… "Missy needs you."

"I'll let you two know if anything changes here," Dad said. "Sabine plans on going to the bail hearing."

Bria and Juliet both nodded. "We'll be back afterward," Juliet said.

"I want to know what happens," Nell said.

"I'll take notes." Bria waved.

"I'd offer to do the same, but we all know Bria won't miss anything." Juliet touched Nell's shoulder. "We'll see you soon."

With that, Nell's two friends left, leaving only her family. Well, minus Sabine, her stepmother, who was a total bonus mom. Dad had married a great woman, one who rescued animals for a living.

Animals.

Cats.

Oh, no. Nell bolted upright. "Who's taking care of Mr. Teddy?"

"Sabine picked him up from your apartment yesterday," Dad said. "He's staying at our house. He misses you."

Nell leaned back against the bed. She loved that old foster cat, who was stuck in his ways. The same as her. It was probably why they got along.

JoJo leaned against the bed. "Do you remember what happened?"

Do I? Nell had to think, and that wasn't easy to do. "It was a beautiful day. Gage was climbing the next pitch. I was with Welles on a ledge. There was a crack. Gage yelled. It was so dusty. Welles pressed me against the rock and covered me. I don't remember anything after that. Other than I think there must have been a skunk somewhere nearby."

"Certain smells evoke memories." Evie's gaze darkened. "That smell might be a trigger in the future."

"Oh, I read something about how scents can trigger memories, too." JoJo shivered. She rubbed her arms. "The rockfall must have been terrifying."

Nell's chest tightened. "It was until it all just stopped. Welles protected me."

Dad nodded. "We owe him for that."

"And we'll tell him once he wakes up," Evie said.

Nell's muscles stiffened. "Welles is unconscious?"

"He came through his surgery just like you did," Dad explained, but the underlying concern was clear.

JoJo nodded. "He's one tough cookie."

Dad half laughed. "I wouldn't call a paramedic firefighter like Welles a cookie, but he's strong and tough."

"Except he's a big ole softy around Nell." Evie touched Nell's shoulder. "He's been crushing on you for more than three decades."

"More like a quarter of a century. He's younger than Nell, remember?" Mom corrected, much to her sisters' amusement based on their grins. "But it's true. He'd do anything for you. Always has."

They lived next door in the same apartment building, too. "That's what friends do for one another. But this was next level."

"That's Welles for you," JoJo said in a matter-of-fact tone.

"Can someone find out how he's doing, please?" Nell asked.

"Of course, sweetheart," Mom said. "His father has been here the entire time. Buddy will make sure his son is receiving the best care."

Nell didn't know Buddy all that well, but Welles looked up to his dad and worked for the family business, Sasquatch Adventure Tours, on his days off from the station. "Thanks, Mom."

Charlene kissed Nell's cheek. "Now, you focus on getting better, and let us worry about everything else. You're not alone. You'll have us with you every step of your recovery."

Tears pricked the corners of Nell's eyes once again. She was grateful for everyone being there with her, but she hated thinking of Missy being alone. *And…*

A deep sense of guilt gnawed at her heart. "This is all my fault."

"No," everyone said over each other.

Mom's gaze narrowed. "Why would you say that, honey?"

"I introduced Welles to Gage." Nell's vision blurred. "If I hadn't, he wouldn't have been with us that day. I probably wouldn't have gone, and no one would have been injured."

"You can't blame yourself for what happened." Evie came closer to the edge of the bed. "It's so easy to blame ourselves when something goes wrong. You had no idea what would happen."

Nell understood the logic behind her sister's words, but the guilt still weighed heavy on her. She'd wanted Welles to take her place on these outings with Gage, to become his buddy and have a bromance. It was hard to let go of the feeling she was responsible for Welles's injuries.

A knock sounded and the door to her room swung open. Gage took two steps inside, appearing almost hesitant. His lips pressed together but curved upward. His gaze locked with Nell's, and his smile wavered. "Hey, babe."

She stiffened, unsure how to react. He'd called her that during the climb, and it had surprised her as much then as it did now.

"Hi." That was the only word she could manage. She saw his bandaged hands and forehead. A mix of emotions swirled through her so fast she couldn't name one of them. She swallowed around the lump in her throat. "How are you?"

His smile widened. "Better now that I can see you and your pretty eyes."

Her friends' compliments had sounded genuine, but his felt cheesy and fake, especially when she must look a mess. But he'd seen her haggard and exhausted during and after one of his outdoor outings before, so maybe this was one of her better looks. "Thanks."

Nell didn't know what to say to Gage. She didn't blame him for what happened. That was her fault for stupidly thinking she could be the adventurous outdoorswoman he believed her to be. She'd pretended—okay, lied—about how much time she spent outside. And for what?

To get Mom off her back about being thirty-seven and single. Stupid.

Even worse, she'd told Mom that she and Gage were dating. And they were, sorta. Then, she'd involved Welles. And now…

This was all her fault.

Tears welled, blurring her vision. Gage stood at her bedside before she could blink twice.

"Hey, it's going to be okay." He carefully put an arm around her and leaned closer. "Everything's going to be okay."

She wanted to believe him, but she couldn't. No matter what Mom or anyone said, Nell blamed herself. "If I hadn't—"

He placed his fingers against her lips. "Shh. Please don't blame yourself. It was an accident. I would do anything to take it back. To have stayed home and watched a movie while we carved your pumpkin."

Oh, man. She must've missed Halloween. That was one of her favorite holidays, but she'd forgotten all about it. Though she was surprised at how sincere Gage sounded. He was showing a new side to her.

"We can have our own Halloween celebration," he said as if reading her mind. He held her hand. Bandages covered his palms and fingers. His gaze focused on her even though others were in the room. "I want to hold on to you and never let go."

Mom sighed. At least Nell thought she was the one, but JoJo was a romantic at heart, too.

The sun streaming through the room's window illuminated the dust particles in the air. For a moment, it appeared as if someone had thrown pixie dust everywhere. Talk about magical.

"When I saw those rocks tumbling toward you…" His voice was hoarse. "I thought my heart would stop beating. I've never been so scared in my life."

"You yelled."

"That's what you're supposed to do when climbing, but you were clipped in, and there was nowhere for you to go." His thumb traced small circles on her skin, and she could feel the tremble in his touch. Even though he was an adrenaline junkie, he was showing vulnerability in an unexpected way. His eyes gleamed with unshed tears. "I'm sorry, Nell. I'm so, so sorry."

As she remembered the horrific sound of the rockfall, of Welles saying he had her, of not being able to breathe because of all the dust, Nell's breathing turned shallow. She forced herself to inhale deeply to try to get her breathing pattern to return to normal. "You don't have to apologize. It was an accident. Thank you for getting the rocks off us."

He flinched, blinked. His bottom lip quivered slightly. "What matters is you're okay."

"Hey," she murmured, squeezing his hand. "I don't remember much about the rockslide, but I remember you trying to save me. That was...incredibly brave of you."

Gage let out a choked laugh, shaking his head. "I don't know how brave. Reckless, maybe." He sighed, looking down at their entwined hands. "But I couldn't just stand there and watch you get hurt. I had to do something."

"Thank you."

His mouth twisted. "I'd do anything for you. You know that, right?"

She nodded.

Relief flashed in his eyes. "What happened yesterday was a wakeup call. I know we only met in early September, but I know..."

The room went dead silent. The only thing Nell could hear was the beating of her own heart. "Know what?"

He raised her hand to his mouth and kissed it. "I love you. More than I've ever loved anyone. I never want to lose you. I thought I had, but I've been given a second chance, and I'm going to take it. Nell Culpepper, will you marry me?"

The automatic blood pressure cuff tightened on her arm. She stared at him in shock. All her life, she'd wanted to be a wife and mom. She thought she'd met the love of her life until he fell in love with someone else and married her two weeks later after dating Nell for years. But still…

She had to ask. "Are you serious?"

"I've never been more serious in my life," Gage said.

Nell had imagined being proposed to, but in a hospital room with her connected to monitors and her family watching hadn't been a part of the scenario at all. Sure, this wasn't a romantic candlelit location like in the movies, but Gage looked serious.

Why wasn't she more emotional? Were the pain meds and her injuries muted her feelings.

Mom let out a delighted squeal. "Oh, this is perfect. A good thing you have a mother and a best friend who are event planners. We'll make sure everything is perfect."

The excitement appeared to be contagious. Her family smiled and chimed in with their wedding ideas. There was one problem—Nell hadn't said yes. She'd never told Gage she loved him.

Did she love him?

He was hot, which was why she'd gone out with him the first time. But love…

Gage squeezed her hand gently, drawing her attention back to him. "Nell," he said softly, his eyes searching hers. "I meant what I said. Being with you is all I've ever wanted, and I can't imagine my life without you. I know this may not be the most romantic setting for a marriage proposal, but I couldn't wait any longer. I needed you to know how much I care, how much I love you."

Nell's breath hitched. She'd waited more than ten years for Andrew to say those words to her. And Gage was saying it after meeting her weeks ago.

A tear slid down her face.

He brushed the wetness away with his thumb. The tender gesture touched her heart, but marriage…

Gage let go of her, reached into his pocket, and pulled out a ring box. "I had to ask the jewelry store owner to open early so I could pick something out for you. If you don't like it…"

He flipped open the lid of the black velvet box to show a gigantic solitaire with diamonds inlaid on the band.

Her chest tightened as if encircled by a vise. She forced herself to breathe.

"It's gorgeous." Something Nell had dreamed about but had never expected a man to buy for her after wasting a decade of her life with Andrew. "It's too much."

"Not for my Nell." Gage removed the ring and held it up. Colorful prisms shot around the room.

Is this really happening?

Gage's hopeful expression overwhelmed Nell. Emotions threatened to swamp her. Everything around her blurred. The faint beep of a monitor in the background merged with the steady thrumming of her heartbeat.

"Will you marry me, Nell?" Gage asked again, his voice barely above a whisper but reverberating through every fiber of her being.

She opened her mouth to respond, but the words were stuck, lodged somewhere between the pain in her body and the conflicting emotions swirling within her.

"Of course she'll marry you!" Mom clapped her hands together excitedly. She practically danced, no doubt already dreaming of color schemes and flower arrangements. "Oh, Gage, this is wonderful! Welcome to the family!"

Nell's gaze darted to Gage, who smiled warmly at Mom's outburst. When his eyes met hers, she glimpsed a trace of uncertainty as if he sensed her hesitation.

"Mom." Nell needed to reel Mom in. "I haven't—"

"Darling, don't worry about a thing." Charlene waved off her concerns, her excitement practically palpable. "You focus on getting better. Juliet and I will handle all the details."

"Listen to your mom." Gage kissed her forehead and then slid the ring onto her finger. "Your recovery is the most important thing. Once you feel better, we'll discuss the wedding details."

Staring at the beautiful ring on her finger, Nell nodded. This was what she'd always wanted, so why wasn't she happier about finally becoming engaged?

chapter six

ON MONDAY AFTERNOON, Sam got out of his truck in the parking lot at the county courthouse. The building loomed before him, and he fought a yawn. The sleepless nights were catching up to him, but how could he sleep with Missy in jail?

Not that any amount of tossing and turning would help her, but that was beside the point. Mom even reached out to her doctor for a sleep aid, but he wouldn't take it. He doubted Missy was sleeping much, either.

Sam spotted Elias, Missy's lawyer, leaning against the building and staring off into the distance.

"Hey," Sam said. "How's it going?"

Elias straightened and walked over, clasping Sam's shoulder. "Missy will be relieved to see you."

Sam couldn't wait to see her. "How's she holding up?"

Elias shook his head. "Not well. She's worried they'll withhold bail."

Sam's stomach dropped. "Is that a possibility for Missy?"

"Yes, but that's always the case in any hearing. The reality is different. Selena's willing to put up the bail. Sheridan DeMarco's fiancé, Michael, also offered to cover the bail. I also have a strong case for Missy's release."

Sam rubbed the back of his neck. "Okay, you had me worried for a minute."

Elias sighed. "I wouldn't relax just yet. Between you and me, it looks like the DA wants to make an example of her, so this won't be easy."

Sam's stomach twisted into knots. "Why would the DA do that?"

"Politics."

Sam had grown up in Berry Lake, and though he hadn't been part of the sheriff's department for long, politics played a role in small towns. He balled his hands. "Sheriff Dooley."

Elias glanced around. "Looks that way."

The guy had always been by-the-book. It made no sense for the sheriff to act this way. "Why?"

"I haven't figured that out, but I hired a PI to see if they can dig up anything. Something more is going on here, given how they arrested Brian Landon first and then arrested Missy after that. That dinner conversation Ian Dwyer heard keeps me awake at night. I mean, who would know she was the latest suspect and why would they even talk about that at a dinner party?"

"It makes no sense." Sam couldn't lose Missy. Not after waiting years to finally get his chance to be with her. She was everything he'd ever wanted. But his feelings for her aside, she was innocent and what was happening to her was a travesty. "We have to get her out of there. She doesn't deserve this."

"You're right." Elias gazed at the doors to the courthouse. "I'll do everything in my power to make that happen."

"Thanks." Sam squared his shoulders. He looked up at the courthouse and took a deep breath.

"I need to get in there." Elias headed toward the entrance.

Sam followed him inside the building and went through the metal detector. Dad waved at him. Sam walked over to where his family and Missy's were gathered. Mom wrapped him in a hug, and his brother, Josh, clapped him on the back.

"How's it looking?" Josh asked.

Sam shrugged, not wanting to worry people. "Elias will take care of her."

He stared at the doors, willing them to open, willing the judge to let Missy out on bail. She belonged with the people who loved her, not locked away in a cell. If the judge denied bail, Sam didn't know what he would do. He'd spent most of his adult life as a police officer. He believed in law and order and justice. But now, seeing the system run amok, he didn't know what to do. All he knew was Missy was his life now. She was his heart, and he wanted her to be his home. He would fight for her and their future, however he could, no matter what it took.

Jenny Hanford, Missy's sister-in-law, came up. "Hey, Sam. We can go into the courtroom now."

His pulse kicked up, and his head swam. He closed his eyes. Lack of sleep was causing him to feel lightheaded.

Jenny touched his arm. "Hey, everything's going to be okay."

Sam opened his eyes. He wanted to believe her, but he worried if justice would be served. He didn't want Missy to be the scapegoat. Not trusting his voice, he nodded.

The entire group went inside the courtroom. Sam headed to the front row of seats right behind where the defendant would sit. He wanted to be as close to Missy as possible. His family flanked him on either side and behind him. Jenny and her husband, Dare, took the two seats nearest the aisle. In the next row sat Sabine Culpepper, Bria, Juliet, and the teenaged boy, who'd been a witness to Juliet's car accident—Bentley. Sam remembered his name.

He couldn't believe that after Missy had grown up in town, working at the cupcake shop since she was fifteen, and volunteering at the animal hospital, only a few people had come to the bail hearing. She'd been a bright light in Berry Lake, yet when she needed support, no one outside of her closest circle had shown up.

A few minutes later, a door opened.

A deputy emerged. Pulse racing, Sam sucked in a breath, and he sat ramrod straight. Next came another deputy with Missy, clad in an orange jumpsuit, her hands cuffed in front of her, limping.

His heart clenched at the sight of her and so did his hands. *Oh, sweetheart.*

Missy looked small and vulnerable, her eyes red-rimmed with dark circles under them, her hair mussed, and her complexion pale. The jumpsuit hung off her slender frame, the pant legs bunching around her ankles. And her feet—she wore a pair of too-big slippers instead of shoes.

Rage boiled up inside him, sending his temperature shooting up thirty degrees. How dare they treat her this way? She didn't deserve to be paraded in front of strangers, didn't deserve to have her dignity stripped away like this. And based on her favoring her foot, her injury seemed to have gotten worse, not better with time.

Sam started to rise, ready to sweep her into his arms, but Josh grabbed his arm, holding him back.

"Don't make a scene," his brother warned under his breath. "It'll only make things worse for her."

Sam forced himself to stay still, but his fists remained clenched as Missy limped to the defendant's table. As Elias held out a chair for her, she lifted her gaze and found Sam's. A flicker of life returned to her eyes, a hint of a smile curving her lips.

His heart swelled, and he smiled back, hoping to convey without words how much he loved her. How he would always love her, no matter what. Yes, things between them had moved fast, but this was over a decade and a half in the making. At least on his end.

Missy gave a small nod as if she understood, and in that moment, his heart told him they would get through this. Their love was strong enough to face any challenge and overcome any obstacle. They would be together.

They just had to get through this hard part.

The bail hearing began. And the DA argued against bail, citing Missy's history of depression, using her journals as proof.

Sam tensed. Bringing up her past struggles after losing Rob was a low blow. The DA made Missy sound like she'd set the fire and the motivation was self-harm. Sam's chest tightened, and his breaths were more like huffs. The corners of his eyes stung, so he rubbed them.

Dare reached into Jenny's purse and handed his wife a tissue. Jenny was Rob's sister, so Sam thought hearing all this must be a double hit to her.

Missy didn't glance back. She didn't even move.

Sam wished he could hold her hand—something. Because having the darkest moment of her life—something she'd journaled about, thinking it was only for her—brought up in front of strangers just piled on to the nightmare she'd been living since Wednesday. It wasn't fair. If anything, this felt calculated, like a public attack rather than any form of justice.

Elias stood, appearing ready to make his counterargument. "The journals you refer to are nearly a decade old. Ms. Hanford received counseling and medication at the time and has shown no signs of mental distress since. I have records as well as a statement from her former therapist."

The judge frowned, his gaze shifting between the attorneys. "While Ms. Hanford's mental state is a concern, the evidence against her seems circumstantial at best." He shuffled some papers. "Bail is granted, but with conditions. Ms. Hanford must undergo a seventy-two-hour hold and psychiatric evaluation. If cleared, she will be released on house arrest and required to wear an ankle monitor."

Sam's heart leapt with relief, but anxiety still gnawed at him. A psych eval and house arrest weren't ideal. Still, it was better than nothing.

"Bail is set at five hundred thousand dollars," the judge concluded. An exorbitant amount in Sam's opinion, but he knew Selena or Michael or a combination of the two would cover it. They believed in Missy's innocence as much as he did.

After the judge left, Sam hurried over to Missy. Her lower lip trembled. "What if they don't release me? What if I'm stuck in a psychiatric hospital for months?"

"That won't happen," he said firmly. "You'll do the exam, and they'll release you after three days."

"But the damage has already been done. Even if I'm cleared, people will always suspect I'm crazy." She swiped at her eyes. "I'll never escape this. Never rebuild my life or my business. The cupcake shop…"

Sam cupped her face in his hands, wiping away her tears with his thumbs. "Forget about what anyone else thinks. This is about us, and I believe in you with all my heart. You're innocent, and we'll prove it. We'll get through this together, and when it's over, we'll face the future side by side. The way it was meant to be."

A fragile smile graced her face. "You always know just what to say." She rose onto her tiptoes to kiss him softly. "I love you, Sam Cooper."

"And I love you, Missy Hanford. Now and forever."

"Let's go, Hanford," one of the deputies barked.

Missy flinched, but she stepped out of Sam's arms without a word and went to the man.

As the two deputies escorted Missy out of the courtroom, Sam watched helplessly. She glanced over at him. Though she tried to appear brave, fear lurked in her eyes. Fear of the unknown. Of what might happen to her in that psychiatric ward.

His hands curled into fists, aching to lash out at someone— at the sheriff who'd framed her, the DA who'd painted her as mentally unstable, the whole messed-up justice system that had failed her. But violence wouldn't help Missy. She needed him to stay strong, to keep fighting for her freedom and her good name.

"Don't worry, son." Dad clapped a hand on his shoulder. "We've got the best lawyer in the county on her case. She'll be home in no time."

Sam nodded, though he wasn't nearly as confident. Elias was correct. The DA seemed determined to make an example of Missy, and even with a top-notch lawyer, exoneration could take months. Months of Missy stuck at home and being viewed as a criminal.

His stomach churned. She didn't deserve this. He'd keep saying that to anyone who would listen. She was the kindest, gentlest soul he'd ever known. The woman who'd brought warmth and laughter back into his life after his messy divorce. Who made him happier than he'd ever dreamed he could be again.

And he would make this right. He didn't know how yet, but he would find a way to free Missy and give her back the life that had been so unjustly stolen from her. They'd had too few days together as an official couple. He wanted a lifetime more.

Sam strode out of the courthouse into the golden sunlight, determination steeling his resolve. The battle had just begun, but he would fight for Missy until his last breath. Because a life without her was no life at all. She was his heart, his home, his everything. And he would never give up on them. Never.

☕ chapter seven ☕

"**I** DON'T CARE IF I'm supposed to stay in bed, Dad."
Welles slapped the hospital bed, his hand thudding
against the bedding. He hated being stuck in this room.
"I want to see Nell now."

Dad rubbed the back of his neck. "So, you just plan on getting
out of bed and walking to her room?"

"Would if I could." Bruises and cuts aside, Welles's leg was
elevated, and his arm was in a splint following surgery, so he
wasn't going anywhere, even though he wanted to. Desperately.
His injuries didn't matter. He'd even risk the chance of a setback.
Only one thing—one person—had been on his mind since he'd
woken up after surgery. He couldn't wait any longer. "I just need
to see Nell for a minute."

If he didn't, his heart might burst out of his chest. He could
barely breathe as it was. Seeing her with his own two eyes to make
sure she was okay would be the best medicine. He didn't think

Dad or Max would lie to him about Nell's condition, but Welles still wanted to make sure for himself.

"I know you do, but you need to rest and heal," Dad said in that growly voice of his. "So does she. Nell had surgery last night, too."

"Which is more reason to make sure she's okay." Yes, Welles was acting more like a thirteen-year-old kid than a thirty-three-year-old man, but he didn't care. He would blame all the pain meds they had him on. Apparently, it wasn't enough if he could be this worried about Nell instead of off in la-la-land. "What if her condition changed?"

He was a paramedic. He knew that could happen. Anything could, which was why he was so concerned. "Can you FaceTime her?"

"She might not have a phone."

"Dad…"

"Let's see how you're doing tomorrow." Dad spoke calmly. "You might not feel like you're drugged up, but they have enough pain medicine in you to knock out Squatchy."

Dad yawned and stretched his arms over his head. The dark circles under his eyes suggested he hadn't slept much in the chair near the window. Typical Buddy Riggs. Sasquatch Adventure Tours inspired a huge summer festival that brought tens of thousands to their small town, but he looked more like a lumberjack—a gruff and grumpy one at that—than a scion of Berry Lake businesses. But Dad's success was two-fold—his kinship with the mythical Bigfoot and throwing himself into the work after Mom died. He not only kept busy but stayed in shape with all the tours they ran. In his fifties, Buddy Riggs was fitter than most thirty-year-olds.

Welles would keep trying until he fell asleep. "Dad, please."

"No."

"But—"

"I'm not rolling your bed into her room." Dad held up his hands, palms facing Welles. "So don't ask me to do that again."

Huh? Welles didn't remember asking, but that wasn't a bad idea. "Five minutes. Or three. I just want to see her."

"You'll see Nell soon enough. Drink. You've got an IV, but a little water never hurt anyone." Dad held the water bottle's straw to Welles's mouth, and he sipped. "Nurses keep coming by to see you. Flirt with one of them. Might end up with a girlfriend by the time you're released."

"Not interested." Welles took another drink, and Dad put the water bottle back on the bed tray. Welles had dated several of the nurses with the sole intention of making Nell jealous. It hadn't worked. He still found himself in the friend zone, the same place she'd parked him after she'd returned to Berry Lake five years ago. He'd decided to only flirt with her coworkers after that. Oh, he still flirted with her coworkers and went out with other women, but ones from the surrounding towns.

Dad eyed him suspiciously. "I don't believe that."

Welles shrugged, not wanting to talk about this when he was struggling to think straight, but he knew Dad could be as stubborn as him. That gave Welles an idea. "Could you at least do me a favor?"

"Anything for you, son."

The emotion in Dad's voice brought a lump to Welles's throat. After they'd lost Mom, he'd tried to be both parental figures. Buddy Riggs didn't always succeed, but he tried. Welles had never doubted Dad's love. "Would you buy a package of peanut M&Ms and take them to Nell from me?"

Dad thought for a moment. "Candy, huh?"

"She has a sweet tooth."

He stared at Welles with an unreadable expression.

"Dad?" Welles asked.

"Take a nap." His voice was firmer than Welles expected. "I'll be back shortly."

"Thanks." He might not get to see Nell, but Dad would give him a full update. That would have to do for now.

Lying in the hospital bed, Nell inhaled the floral fragrance lingering in the air. JoJo had set the many floral arrangements around the room to brighten the space, but with everyone there earlier, Nell had been too overwhelmed to notice. Now that she was alone while people went to eat so she could nap, she took the time to look at each one.

Wildflowers, a mixed bouquet, lilies, carnations, even an arrangement of daisies with a small mylar balloon on a stick that said *Get Well* brought a smile to her face. What had happened on the climb sucked, but the thoughtfulness of people touched her heart.

Too bad I can't take them home.

Well, except for the little balloon thingy. Mr. Teddy would demolish all of the flowers and then end up vomiting on her carpet. She didn't need to deal with that while healing. Before she was released, she would ask Cami to distribute the flowers to patients who didn't have any. That should bring smiles to some faces.

Home.

She couldn't wait to be there.

Even though the ER was like a second home, Nell wasn't used to the upper floors of the hospital. More importantly, she didn't like being a patient. She'd barely slept since waking up this morning or had a minute to herself.

She appreciated having her family's and friends' support, but if Mom mentioned wedding planning one more time, Nell might scream. The pain meds were messing with her head. Being this annoyed over the topic surprised Nell since she'd been imagining a wedding of her own since she was a little girl dreaming of her future.

Five years ago, she'd planned her and Andrew's wedding, expecting him to propose after their "break." She had magazines filled with ideas for color schemes and styles of gowns she'd been drawn to. Since she'd grown up as the daughter of an event planner, a wedding had become the pinnacle to her. That was why Nell had been ready and waiting for the ring. And then Andrew proposed to and married a woman he'd known for only two weeks.

I've known Gage for longer than that.

That realization didn't make her feel any better. Oh, it had taken Nell time to get over Andrew and being dumped the way she had, but she still wished to be a bride, to have the wedding of her dreams, and live happily ever after.

So why did everything feel off about Gage's proposal and the ring she now wore on her left hand?

Nell held out her hand. The diamond sparkled, but the platinum ring felt heavy with uncertainty. Gage had proposed to her, but Mom had said yes. Did that mean Nell was actually engaged?

Everyone seemed to think so, but a part of her still seemed to be standing on that ledge with Welles, joking around and having fun.

Guilt coated her mouth. She was to blame for Welles getting hurt. She never should have dragged him into doing things with Gage. That was totally on her. And she shouldn't have gone herself.

If she'd gone to see Missy...

Sweet Missy, who was in a room several floors above her in the hospital's psych ward on a seventy-two-hour hold. Nell prayed her friend would be okay. Being arrested and then sent for observation could end up being traumatic enough to affect the rest of Missy's life. Nell hoped that, after everything, Missy had been through, she'd be strong enough to withstand this.

When Sabine had told her the DA had suggested "self-harm" as a motive for Missy to have set the fire, Nell had been incensed. Nothing could be further from the truth.

Did Missy suffer from depression?

Yes, no one would say otherwise, but she'd also been through so much: disowned by her parents when she married Rob and then lost her husband five years later. Most people would have trouble coping. But anyone with half a brain knew that being depressed didn't turn a person into a felon. Missy was innocent of arson.

Thinking of all Missy had been through brought the love story of Rob and Missy to mind. Nell considered her feelings for Gage. She liked him and thought he was hot, but were those good enough reasons to get married? She thought back to Andrew, who she'd believed to be the love of her life. She'd been head-over-heels in love with Andrew by their second date. They'd met when she was twenty-two, and during each of the ten years they were together, her love for him grew.

Nell barely knew Gage, which raised so many questions.

Had he proposed out of guilt? The hospital room seemed to close in around Nell as she fidgeted with the engagement ring, which felt like a foreign object on her finger. Gage had never mentioned wanting to settle down. They were only casually dating. Exclusivity had never even come up.

A gentle knock sounded at the door.

"Come in," she said, even though most people just waltzed right in.

The door opened slowly.

She glanced over to see Buddy Riggs, Welles's dad, lumbering into her room. He was tall, at least six-four, with salt-and-pepper hair and a beard. His kind, blue eyes mirrored his son's, and he had the same thick, lush lashes most women would kill for.

"Hey, Nell." Buddy's smile was warm, but lines of worry were etched into his face. His clothes were wrinkled and his hair messy, suggesting he'd spent the night at the hospital. He approached her bedside. "How are you feeling today?"

"I've been better, but it could be worse, so no complaints." She sat straighter. The ache in her gut had nothing to do with her injuries. Dad had given her a report on Welles's condition, but she knew how fast that could change. She swallowed. "How's Welles?"

"Stubborn as always and driving your coworkers crazy." Buddy shook his head. "That boy isn't used to sitting still, but he needs to do that in order to heal and get released for duty."

She remembered Welles being put on probation for going into the cupcake shop when it was on fire to pull Missy to safety. "How long is he out for?"

"Six to eight weeks, but he'll be at the desk for a while after that."

Nell grimaced. "Oh, man. Welles will hate that."

Buddy laughed. "He used a bit more colorful language when the doctor gave him the news."

She smiled. "Sounds like Welles."

Buddy pulled something yellow from his coat pocket. He handed her a bag of peanut M&Ms. "Welles asked me to bring these to you, said they were your favorite."

"They are. Thanks." Nell took the candy and cradled it in her hands. Welles had given her a similar bag right before the rocks tumbled on top of them. She had no idea where that bag had ended up, but she wouldn't lose this one.

"Are you okay?" Buddy asked.

Her throat tight with emotion, Nell nodded.

Buddy's gaze focused on her ring. "I heard about the proposal. Didn't realize you two were that serious."

Me, either. Nell sighed, her eyes filling with tears. "Gage proposed, but...I didn't say yes. My mom did."

Buddy chortled. "Sounds like Charlene Culpepper." Mom and Buddy had never gotten along, but that often happened in small towns.

"She's wanted me to get married for a long time."

"That might be the case, but Charlene isn't the one getting married." The edge to his voice wasn't surprising. "You are, if that's what you want."

Nell stared at the ring as if it held all the answers. "I don't know. I should know, right?"

"Not always, so don't let anyone rush or push you into something you don't want," Buddy said gently, reminding her of Welles. "You don't have to make any decisions right now. Those pain meds must be messing with you the way they are with my boy. Focus on getting better first."

"Thanks, Buddy," she whispered, grateful to have someone on her side. Still, guilt gnawed at her insides, making her wish she could turn back time. "I'm so sorry about Welles getting hurt. I never meant for anything to happen to him."

"I know, and he knows that, too." Buddy brushed his hand through his hair. "And he didn't want you doing anything alone with that idiot where you could get hurt."

"You mean Gage."

"Yep." Buddy shifted his weight between his feet. "We both know Welles has had a crush on you since elementary school. I think he actually looks forward to bringing a patient to the ER so he can ask you out."

That made her smile. Dads were always the last to know. "He does ask me out, but he's just joking around. That's how Welles is. Friendly."

Buddy took a breath and exhaled slowly. "I know my son, and he's not joking."

The words seemed to float between them. It took Nell a minute to comprehend what Buddy was saying.

"Oh." Her face heated. Cami had said something similar, but Nell hadn't believed her. Why would she? Welles was a hot paramedic who was in the best shape of his life and could date anyone, and she was a nurse who was four years older and never said no to anything sugary, which showed. "I-I don't know what to say."

A small smile tugged at the corners of Buddy's mouth. "My son thinks the world of you. I know it's a lot to take in right now, but I thought you should know."

Nell stared at the bag of peanut M&Ms in her hands, her mind racing with conflicting thoughts. She'd always considered

Welles a good friend. They'd become neighbors when he moved into her building, but she'd never really thought of him as anything more than that. Firefighters and paramedics seemed to be red flag occupations, and after Andrew, she'd been extra careful about the men she dated. Not that she'd had many dates over the past five years.

"Since Welles woke up, he's been asking for you nonstop," Buddy continued, his gaze steady and sincere. "He wants to make sure you're okay. It's all he can think about."

The determined glint in Buddy's eyes mirrored what she knew to be true of his son—Welles Riggs never gave up. He'd risked his life to save Missy and Nell. These Riggs men were made of different stuff.

"Thank you for telling me, Buddy." Nell's throat constricted. She swallowed. "If you can find a wheelchair, I'd love to visit Welles, if you don't think he'd mind."

Buddy grinned. "He would love that. I'll be right back." With that, the man hurried out of the room.

Nell lay there surrounded by the gentle hum of hospital sounds. Her fingers wrapped around the candy. She would thank Welles for saving her life and giving her candy. That was the least she could do, right?

Then she would take that nap her family wanted her to take so she could heal. The rest would sort itself out. At least she hoped it would.

With the help of two nurses, Nell sat in the wheelchair. Someone covered her with a blanket.

"Her IV needs to go with her," Danielle, her day RN, said, attaching the bag of fluids to the wheelchair's IV stand. "And this needs to be a quick visit since she's still recovering, so keep that in mind."

Nell felt as if she were seven, not thirty-seven. "I will."

"All right, let's get you to Welles's room." As Buddy's strong hands gripped the handles of her wheelchair, he pushed her through the maze-like hallways of the hospital, navigating the bustling corridor with ease.

"Watch out for that cart," Nell warned as they approached an overflowing laundry cart in the middle of the hallway.

Buddy deftly maneuvered around the obstacle, making it look like a well-practiced dance move. Nell couldn't help but smile at his agility and grace.

"Nothing can keep me from getting you to my boy." Buddy laughed heartily. The sound was infectious, and Nell found herself joining.

When they reached the door to what she assumed to be Welles's room, Buddy paused, giving Nell a reassuring nod before pushing the door open with a gentle creak. The room was dimly lit, the curtains drawn to block out the daylight. In the bed on the left, surrounded by monitors and medical equipment, lay Welles Riggs.

Nell's breath caught in her throat. He looked so pale and fragile beneath the sheet and blanket with his leg and his arm elevated—a stark contrast to the strong, vibrant paramedic she knew him to be. His usually bright eyes were heavy with exhaustion, dark circles shadowing their brilliant blue.

"Hey there, Paramedic Welles."

As his gaze met hers, a spark of life seemed to ignite within him. A slow, weary smile spread across his face, lighting up his handsome features like the first rays of sunshine after a storm. "Nurse Nell." Relief and gratitude sounded in his voice. "You're here. You're okay."

"I am." Her heart swelled with an overwhelming mix of emotions. "Thanks to you. You saved me."

He blinked and then swallowed. "Well, ya know, I have three more to go."

"Huh?"

"There are five Cupcake Posse members. I figure saving all of you will get me free cupcakes for life."

She laughed. "Probably."

"Come closer, please."

With the steady beeping of the monitors as background noise, Buddy carefully positioned her wheelchair beside Welles's bed.

Nell reached out to take his free hand. "I'm so sorry."

"It's not your fault."

"But it is."

"You can't blame yourself for any of this. We make our own choices. What happened was an accident, and I don't regret being there for you." Welles gently squeezed Nell's hand, his touch warm and steady.

His gaze, however, zeroed in on her left hand.

"So, is that what I think it is?" he asked, his voice strained but teasing.

Nell stared at the ring on her finger, a heavy weight settling in her chest. Being with Welles had made her forget about the ring. "Yes."

"Gage?" Welles kept his tone lighthearted, but the underlying tension was hard to miss. He offered her a small smile that didn't quite reach his eyes.

"Y-yeah." Her face burned. "He proposed last night, but I haven't... I mean, I didn't say yes. My mom jumped in and accepted for me."

"Ah, Charlene." Welles's brow furrowed with concern. "Always looking out for her little Nell."

The hint of sadness behind his words sent another pang of guilt. Though she didn't know why. Maybe he did have a crush on her as Buddy had said, but they'd always been just friends. It wasn't as if they'd done anything together outside of the ER or passed each other at their places until Gage had entered the picture.

"For being newly engaged, you don't look that happy."

"It's just..." Nell's gaze dropped to their hands. "The ring is gorgeous, and Gage appears sincere, but we haven't even known each other that long. We weren't even exclusive."

"True."

"And then there's all the guilt I feel about you getting hurt."

"I told you—"

"But if I'd gone to see Missy in jail instead of climbing, none of this would have happened."

"It still could have happened to me and Gage."

"Would you have gone if I hadn't?" she asked bluntly.

"Hey, what's done is done." Welles brushed his thumb against the back of her hand. "You can't blame yourself for what happened. It was an accident. And as for the proposal... Take your time. You deserve someone who makes you happy, who supports you and loves you for who you are. Don't settle for anything less. If that's Gage, I wish you the best. Just don't settle to make your mom happy, okay?"

She nodded. Welles's kind, understanding gaze brought a lump to her throat. Nell swallowed hard.

"Remember Selena T's wise words: just remember to follow your heart. You'll make the right decision."

"You're right," Nell admitted. "Thanks."

"I'll always be here for you."

She couldn't shake the feeling that there was something more between them, a connection she'd never truly acknowledged before. But with the weight of the engagement ring on her finger and the uncertainty of her future looming over her, Nell knew she couldn't allow herself to entertain such thoughts.

"You're a good friend."

"You mean a *great* friend," he teased.

That made her laugh. "Oh, sorry. Yes, a great one, who gives me my favorite candy."

"What can I say?" Welles joked. "I know you well."

He did, and that made her wonder how well Gage really knew her. Though anyone could pick a shiny ring and guess a ring size. But again, was that enough?

Her heart wasn't so sure.

chapter eight

AFTER HIS SHIFT at the Berry Lake Animal Clinic on Tuesday, Roman Byrne stood on the front porch. A slight breeze blew, rustling the leaves strewn across the yard. He yawned, his early morning catching up with him.

He'd switched shifts so he could be at home today when his niece got out of school. Katie had turned twelve last month and could be on her own, but she seemed down. That happened given her grief, but this seemed different. His gut told him there might be a new problem, and he didn't want her to be alone today.

Yesterday, he'd phoned her therapist, who'd been working with Katie for the past month on processing the loss of her parents earlier in the year. He missed his twin sister, Katie's mom, so much. She'd not only been family, but they'd owned a veterinary clinic together. Sometimes he still picked up the phone to call her. But between relocating, his new job, and niece, Roman hadn't had time for therapy. Sometimes, he barely had time to sleep. But one of these days...

Roman glanced down the street, past the tall maples lining the road, but the sidewalk was empty. No sign of his niece. Maybe he'd showered and changed faster than he realized.

Katie trudged up the driveway. With her hunched posture, her backpack hung off one slim shoulder. "Hey, Uncle Roman."

The tremble of apprehension in her voice hit him right at his heart. He was still learning to be a parent, but he knew without a doubt something was wrong from the way she sounded.

He needed to stay calm. "Hey, kiddo, how was school?"

She shrugged. "You're home early. You even changed clothes."

Shorts and a hoodie were his typical Sunday wear. "I thought I might do some work in the yard. I also made cookies for us."

He expected her to react to that. A smile, at least. Katie loved homemade cookies. Her expression didn't change.

He opened the door. "Come inside."

Her footsteps dragged, but Roman would wait to talk. She stepped inside and he followed her, closing the door behind him. The sweet aroma of homemade chocolate chip cookies filled the air, but Katie didn't even notice. Her backpack plopped against the floor, and she shrugged out of her jacket in silence.

That wasn't normal at all. "Let's sit down for a minute."

She went to the couch and sank into the pillows, not saying a word.

"You haven't seemed yourself." He waited for a response, but she didn't even blink. "What's going on, kiddo?"

Katie wouldn't meet his eyes. She took a breath and then blew it out.

"Hey, talk to me. You and me. Partners in crime."

"Are we still?"

Her question surprised him. "Of course. Why would you think otherwise?"

Katie bit her lip.

"You can tell me anything," he urged.

She rubbed her hands over her arms. "Fleur said something that upset me."

Heather's daughter? That was unexpected. "What did she say, sweetheart?"

"She...she said that when you get married to her mom, you and Heather are sending me to boarding school. I didn't know if I should believe her, but she said it again," Katie confessed, her lower lip trembling as she held back tears. "This time Heather overheard her and said that was correct."

Roman's heart dropped, but he offered Katie what he hoped would be a comforting smile. "Oh, Katie, you must've misunderstood her. Heather wouldn't want to send you away—we're a family."

Roman hoped that would be enough to reassure Katie, but she shrugged again, appearing unconvinced. That gave him an idea. "Why don't we move this conversation to the kitchen table, where there are cookies?"

Katie got up and went to the table. His bookish niece seemed like a different child.

Roman placed a cookie on a plate for her, poured a glass of milk, and set both in front of her. But she didn't eat them. He ate a cookie.

Not bad, if he said so himself.

Maybe he should call the therapist again or ask Juliet. Though she was likely still at work. But she understood Katie in a way others didn't. If only things had worked out differently... He missed dating Juliet, but he understood she needed time with her divorce. Still, finding a mother for Katie was his priority, no matter that if he wrote a list of the qualities of the perfect woman, Juliet Jones Monroe checked each one.

Katie sat at the table, her untouched cookie resting on a plate. That wasn't like her at all.

Roman gently pushed the plate closer to Katie. "Here, have another one."

Her gaze flickered to the untouched cookie on her plate. "I haven't even eaten this one yet."

"Then you get two."

She inhaled. "Are you planning on marrying Heather, Uncle Roman?"

Roman stilled, surprised by her question. He didn't know if this had something to do with what she'd told him about boarding school, but he wanted to tread carefully. "Heather and I haven't been dating long, sweetheart. But wouldn't it be nice to have a sister like Fleur?"

A shadow crossed Katie's face. She lowered her eyes to her lap, fingers nervously playing with the napkin edge. "Fleur is one of the mean girls at school."

This was news to him. He'd assumed Fleur was a sweet girl like her mother. "I didn't know that, Katie."

"If you get married and Heather doesn't want me, can Juliet adopt me?" Katie's voice was thick with emotion. "That would be better than being sent away to boarding school."

"Katie." Roman wanted to ease her fears. He offered her a smile, though his heart ached at the pain in her eyes. "You've read too many books. Your imagination is running away with you."

She nodded dejectedly, her spirit visibly dimmed, and she seemed to shrink. She stared at her cookie.

"Everything will be okay, Katie," Roman reassured her softly, squeezing her hand gently, trying to comfort her. But doubt lingered in his heart, making it harder to sound convincing. "I promise."

"Sure, Uncle Roman." She picked up her cookie, taking a tentative bite, but her eyes held a touch of sadness.

Things weren't even close to being okay, but Roman had no idea what to do. But he had to find out why Katie thought Heather wanted to send her away. That made no sense when she had a daughter the same age. So what had Katie heard, and how had it spun this far out of control?

At Events by Charlene, Juliet focused on preparing supplies for an upcoming princess tea party she'd be hosting on Saturday. They were her favorite events to do because she got to put on a gown and tiara and act like a princess. Some might think thirty-five was too old, but everyone had a princess inside them, no matter what age.

She tied a ribbon around the box containing a complete miniature ceramic tea set that would be given out to each party guest as a favor.

Charlene scrolled online, looking at wedding dress designers. She pointed at the screen. "Can you imagine Nell in that stunning gown? She'll be a picture-perfect bride."

"She will." A smile tugged at Juliet's lips. Charlene had dove into planning her daughter's wedding even though Nell and Gage had given her no direction. "Though she'll likely want to try on her own dress. Bria mentioned a dress shop in Wishing Bay that sounds wonderful."

Bria had discovered the place while researching the beach town where Molly's facility was located. More than once, the light in Bria's eyes talking while about wedding gowns suggested she saw herself and Dalton ending up together. Juliet crossed her fingers for Bria's sake that everything would work out.

Charlene did a little dance. "Road trip!"

Her excitement and anticipation over her oldest daughter's wedding were palpable. The Posse would have so much fun doing that except...

Missy.

She was only twenty-four hours into her stay at the hospital with forty-eight more to go. The image of her in the courtroom, appearing so fragile and exhausted, haunted Juliet. She'd texted Jenny, but she didn't have any updates. Charlene was gossip central in town. Maybe she knew something.

"Have you heard anything about Missy?"

"No, but due to HIPAA, nothing can be reported." Charlene's expression softened. "Missy's been through so much. She'll pull through this."

Juliet understood, but she found little solace within. Ezra's image appeared in her thoughts, along with his desperate pleas and promises. His transformation from a cheating husband to a remorseful suitor was both confusing and disheartening. "It looks like all of us have to be fighters."

She'd never had to fight before—or rather, she'd been too afraid to speak up to Ezra. But Tamika, her divorce attorney, said his lawyer was dragging his feet about the divorce. Thank goodness Juliet had a job, or she would have no money to live on. If Ezra truly cared about her, he wouldn't be making her count every penny, living paycheck to paycheck. She sighed.

"What's that sigh for?" Charlene asked. "Worried about Missy?"

"Yes, but I was also thinking about Ezra."

"It's too soon for the divorce to be finalized."

"Yes, but he showed up at the house on Sunday night. He brought over dinner for me and Bria, which was nice after being at the hospital, but then he asked for a second chance to make things right."

"That takes nerve after what he did with Remy Dwyer."

"It was so frustrating." The incredulity in Juliet's voice barely veiled her hurt. "I just can't believe him. He's nothing like the man I married. Or maybe he just pretended to be a nice guy back then."

Charlene set the fabric samples on the table. "Well, divorce worked miracles for Max and me. Perhaps someday, you and Ezra will be the same."

"Unlike my soon-to-be ex, Max is a great guy. He never betrayed you the way Ezra did me." Juliet's voice hardened. "I don't want him back in my life at all."

Understanding shone in Charlene's eyes. "I understand. You don't have to want him back. You're entitled to happiness. Just don't let the past with him dictate your future."

Juliet nodded, grateful for Charlene's support. As she stared at the crystal tiaras sparkling underneath the lights overhead, a flicker of hope sparked within her that she was on the path toward healing. It would take time, but she was taking the first steps.

That felt so good. All she wanted was to put her heartache behind her, even if an uncertain future awaited her. She no longer had her grandmother in her life, but she had a family in Berry Lake—not one of blood, but of the heart. And it was more than enough.

An hour later, with her workday over, Juliet left and stepped onto Main Street. The sun had started its descent to the horizon, casting warm hues of orange and pink across the sky and leaving an autumn nip in the air. Berry Lake, with its quaint shops and friendly faces, provided a soothing balm to her frazzled nerves. She breathed in the familiar scene, noticing the sharp scent of pine, and then headed away from the little downtown toward home.

In the park, teenagers hung out at the gazebo, while a little kids' soccer team practiced on the grass. Someone scored a goal, and everyone cheered.

She continued toward her street, trying to decide what to make for dinner. There'd been enough leftovers from Ezra's meal that they hadn't had to cook last night. Maybe Bria would have an idea. Her car was parked in the driveway.

"Juliet!"

She turned toward the sound of her name to see Katie waving from her front porch. Juliet walked over there and wrapped the girl in a comforting hug. "I hope you had a great day at school."

Katie shrugged, which wasn't like her. "Thanks."

Juliet hadn't known Katie long, but she wasn't her usual self. "Are you okay?"

"You know how you said I should talk to Uncle Roman about boarding school?"

That had been last month. "Did you?"

Katie shifted her weight between her feet. "I...tried. He said I must've misunderstood, or I'm letting my imagination run wild."

Taken aback by the unexpected revelation, Juliet felt a wave of sympathy for Katie. Roman hadn't handled that well at all. "I'm sure your uncle didn't mean that. But I hope you know he'd never let anyone send you away," Juliet reassured her, even as she remembered her brief relationship with Roman, fraught with complexities and misunderstandings.

"It doesn't matter, since he won't listen to me." Katie's voice trembled. She looked so lost and alone that Juliet was immediately reminded of being orphaned herself.

"I understand how you're feeling, Katie." Juliet touched the young girl's shoulder. "I know how scary it is with your parents gone and feeling like you're all alone. But remember, you're not alone."

Katie's hopeful eyes bored into Juliet. "Would...would you talk to my uncle, please? He won't accuse you of making things up."

The plea resonated deep within Juliet, stirring her own memories of feeling out of place and unwanted, even though she'd lived with her grandparents most of the time while Mom and Dad had traveled. But in her heart, she'd always believed they would want to be a family, just the three of them.

Until that became an impossible dream.

Roman wouldn't like Juliet getting involved, but one look at Katie's teary-eyed face steeled her resolve. Juliet empathized and wanted to be there for Katie. "Of course. I'll help you however I can."

Relief washed over Katie's face, gratitude shining in her eyes. "Thank you. He came home early if you have time now."

Oh, Juliet hadn't expected that. "Well, you know what they always say... No time like the present."

"Uncle Roman is in the backyard." Katie motioned for her to follow. "We can go around the side."

Juliet had a few things to say to him that she didn't want Katie to hear. "Why don't you go inside and let me talk to him alone?"

"Okay. I have some homework I need to finish."

"This won't take long." At least Juliet hoped it wouldn't. She made her way around the side of the house. She found Roman putting leaves into bags. "Hey."

Roman straightened, his eyes widening in surprise. "Juliet. What are you doing here?" With his hair messy and leaves clinging to his hoodie, he shouldn't look as handsome as he did.

She lifted her chin, forcing herself to meet his gaze. "We need to talk. It's about Katie."

"Sure." He brushed his hands off and motioned to a picnic table. "You sound concerned."

She sat. "I am. Katie's talked to me twice now about something. She's scared."

His eyebrows furrowed. He took a seat opposite her. "Scared of what?"

"She's worried Heather will send her away to boarding school." Juliet tried to keep the emotion out of her voice, but it wasn't easy.

Roman shook his head. "She mentioned that to me, but she has to be mistaken. Heather would never do something like that."

"Are you sure?" Juliet challenged, her eyes narrowing. "I can't imagine Katie making something like this up on her own. She said Fleur mentioned it first. And then how Heather overheard them the next time and didn't correct her daughter."

Roman fell silent, a hint of doubt creeping into his eyes.

"Katie's worried. You're all she has left, and even though you two haven't been in Berry Lake that long, she's afraid she'll be sent away."

"I just don't think Heather would do that."

Juliet couldn't believe how dense he was being. He really must have fallen for Heather. But that was beside the point. Juliet was here for Katie.

"It doesn't matter what you think. Katie feels like Heather is trying to push her out of your life." Juliet's voice shook with emotion. "And based on what Katie told me, I believe her."

"You've always had Katie's best interests at heart, haven't you?" Roman's voice was soft, regret evident in his words.

"I've been in her shoes," Juliet admitted, her voice barely above a whisper. Her own experience made her even more sympathetic to Katie's plight. "Losing my parents made me appreciate how precious the bond of family is. I don't ever want Katie to feel as alone as I did."

"I never meant to hurt Katie. She means everything to me." Roman raked a hand through his hair, his face pained. "Maybe I've just let myself get so caught up in Heather I'm not seeing things clearly. I'm sorry."

"You don't need to apologize to me. Promise me you'll do right by Katie. She deserves so much more than to be afraid of being pushed aside like that."

"I will. You have my word." Roman's voice was firm, his eyes meeting Juliet's with newfound determination. "I'll talk to Heather, too."

"Great." Juliet's eyes locked onto his. Time seemed to stop until she shook herself out of the trance. "Goodbye."

Roman reached out and touched her arm. "Thank you. I really appreciate you being there for Katie and for me."

Juliet's breath caught in her throat. The spot where he touched her tingled. "You're welcome."

As she headed to her house next door, Juliet ignored the warmth flowing through her. She hated her body for reacting to Roman. They were friends. That was all they could be.

She only hoped he kept his word. Otherwise, Katie would pay the price. At least Juliet had tried. She hoped she'd helped Katie. And maybe by doing so, she had taken another step toward also helping herself.

chapter nine

TUESDAY NIGHT, THE hockey game was tied in the third period. The arena was sold out, and tense fans wrung their hands. A few bit their nails.

Selena, however, didn't understand why they were so worried this early in the season. She held little Murphy on her lap while Roxy ran to the bathroom. "There's too many games left to be this concerned."

Murphy waved his hands. He wore a tiny jersey with his daddy's number on it and a small pair of noise-canceling headphones.

Those didn't keep Selena from talking. Even though he wasn't listening to her, he could see her lips moving. "Yes. They should be cheering and not worry about the outcome."

She'd been trying to decide whether to stay in Seattle or drive to Berry Lake after Nell's accident. Both Charlene and Juliet had told Selena to wait because Nell was improving every day and would be home soon. That had been such a relief to hear because Selena wanted to spend time with Logan during this home stand, too.

The ref blew his whistle after a rough hit.

"Ouch. And that's going to send someone to the penalty box." Selena rocked Murphy. "That'll give us the advantage. I have a feeling the team will pull out a win."

Murphy stared at her.

"Do you think you'll grow up and play hockey, too?" she asked.

Murphy cooed.

Her heart bumped. So sweet.

Something told her that Murphy would be a heartbreaker like his daddy, Clovis Grable. Clovis went by Grable and was an Ivy League graduate who'd been married with kids but was now divorced and engaged to Roxy. While most people thought he'd cheated, Selena found out from Logan that his wife had and not one of their kids was biologically his. Grable was trying to take the high road until the media found out, which they likely would at some point.

Selena only hoped Grable found peace with his new family. Logan had asked her if she had anything that might help Grable. She gave him a copy of her book with sections marked, specific podcasts, and her cell phone number if he wanted to talk. No call yet, but she had a few male clients and knew sometimes it took them longer to come around.

Murphy laughed. The sound wrapped around her heart. She had no idea what he found so funny, but he really was a cutie.

She laughed. "Whether you play hockey or choose to do something else, make sure you have fun and always give it your all. Success will come easier."

Roxy, who wore a matching jersey to her son's, plopped into the empty seat next to them. "Sorry, the line was so long." She looked like she was eighteen, but Selena had found out Roxie was twenty-three and had a degree in marketing. "Listen to her, Murph. People pay big bucks for one-on-one coaching with Selena T."

Even though it was true, Selena laughed. "You can never start them too young."

"That's for sure." Roxy's eyes softened. "You're so good with him."

As Selena rocked the baby, the compliment took root in her heart. Nell was the one who had always wanted to be a mom growing up. Selena's goal had been to escape Berry Lake, but she'd wanted kids someday, too. Only that dream had died on an operating table after she'd suffered from debilitating cases of endometriosis and adenomyosis. She still had her ovaries, but she'd had a hysterectomy.

When they started dating seriously, Logan had told her he didn't want children, it wasn't a dealbreaker for her at all. He'd seemed so relieved when she told him that she was unable to have kids. Even though she couldn't have children, that didn't mean she didn't love them. And thanks to Roxy, Selena had a way to get her baby fix. Now, if she could just convince Logan to let her have a pet.

She smiled at Roxy. "Murph makes the games more fun."

Murph went to grab her hair, and she flipped it behind her shoulder. "I enjoy this young human so much."

Roxy grinned. "I'd say the feeling's mutual."

"Smart kid."

Roxy nodded. "So there's some middle-aged dude in the owner's box who keeps staring this way. Pretty sure he's looking at you."

She glanced that way and saw Ted with his arm around a woman at least half his age. She couldn't see his beady eyes from where she sat, but the guy creeped her out. The guy was the definition of slimy. "That's Logan's agent."

"Oh, I wasn't expecting that."

"They go way back." Unfortunately. Selena hoped Logan opened his eyes to the guy's sleaziness sooner rather than later. She'd been telling her husband to dump his agent for more than a decade. And lucky her got to have dinner after the game with Ted and Logan.

"Want me to take Murph?" Roxy asked.

"Nope." Selena tapped the tip of Murphy's nose. "I'm enjoying him too much."

Alek Ramson stole the puck and passed it off to Logan, who took the puck across mid-ice and then passed it back to Ramson, who took a shot.

The red light on the net illuminated, and the horn blasted. Goal.

Roxy jumped to her feet. Everyone else did the same, going crazy now that the Volcanoes were in the lead. Selena remained seated to keep from disturbing the baby. It was still early in the season, and many more games would be played over the coming months, but she understood.

Everyone was dreaming of the playoffs. Not Selena. All she cared about was the season ending. Maybe some would call that sacrilege, but she wasn't sure she wanted the Volcanoes to make the playoffs because that would mean Logan putting off retirement that much longer.

Selfish? Yes, but she'd put their future on hold each season he'd changed his mind about hanging up his skates. She glanced at Ted, who clapped along with everyone else. He'd convinced Logan not to retire in the past, and something in her gut told Selena that Ted would try the same this time around.

She just hoped Logan didn't listen to him this time.

After the game, Selena went to an Italian bistro to wait for Logan and Ted. A candle flickered on the linen covering the table in the cozy booth next to the front window. The flame's soft glow provided a romantic vibe, but with Ted there, this wouldn't be a date.

Raindrops tapped against the glass. Typical for Seattle in early November or throughout the year. Berry Lake got rain but had four distinct seasons. She watched water stream down the window like tears, hoping that wouldn't be an omen for how this night would turn out.

Stop.

Selena knew better. The story in her mind wasn't true. She needed to focus her thoughts on what she wanted—namely for Logan to tell the team this was his final season like he'd already told her so they could enjoy the rest of their lives the way they'd planned.

After taking three deep breaths, she imagined them in their new home on Berry Lake and let the happiness in her heart at their life spread through her. Okay, that was better. Speaking of Berry Lake…

She checked the Posse's group chat to see if any new messages had appeared, but none had. No news is good news, so she hoped Nell's recovery was continuing. Missy's seventy-two-hour hold and the blackout of information during that frustrated Selena. Unfortunately, no one could do anything about that.

A male server dressed in black brought over a basket of breadsticks and a plate of olive oil drizzled with balsamic vinegar. The aroma of garlic and freshly baked bread wafted in the air.

"For while you wait." He shifted his weight between his feet. "And I just want to say, I never miss one of your podcasts. You kept me from making a huge mistake with my ex. I owe you."

"Thanks for the breadsticks, and I'm happy I helped, but you're the one who took the action, so the credit belongs to you."

"Never thought of it that way." He stood taller. "But you're right. Still, thanks."

"You're welcome." As he walked away with a bounce to his step, she grabbed a breadstick, dipped it into the oil, and took a bite. Delicious.

Logan hurried in, shaking off his jacket. His tie was jammed into the front pocket. He kissed her cheek and slid beside her into the booth. "Sorry I'm late. Got stuck in media, the trainer wanted me to ice, and then there was traffic out of the arena."

Ted sauntered behind him, grumbling about the rain.

"Feeling okay?" she asked Logan.

"Sore as usual." Logan's nervous energy was almost palpable. His leg jittered under the table. "Not getting any younger."

"You're playing as if you're ten years younger." Ted picked up his menu. "That rookie was icing, too, and he's still a teenager."

Selena pressed her lips together. She'd heard this from Ted before.

After they ordered, a bottle of red wine arrived and their glasses were filled. Ted raised his glass. "To a stellar game. Ramson scored the goal, but if not for you, the team would have lost."

Logan's fingers drummed an uncertain rhythm against the stem of his wine glass. He usually drank slowly since he never had more than one glass.

Selena raised her glass, gazing into his eyes. Logan had never kept anything from her, so she had no reason to believe Ted knew something she didn't. Besides, Logan had already told her he was ready to retire at the end of the season.

She had no reason to doubt him. "To Logan."

They each drank.

Logan reached under the table, took her hand, and squeezed it. "I told Ted about wanting to retire after the season."

Her heart pounded in her chest. She barely dared herself to breathe, but she had to ask. "And?"

Ted rolled his eyes. "Logan will be an All-Star again. There's no reason for him to retire yet."

He sounded more like a teenager with an attitude than a fifty-five-year-old agent.

Logan looked at Ted pointedly. "This body might still work, but it's needing a lot more TLC. It's time to stop pushing this off every year the way I have in the past."

Ted snorted, but Selena ignored him, her focus on Logan.

"Going out while I'm still on top makes sense," Logan added. "Selena and I have been talking about what the future will look like, and I can't wait to see it."

The joy bubbling inside Selena nearly overwhelmed her. The real thing felt so much better than her visualization. Tears prickling her eyes, she hugged him. "It does make sense."

Ted's lip curled into a sneer, making him look more like a cartoon character than a human. "You're leaving millions on the table."

"Selena makes more than me as it is," Logan said with no hesitation. "We'll be fine."

A vein pulsed on Ted's jaw, confirming for her that Ted was more worried about his wallet.

She searched Logan's face for any sign of doubt, finding only unwavering love. Her heart swelled with affection and gratitude for this man, her husband. "Your well-being is the most important thing. I want you to be sure about this decision, Logan."

His smile was warm, full of love. "I am."

She wiggled her toes but didn't want to rub her victory into Ted's face. He'd done that the last couple of years when Logan decided to keep playing, but she would take the high road.

With a determined set to his jaw, Logan flicked his gaze over to Ted, who sulked across the table from them. "I know you disagree, but I want your support on this."

"I'll do whatever you say." Ted's eyes darted between her and Logan. "But as I said earlier, there's still money to be made, contracts to sign, endorsements to cash in on."

His words held a hint of desperation, but this was Logan's career. She didn't want to interfere.

"We have more money than we'll spend in this lifetime," Logan said, his voice firm. "I've been neglecting Selena for too long, and I feel out of alignment with myself. It's time."

Thank goodness. She'd felt out of alignment and like a fraud herself. But now everything would fall into place. "It is time."

Ted shrugged, but he seemed to have something on his mind. He was probably thinking about all that commission he'd be losing. "Before we go to the team, I want you to sleep on this. Really think hard about your life after hockey. Then we can make plans going forward."

"Sounds fair." Logan looked at her. "Do you agree?"

Not really, but she didn't want to be unreasonable. This was the biggest decision he'd make about hockey. "There's nothing wrong with sleeping on a decision."

Even if they'd already discussed it for a few years now and he'd agreed it was time to retire only a few nights ago.

Logan exhaled as if he'd been holding his breath. "I don't know what I'd do without you, Selena."

"Let's hope you never have to find out," she teased.

Ted seemed to splutter into his wine glass, at a loss for words. He lowered his glass and refilled it. She didn't want to gloat, but still a victorious smile tugged at her lips.

"You need to be patient, Selena. This is a big decision, and we need to make sure it's the best one for Logan." Ted's voice was as smooth as a practiced salesman's pitch.

The guy was such a jerk, but she wasn't about to lose her temper. That was what Ted wanted. He'd been trying to get her to react for years.

"I know."

"Selena understands." Logan didn't miss a beat. "She only wants the best for me. The same as I want for her." He leaned over and kissed her.

"That's right." Selena took a sip of wine. And her instinct told her the best thing for Logan was to get him away from his shady agent. The sooner, the better.

After dinner, Selena arrived home before Logan since he needed to drop off Ted at his hotel. She kicked off her shoes in the mudroom and went into the kitchen to the windowsill where her succulents were. "Looks like Berry Lake is a go. You'll love it there. More sunny days."

She removed her phone to check her messages. The first one made her laugh.

> **TAMIKA:** *How was dinner with the slimy snake?*
> **SELENA:** *Ted doesn't want Logan to retire.*
> **TAMIKA:** *Nothing new. Do you think he'll talk Logan out of it again?*
> **SELENA:** *No. Logan said he would retire, and I believe him.*
> **TAMIKA:** *He's said that before.*
> **SELENA:** *This feels different.*
> **TAMIKA:** *Hope you're right.*
> **SELENA:** *Me, too. I can't go on like this.*
> **TAMIKA:** *You could, but Selena T wouldn't want to.*
> **SELENA:** *Truth. And I'm feeling more like Selena T every day.*

Selena didn't see any new messages on the Posse group chat. She took that to mean everything was going well, but she wanted to make sure. She typed a message.

> **SELENA:** *Just checking in. Any updates?*
> **JULIET:** *Nell is doing so much better. She's more like herself.*

BRIA: *I spoke to Jenny, and she hasn't heard anything about Missy. That's normal in situations like this, even if we all want news.*

SELENA: *Let's hope we hear something tomorrow.*

BRIA: *I drove past your lake house today. The renovations are going well.*

SELENA: *Yes! The contractor messaged me about that. I can't wait until we move to Berry Lake permanently.*

JULIET: *We can't wait to have you. So will this be Logan's final year?*

SELENA: *He hasn't made an official announcement, but you all will be stuck with us soon! I'll be on my way there for another trip after Logan leaves for his next away game.*

JULIET: *Can't wait to see you.*

SELENA: *How are you and Dalton, Bria?*

BRIA: *I haven't heard from him since Missy's arrest.*

SELENA: *I'm sorry. I thought things had changed after that.*

BRIA: *Me, too, but I'll just have to see what happens.*

JULIET: *I'm keeping her mind off things.*

BRIA: *And doing a great job. Plus I've taken on three more clients.*

SELENA: *That's wonderful. Have you spoken to Tamika, Juliet?*

JULIET: *Yes. Ezra's lawyer isn't playing nice, but she's handling it. Thank you for introducing me to her.*

SELENA: *She's not only a great friend, but a shark divorce attorney. You're in good hands.*

The garage door opened, and Selena's pulse skittered.

SELENA: *Logan just got home. TTYL.*

She plugged her phone into the charger on the counter and waited for Logan.

He entered the kitchen, his feet dragging a little as if he were sore from the game. "Sorry it took so long."

Selena kissed Logan. "Let me guess. Ted wanted to discuss your future."

"Yeah." Logan wrapped his arms around her. "Even though we discussed it earlier today. And yesterday."

"He doesn't want to lose his cash cow."

"Not a cow."

"Bull, then," she teased.

Logan laughed. "Ted's worried about my financial future."

She stepped back and motioned to the kitchen. "If we sold this place, we could live a long time off the profits. And we have all our other investments and savings and my company."

"I know, but he thinks of me as a son." Logan put his finger against her lip. "And before you say anything, I know I pay him. But I tend to see him as a father figure, too."

One who wasn't much better than his original dad, an alcoholic who used to beat Logan. His biological dad was a monster, but she got the feeling Ted was similar, only he dressed nicer and didn't punch Logan. "My gut tells me Ted isn't going down without a fight."

Logan embraced her. "Then it'll be two against one. We're a team."

She snuggled against his chest. He was so solid and strong. The scent of his soap tickled her nose. "Yes, we are."

He rubbed smoothing circles against her back. "Thank you for not agitating Ted. You surprised him."

"Not you?"

"I knew you wouldn't."

She kissed him. Hard. He tasted warm and salty with a hint of wine from the one rare glass he'd allowed himself earlier to celebrate the win. "I love you."

"I love you more." With a soft laugh, Logan pulled her hand to his lips. Desire lit his eyes. "Now, enough talk about the future. Let's head upstairs. We have more important things to do tonight."

"Laundry?"

He laughed. "Well, if by laundry, you mean me undressing you and tossing your clothes on the floor, then yes."

"Come on, big guy." She grabbed his hand and pulled him with her. "I have a feeling I won't look at laundry the same way after we're done."

chapter ten

WEDNESDAY MORNING, NELL woke feeling much better. Sunlight streamed through the blinds. JoJo must've forgotten to close them all the way when she'd left last night. Mom had wanted to stay overnight again, but Nell had said no. Her friends and family had been spending too much time there, including Gage, who'd been working from the waiting room. They had their own lives to live, and she was improving quickly, even if she was tired after the imaging, taking short walks around the floor, and a constant stream of visitors yesterday.

Nell yawned, and a sharp pain sliced through her abdomen. *Oh, man. That hurts.*

A good thing she hadn't needed to sneeze. So maybe she felt better, but she still had some more healing to do.

She glanced around the room. The IV drip continued, the narrow tube snaking along her arm, but her pain medication had been lessened, so she didn't feel as foggy or loopy. She'd alternated between the two at times. The bright floral arrangements contrasted against the stark beige walls that not even the natural lighting could make warmer. And her breakfast tray sat on the bedside stand. Guess no one had wanted to wake her.

She wasn't hungry but knew she needed to regain her strength if she wanted to go home—and that was all she wanted to do. Mr. Teddy needed her home, which was why she'd turned down offers to stay with Mom, Sabine and Max, and Bria and Juliet. Oh, Nell appreciated everyone wanting to help, but she could take care of herself, thank you very much.

"Oatmeal or Cream of Wheat?" She reached for a bowl and removed the plastic lid. "Of course it's not oatmeal."

Though what would have been even better was a cupcake. One of Missy's.

Nell's chest tightened. Clutching the bedsheet, she glanced at the ceiling, thinking of her friend only a few floors above her. But soon, everyone, including Welles would be out of there.

Nell forced herself to take three bites. Not bad, but she didn't want any more of that. She opened the container of yogurt—strawberry flavored. The first spoonful went down easy. The second one, not so much. Maybe she'd just drink the juice and tea.

The door opened, and Gage entered. He wore cargo shorts and a Henley and looked attractive as ever with his hair casually styled. He'd shaved, and his eyes seemed brighter today. Not as many bandages were on his hands and arms, and that made her happy. He was healing, too.

Carrying a shopping bag, he came to the side of her bed. "Good morning, beautiful."

"Hey." Her smile wasn't forced, so she took that as another good sign. "You're here early today."

"Am I your first visitor?"

"You are."

He pumped his fist. "Finally! I never thought I'd beat your mom."

"Well, she has some work to do today so she's going to drop by when she can."

"Then it's good I'm here." He kissed her cheek, which was sweet given her breath had to be rancid. "I brought you something."

"Thanks." Nell took the bag from him and looked inside. She did a double take. "Whoa. A cell phone."

"You don't have yours, correct?"

To be honest, she hadn't a clue where it was. "For all I know, it's still on that rock wall."

He grimaced slightly. "Well, you have one now. After you're out of the hospital, we'll get the number switched over and see if there's a way to retrieve what was on the old one, but at least this way you're not disconnected from people."

Nell's breath hitched. Tears stung her eyes. She blinked.

This was the longest she'd been without a cell phone. Not that she'd felt like calling anyone, but she missed having access to the Posse's group chat.

"This is…" Her voice cracked. She would have never expected Gage to do something like this. One of the Posse or her family, yes, but not him. She stared at the box in disbelief, but then warmth pooled at the center of her chest. Nell glanced up at him. "This is so sweet and perfect. I missed not having mine."

"In full transparency, I have an ulterior motive—a way to get in touch with you if I'm not here." He cupped her face gently. "But mainly, I know your friends mean a lot to you, and this way, you can contact them, too. I want to make you happy, Nell. I hope I have."

His sincerity wrapped around her heart like a well-worn quilt. "I'm happy."

Nell held the phone box against her chest. But was that enough?

Ugh. She wished the questions about him would just stop streaming through her brain so she could enjoy the moment with him.

As he glanced at the breakfast tray, a frown flickered on his lips. "How are you feeling?"

"Better than yesterday." She motioned to the food. "But I don't have much of an appetite."

Gage cradled her hand with a delicate touch and brushed his lips lightly over her knuckles, his gaze riveted on hers. "I don't blame you. That doesn't look appetizing at all. When do you think they'll let you out of here?"

"Possibly today, but I'm hoping by tomorrow at the latest."

"Eat a little more so they don't hold not eating against you. I want you home."

Hearing him say "home" was unexpected. That word was more her than Gage. He loved being out and about in nature, and though he had watched some movies with her, home to him seemed to be wherever adventure lay. Had the accident changed him?

"I want to be home."

"Same," he said, "but I have to go on a short work trip in a few days. I already spoke to my boss, and once I get back, I'll be working remotely as much as possible. I'm looking forward to cuddling with you on the couch and watching those rom-coms you love all day."

Gage was saying all the right words. He sounded like a real fiancé. Only how long would watching movies and hanging out at her place be enough for him?

Nell didn't want a marriage full of thrills. She longed for a partnership, companionship, and commitment that didn't involve an adrenaline rush. She needed to make sure Gage was on the same page. "Thanks."

Relief shone in his eyes. "We'll make sure you're comfortable."

As she nodded, her heart pounded against her rib cage. She needed to ask a question, but she didn't want to offend him. "I…"

"What?"

Her shoulders tensed. It was now or never. "I need to know something, but I don't want you to take it the wrong way."

"You can ask me anything." His warm voice comforted her. He gently squeezed her hand. "I'll answer it."

She swallowed hard, meeting his gaze. "Did you…did you propose to me because you felt guilty that I got hurt?"

Gage startled and then shook his head. "No, absolutely not. The accident just made me realize what's truly important. And that's you."

His answer provided some relief. "Thanks."

"Look." Gage leaned over the bed. "I know all of this is sudden, but everything became so clear that day. I want to spend the rest of our lives together, going on adventures, growing old together. Okay?"

His "going on adventures" brought a shiver, but she nodded. "I needed to know this is about us and not the accident." Her voice quivered with vulnerability and hope.

"It's us. You and me." Gage pressed his forehead against hers. "I promise, Nell. I love you. That's why I proposed. No other reason."

His words, heartfelt and gentle, hung in the air as he released her hand. Not trusting her voice, she nodded.

"Now eat," he urged. "I want you to get better so you can go home."

She took another bite of yogurt and swallowed. "There's something else I need to say."

"Shoot."

Nell blew out a breath. "I've only been pretending to be outdoorsy and athletic because I thought that's what you wanted. I didn't want to disappoint you that I'm more of a couch potato."

Gage blinked as if taken aback. But then his face softened. "Nell, knowing you'd do that for me makes me love you even more."

"You're not upset?"

"Nope." He didn't hesitate to answer. "We can do other things. Skiing, bungee jumping, skydiving…"

He meant to comfort her, but his words sent a wave of anxiety washing over her. The thought of more adrenaline-filled activities left her feeling unnerved and afraid. "Gotta be honest. Hearing that doesn't make me feel any better."

Gage's blue eyes searched hers. His lips opened as if realization had finally dawned. "I'm being an idiot. You were hurt doing something I wanted to do. Of course those things would scare you. But no matter what we do in the future, the most important thing is that we're together, right?"

"Right." But the word felt heavy on her tongue.

Pulling her close, Gage brushed a tender kiss across her lips. "I have a conference call, but I'll be back later. We can talk more then."

"Okay." Her gaze lingered on him as he left the room. The door clicked shut, and she stared at the glimmering engagement ring on her finger. The diamond seemed to mock her, or her attitude was so glum it felt like everything else was too.

Gage acted more like a fiancé than someone she hung out with, which was nice. He was doing the right things, too. Bringing her a phone was so thoughtful. But her heart weighed heavily in her chest and didn't seem convinced.

Nell believed in love at first sight. She'd been that way with Andrew. Her entire future had been so clear in her mind. Only he'd kept saying the timing wasn't right to get married with medical school and then his residency. He'd always had an excuse—ten years of excuses. But he hadn't hesitated when he met someone else. Nell's devotion and love to him for more than a decade hadn't mattered. He hadn't wanted to marry her. She'd been a placeholder, someone comfortable, until something better came along. That had been a hard truth to accept.

But she had.

Now Gage was doing what Andrew had done with that other woman by not waiting years, or even months, to propose. That had to count for something, right? And Gage hadn't hesitated when he told her the proposal had nothing to do with guilt. His response made her feel better. But was that enough? Was what they'd shared over the past month and a half enough to build a marriage—a life—upon, especially one filled with adventures she wasn't sure she wanted?

Unfortunately, Nell didn't know the answer.

The door opened again. Cami appeared in her scrubs and blond ponytail. She pointed at the cell phone box. "Wow. That's the latest model."

"A gift from Gage."

Her eyebrows shot up. "The guy keeps surprising me."

"Me, too."

Cami walked to the side of her bed. "I'm on break and thought we could take a walk. You need to be on your feet."

"I know," Nell admitted, even though her stomach was still tender from the surgery. "A change of scenery will be nice."

"We'll go slow." Cami helped Nell out of bed and wheeled the IV stand near her. "Your color looks better, and you're moving easier."

"Bet you say that to all the patients," Nell teased.

"Only my favorite ones."

Nell focused on putting one foot in front of the other, slowly making her way to the door and then out into the hallway. Walking wasn't pain free, but it didn't hurt as much as it had last night when she'd done a stroll around the surgical unit with Dad. "Which way?"

"Let's go to the right." Cami grinned. "We can poke our heads into Welles's room and say hi."

"If he's awake."

"Oh, I'm sure he is." She laughed and made sure Nell could navigate safely around a gurney. "He's been giving the nurses a hard time up here, so rumor has it they've been taking vitals every hour."

"Ouch." But Welles spent enough time at the hospital that he should know better. "I guess he's going to learn a lesson."

"Maybe a couple," Cami said mysteriously.

Nell must have been a little out of it still. That went right over her head. She glanced at her friend. "What do you mean by that?"

🧁 🧁 🧁

Being in the hospital sucked. Welles was supposed to keep his leg and his arm above his heart, but he couldn't get comfortable. It didn't help that the nurses had woken him up all night long. They'd even been smiling while torturing him.

Okay, taking vitals was far from torture, but they'd poked and prodded him way more than they had Monday night. He would have much rather been at the station. No matter how many runs they made overnight, he slept better there. Though he had a feeling it would be a while before he was at the station again. Or at home. He thought about what he and Dad had been told last night.

Welles needed someone with him at all times for the first week at least.

That wasn't possible for Dad, which Welles understood, or any of his friends, who all had jobs. And he didn't have a girlfriend, so that meant he would be leaving this hospital for another facility.

His cell phone buzzed. Somehow it had survived in his pocket when his left arm and leg both suffered fractures.

He glanced at the screen—a dating app notification.

Ignore it.

That was what he should do, given he wouldn't be able to drive for a long time. Dating made no sense. And his heart needed time to heal over Nell. He'd truly believed he had a chance with her. Sure, he'd never stopped dating for her, but he was just giving her time to see him as more than a friend. He always kept things casual to the extreme in case Nell ever agreed to go out with him. Now…

He swore under his breath, opened his phone, and read the message.

> **SKYEBLUEYES:** *Hey, what's going on? You disappeared on me.*
>
> **PARAMEDUDE:** *Hey. Sorry for not replying. Had a little accident.*
>
> **SKYEBLUEYES:** *Oh, good. I wasn't sure if you were ghosting me.*
>
> **SKYEBLUEYES:** *Not good that you were in an accident. You okay?*
>
> **PARAMEDUDE:** *I will be.*
>
> **SKYEBLUEYES:** *Doing firefighter stuff?*
>
> **PARAMEDUDE:** *Paramedic, but no. Climbing.*
>
> **SKYEBLUEYES:** *Ouch. Bet I could make you feel better.*
>
> **PARAMEDUDE:** *Bet you could, too, and I might take you up on it when I'm a little better.*
>
> **SKYEBLUEYES:** *You know where to find me. Don't be a stranger.*
>
> **PARAMEDUDE:** *I won't be. Thanks.*

Welles lowered his phone. The woman's photos were gorgeous, but they were still just talking. He hadn't wanted to move too quickly. Not while he'd waited to see what happened with Nell and Gage. He'd thought they would have ended by now because Gage was so not right for her. Welles wasn't sure how he had gotten this so wrong.

Maybe if Welles had tried another tactic instead of badgering Nell to go out with him every time he'd brought a patient to the ER, he'd have been the one engaged to her instead of Gage, who Welles didn't even like. The only reason he went out with them was to keep Nell safe. He didn't trust Gage, and man, did that prove to be true.

Welles stared at his leg and then his arm. He pushed away the sinking feeling in his gut. With rest and physical therapy, he'd be good as new soon. Nell would be okay, too. That was all that mattered to him.

He checked his messages and laughed at a video Jordan, his medic partner, had sent him. The next text said Jordan's wife would be making some freezer meals for Welles for when he got home.

Whenever that turned out to be. He tossed the cell phone on the bed.

The door opened. Cami poked her head in, her ponytail swinging forward. "Up for a couple of visitors?"

Maybe she had an update on Nell. "As long as you don't plan to take my blood pressure or temperature, you're welcome."

"I'll hold the door for Nell."

Nell? Welles couldn't sit up, but he quickly brushed his fingers through his hair. Whiskers covered his face, so there was nothing he could do about that now. He didn't know if Nell preferred facial hair or the clean-shaven look. That first guy, Andrew, the jerk who broke her heart, didn't have a beard. Gage didn't, either. A beard had never been an option for Welles because of his job. Facial hair got in the way of the respirator making a solid seal.

He inhaled. *Play it cool.*

Nell walked slowly into the room. Her hair was tangled as if she'd just rolled out of bed, which was likely the case, but her face had more color than when she'd visited him before. That time she'd been sitting in a wheelchair, so he hadn't gotten a good look at her. Today, she wore two hospital gowns, so she was fully covered, front and back, and the same hospital socks he wore on his good leg. He'd known her most of his life, and she'd never looked more beautiful.

Freaking butterflies flapped in his stomach. Okay, they usually did around her, but she was engaged to someone else. What he felt for her was nothing more than a crush. They would never be more than friends. Somehow, he would have to be satisfied with that.

She smiled at him, transforming the boring, cold hospital room into something bright and warm as the sun. "Hey, Paramedic Welles."

His temperature spiked ten degrees. A monitor beeped. *Uh-oh.* He needed to stay calm or those stupid machines would give him away. "Look at you, Nurse Nell. You're walking."

She nodded. "Getting in my morning laps."

"She's doing great," Cami agreed. "Might get to go home today. If not, tomorrow for sure."

Thank goodness. The relief washing through him made it hard to breathe, but he could see the two nurses waiting for him to say something.

"I'm jealous." He looked at her engagement ring. "Really jealous."

Nell didn't come as close to his bed as before and he missed that. But he had to remind himself she wasn't his, even if that was what he'd wanted for most of his life.

"You'll be there soon enough," she said.

If only… "Not sure about that."

Nell took a step toward him and then stopped. "What's going on?"

"No big deal." He wanted to downplay this to not worry her. "But I might have to go into SNF." Which sucked, but he didn't want to be a burden to anyone so going to a skilled nursing facility while he recovered made the most sense.

Lines formed around Nell's mouth, and he didn't want her to blame herself.

"It'll be easier this way," he added. "I'm sure I won't be there too long."

She nodded but didn't look convinced. "You need to make sure you don't overdo it, so you heal."

The concern in her voice smacked right into his heart. Man, he wished she cared for him in a way that wasn't just neighborly. Yes, they were friends, but despite his efforts, they'd never been more than that. "I won't. Healing is number one on my to-do list."

"Well, once we're both home, if you need anything, please let me know."

"I'd say the same to you, but I won't be much help for a few more weeks." *At least.* He hated that.

Her gaze softened. "You already did your part."

His heart thudded. Welles hadn't thought about what he was doing. He'd simply reacted to keep her safe. That had been his driving instinct, his only goal. "Wrong time, right place."

But his joke fell flat. It wasn't the first time.

"But I'd do it all again in a heartbeat."

A V formed above the bridge of her nose. "Even knowing you'd break bones and end up in an SNF and off work for weeks, maybe months?"

"Even then." It was too late to take his shot, but he could tell her something. "I care about you, Nurse Nell. And I wouldn't be able to live with myself if something happened to you on my watch."

Nell's mouth formed a perfect O, and no words came out.

He grinned. "Nothing to say."

"Dare I say, you've surprised both of us, Welles." Cami put her hand on Nell's shoulder. "Let's get you back to your room before you get too worn out."

Welles liked surprising Nell. He would try it again sometime.

chapter eleven

DALTON PARKED AT the curb in front of Bria's house. He turned off the ignition but didn't get out. Instead, he stared out the windshield and drummed his left thumb on the steering wheel. He'd comforted Bria after Missy's arrest, gotten dinner for her and Juliet, and then tucked in Bria when it was time for bed.

That was the last time they'd seen each other or spoken. Dalton hadn't replied to her Halloween text, and she hadn't sent more. He didn't blame Bria. Two of her friends were in the hospital for very different reasons, and that made him a jerk for not checking in with her, but what would he say?

Hey, have you gone no contact with your dad?

That wouldn't go over well.

Nor would telling her that Mom and Sal had paid off his car loan last Friday and offered to help him pay down the mortgage on the Pinewood Lane cottage Dalton would take possession of in January as well as give his company an exclusive opportunity to purchase the art gallery when the time came for Sal to sell. Dalton knew how much Mom valued her money. Her willingness to part with it and her assets proved how much she loved him and wanted him to be part of the family again. Something he hadn't been for years until recently.

Money and favors aside, he liked being back with his family.

Things were going well. He'd been staying at their house since leaving Bria's house on Wednesday. The abundance of alcohol they'd offered had helped him not think about Bria so much. He'd never been one for day drinking, but starting out each morning with a mimosa or Bloody Mary didn't suck. It quieted those dark thoughts of being alone and made him feel better.

Still, Dalton hadn't ignored his situation with Bria, and that was why he had a reason to be there now. He picked up the manila envelope on the passenger seat. Dalton hadn't looked at the report yet, but the PI said what had happened should be clearer based on what he'd found in the old police file.

Maybe this evidence would convince Bria that she needed to cut off her father. He hoped so.

Dalton slid out of the cab and made his way to the front door. The red and gold leaves signaling autumn were in full force, but the chill in the air suggested winter wasn't that far away. He was looking forward to spending Christmas with his family. It would be his first with them in more than a decade.

Through the front window, he saw Bria seated at the kitchen table, staring at a laptop. Dalton admired her industrious spirit, her pragmatic approach to her work, and her practicality on how she handled whatever came her way, but right now, he wished she would glance his way.

When she didn't, he pressed the doorbell.

She rose, headed to the door, and opened it. Her mouth dropped open. "Dalton?"

"Hey, Bria." Dalton's gaze lingered on her, his heart clenching at the sight of her. He'd missed her so much.

Her expression morphed from surprise to guarded apprehension. "What are you doing here?"

His fingers rubbed the back of his neck. "I, uh, wanted to talk about…us."

"Us?" Bria echoed, the question hanging in the air like a storm cloud. "You made it clear that day in the park there isn't an us. I thought you'd changed your mind after Missy's arrest, but then you ghosted me."

Dalton winced at her words, the harsh truth slicing through him like a knife. Mom had forced a wedge between him and Bria when they'd been in high school. Then, he'd done what he'd thought Dad would have wanted as well as at the park, but now…

"The last thing I want is for history to repeat itself. That's why I'm here." Only he didn't want to talk about this under the watchful gazes of her neighbors. Gossip in Berry Lake was bad enough without adding to it himself. "Can I come in?"

Bria hesitated, clutching the door handle until her knuckles turned white. She bit her lip.

He had never expected to be stuck standing on her welcome mat, but he remembered her face that day in the park. Yeah, he had some groveling to do. "Please."

"Okay." She opened the door wider and motioned him inside.

He sat on the sofa as he'd done so many times before and expected her to join him. She, however, sat on the chair.

Probably deserve that. Dalton exhaled. He forced himself not to wrinkle the envelope. "Where's Juliet?"

"At Nell's. She and Charlene are making sure everything's ready for Nell to come home from the hospital tomorrow."

"Glad to hear she'll be released." He rubbed his palms against his pants. "That's good."

Bria clasped her hands in her lap. "What did you want to say?"

"I know things seem complicated, if not impossible, right now." The desperation in his voice made him cringe. Still, he kept going. "But I want to see if there's a way through this."

"I wish I could believe that, Dalton. But how can we move forward when your loyalty lies with your mom who hates my dad and by default me?"

Dalton's heart seized at her resigned tone. "I didn't mean to hurt you." He reached out toward her, his hand hanging between them as if in a silent plea. The words that had been stuck in his throat begged to come out. "I love you, Bria. I always have. But I also love my mom, and I want to believe she's changed after all these years."

"Changed?" Bria's bitter laugh was devoid of any real humor. "Deena's doing the same thing she did back when we were in high school, tearing us apart because of her grudge against my parents. How has she changed?"

His mother's actions were too familiar, too painful. But Mom was different. She never would've given him money or spent hours being with him. She was so much sweeter to Sal than any of her previous ex-husbands.

"She's changed," he said, "and I'm sorry for hurting you. I want to be with you, and I believe she'll come to accept us together. I'll do whatever it takes. Being without you has been hard."

Bria's gaze locked with his, their shared history reflecting in her eyes. A single tear slipped down her cheek. As his chest tightened, she brushed it away. "You know what's been hard? Having two of my best friends facing horrible situations and not having someone to hold me while I cry and tell me they'll be okay."

He stared at his shoes. "I'm sorry I wasn't here for you."

"You didn't even call."

No, and telling her he'd spent the weekend buzzed or drunk wouldn't help his cause, even if it had made getting through the days easier.

"I know, and I'm sorry for that, too. But I'm here now. I hired a PI." He waved the envelope. "I thought we could review the report together. The guy said what he found should clear up some of our questions."

"Why did you hire a private investigator?"

"To see if I could find something—anything—that happened in Hayden Lake, so we can be together. Please look at this with me."

Bria shrugged. "I'm willing to look at the report, but you've hurt me. I'm not promising anything more than that."

Relief swamped him. "That's enough." *For now.* "I really meant what I said about making this work. Whatever it takes."

"Including going all-in with me, if it comes to that? And that's a big *if* right now."

That was more than Dalton had expected to get. He wouldn't blow the chance if she gave it to him.

"I'm willing." He patted the cushion next to him. "Come over here, and let's see what's inside."

Dalton showing up out of the blue was unexpected, and Bria had to keep from letting herself think something had changed between them. She appreciated him hiring someone to look for proof from thirty years ago—talk about a needle in a haystack. Maybe she would get some closure and be able to share information with Dad, but she wanted—needed—to protect her heart. A person could only take so much, and right now, with everything going on with Missy and Nell, her nerves were on edge.

No matter what Dalton said, she didn't believe Deena had changed. The woman wasn't capable of it.

Still, Bria read over the list of items in the report the PI had included. "I don't see a smoking gun on this list."

"No, but this is way more than I expected him to find."

Papers covered the coffee table. Some were newspaper clippings. Others were more official looking documents, including police reports.

Dalton's forehead creased. "Look at this."

She leaned closer, trying to ignore how good having her thigh against his felt. Like it or not, she missed being with him. "What?"

"A gas station receipt."

He showed her a piece of paper. The receipt was a photocopy, but it seemed to have been wet and then dried at some point. That would make sense with the car going into the lake.

She remembered something. "My dad mentioned my mom stopped at one."

"Your mom filled up the car and bought a soda pop and a toy." Dalton's gaze met hers. His lips twisted. "Why would Molly do that if she was planning to kill herself?"

Bria had had this same conversation with Dad. This was the smoking gun, only she'd already heard that story, so why hadn't it jumped out when she read the report? She straightened. "My dad is telling the truth. She was planning to come home to us."

Dalton said nothing, but he stared at the receipt as if trying to see if it were real or not.

She recalled something else from the report and sorted through the papers until she found the police report and pointed at a photo and then a hand-drawn diagram. "Look at this. They mention an animal and swerving. See how they drew the road with the tire tracks and the lake? The way the car swerved, she didn't just gun the accelerator and drive off the road into the water."

Dalton rubbed his neck. "That's a weird angle."

Not if a car didn't purposely drive into the lake. The pieces clicked together in her mind. She didn't need to look at anything else. "Everything the PI found supports what my dad told me. You see that, right?"

"I wasn't expecting to find any of this."

"It contradicts what your mom said."

He reread the report again. "There must be an explanation for that."

At least Dalton wasn't shutting the proof down, but the way he kept shifting on the couch told her what the PI had found was a surprise. And that meant one thing—he'd expected his mom to be vindicated, and he was trying to prove his side right again, not discover the truth.

She took a breath. "If you meant what you said earlier about us getting back together, we'll never be able to see where we are as a couple until we clear up what Deena's been saying about my parents."

He bit his lip. "We need to settle this. Want to go now and ask her?"

Bria glanced at her laptop. She could finish her work later. Nothing was due to her client until tomorrow afternoon, and even though he'd hurt her, she wanted to get back with Dalton. She loved him. "I do."

"I have to be in Portland tonight. Do you mind driving yourself so I can take off from there?"

"I don't mind." She thought it might be better that way depending on how Deena reacted. Dalton might have to do some damage control before his mother accepted Bria once and for all. "But this proof should be enough to stop her from interfering with us anymore."

"I won't let her come between us," he said earnestly.

A spark of hope ignited within her. He sounded so sincere. Even though she should know better, Bria wanted to believe him with her whole heart. She would be lying if she didn't admit she wished she would be getting a proposal like Nell. Yes, it was too soon given their situation, but wishes didn't always make sense. "I'll see you there."

Fifteen minutes later, Bria parked her car next to Dalton's. She didn't want to go into Deena's house all bright and bubbly, but Bria couldn't help but smile. She had to give him credit for hiring the private investigator. Now they would finally get past everything and be together. She couldn't wait to get their relationship back on track.

Dalton carried the manila envelope, but he didn't appear as happy as she was.

Bria understood. He thought the proof would support his mom, not her father. "You okay?"

He nodded. "I'm still a bit surprised."

"Thank you for looking more into this." She touched his arm. He'd done this for them and their future, even if he'd thought they'd find something that supported Deena's lies. "It means so much to me."

When they reached the front door, he didn't ring the bell or knock. He opened the door and walked right in.

Guess things have changed since the last time I was here.

She followed him toward the back. A hockey game played on the TV. Sal and Owen sat on the couch. Two bottles of wine sat next to wine glasses on the coffee table. She glanced at the kitchen and saw another wine bottle that appeared to be empty.

Owen's eyes were glassy, his face flushed. He refilled his glass, his hand shaking. "Yo, bro. Didn't expect you to bring her home. Someone's going to end up in the penalty box."

"Hello, Dalton. Bria." Sal's words slurred. "We're watching hockey and enjoying happy hour. Care to join us? I can open another bottle of wine. The cellar is full of them."

"Open another anyway. This one's almost empty." Owen laughed and then burped. "We've had a few."

It wasn't even dinnertime and both men appeared plastered. She took a step back.

Sal filled two of the empty glasses sitting on the table. It appeared they kept a supply handy. He handed one to Dalton.

He took it and sipped. "Thanks."

Bria waved Sal off. "No, thanks. I have work to do tonight."

Dalton drank more. "Where are Mom and Ian?"

Owen swayed. "Ian's at a study group at the library. Kid's turned into a nerd."

Sal downed the remainder of his glass and refilled it. "Your mother's in the library reading. She got bored with the game."

"Come on." Dalton held on to the envelope with one hand and his wine glass with the other, and Bria followed him down a hallway. The door was ajar, so he pushed it open. "Hey, Mom."

Deena brightened and lowered her book. She saw Bria and frowned. "I didn't expect you to bring home company tonight."

Bria glanced at him, not knowing if she should say anything. He shook his head slightly.

Alrighty then. She would be quiet.

Dalton handed her the envelope. "We wanted to ask you about some things we found."

Deena rolled her eyes and placed the envelope on her lap. "I thought we already went through everything."

He stared over the rim of his glass. "We found a few more things. Would you please look at them?"

Every time he said "we," Bria's hope kept growing. Yes, Dalton had hurt her, but he'd seen the evidence and knew what Dad said was true. Brian Landon would finally be vindicated, and the Dwyers wouldn't be able to make up lies about him or Molly. Bria and Dalton would finally be together.

"What things?" Deena's response was cool, dismissive. She set her book aside, crossing her arms defensively.

"About what happened in Hayden Lake." Dalton's voice sounded strained. "It raises some questions about what you told me."

Deena scoffed. "Don't tell me you're taking her side again. I thought we were past that."

"Mom—"

"Fine." Deena removed the paperwork from the envelope and scanned the pages. "What questions does this raise?"

Dalton downed his wine and set the empty glass on a nearby table.

Bria fought the urge to reach out to Dalton. The one thing she could do was speak up for them. "Like why Molly would stop at a gas station to fill up the car, buy herself a can of pop, and a toy for me if she was planning to kill herself."

Deena shook her head. "You have no proof."

Dalton motioned to the paperwork. "I hired a PI. He got access to the police records and made copies. The receipt is there."

Deena glanced at the report and then shoved everything at Dalton. "Someone is lying, and it wasn't your father."

Oh, no. Bria hadn't expected Deena to doubt their proof. "How do you explain what was in the police records?"

"Whoever was digging for evidence got confused," Deena said in a matter-of-fact tone.

Dalton showed her the photo and the sketch of the accident. "If you look at how the car went into the water, it doesn't add up to what Dad told you."

Deena's face reddened. "Are you calling your father a liar?"

"No," Dalton replied quickly. "Dad would never lie. But Bria and I need to know the truth about what happened."

"I told you what happened, and this needs to stop right now, Dalton Paul Dwyer." Deena pointed at Dalton. "How do you even know your so-called proof is real? What if it's from some other accident or completely made up?"

"It matches what my father told me," Bria offered.

Deena snorted. "Which explains everything. Brian must have found a way to plant evidence."

Bria wouldn't let anyone talk about her father that way. "No. My—"

"Oh, don't you try to defend Brian Landon." Deena's gaze pinned Bria. "We all know exactly what your father is and what he isn't."

Dalton clenched his fists. "Mom—"

"No, Dalton." Deena shook her head as if to emphasize the point. "This has gone on for far too long. Sal and I have welcomed you back into the family. Having you here this past week has been wonderful. That's why we paid off your car and want to give you so much. But now you bring her into our home to sully your father's reputation…"

Bria didn't quite understand what was going on. It almost sounded like Deena was trying to buy Dalton's loyalty, but she knew that wouldn't work. He would never fall for that. "We just want to—"

"I know, Mom," Dalton said, interrupting her. "I'm grateful, but Bria deserves to know the truth."

"I told you the truth, but you're letting your heart get in the way." Deena's gaze bounced between Dalton and Bria. "I didn't want to have to do this, but you've left me no choice. It's time for you to make a choice."

Bria's stomach dropped to her feet.

His face paled. "What do you mean?"

"Choose, Dalton." Deena's demand came out ice cold. "Choose between your family or this girl who's only brought trouble to our lives."

"No," Bria whispered.

"Get out." Deena dismissed Bria as if she were a bothersome gnat. "Now."

"Mom…" Dalton choked. "You can't be serious."

Deena remained unmoved. She didn't even blink.

Bria stood frozen. She wanted to take a step back, but she couldn't.

Deena's face hardened. "I am quite serious. But before you make your choice, consider what your father would do in this situation." The finality in her tone echoed through the library.

The anguish on Dalton's face tore at Bria's heart. Deena was asking him to make an impossible choice, but his mother had stacked the odds in her favor by mentioning his dad. Still, Bria hoped he picked her.

"Mom." Dalton's voice cracked. "I…"

Me. Bria had to be the choice. Dalton had seen the proof. He knew Dad was telling the truth.

"I can't choose," he said finally. "I…can't."

Huh? The ground beneath Bria's feet shifted. How could he have not chosen her?

Deena grinned, victorious. "Well done. No choice is a choice. And in this case, the correct one based on how defeated *she* looks right now. Please see *her* out. She's not welcome here."

With that, Deena sauntered out of the room like a queen on the way to a beheading.

Get out of here. But Bria's feet remained rooted in place, a cold shiver of realization creeping up her spine. She forced herself to breathe.

"Are you okay?" Dalton's voice came out strangled, thick with pain and regret. He stood next to her, but he might as well have been in another room.

"Am I okay?" Bria echoed his words, her voice barely above a whisper, hollow and broken like her heart. She turned toward him, her vision blurring with unshed tears. "No. No, I'm not okay."

The expression on Dalton's face was etched with guilt and helplessness, making her heart tighten further in her chest. "I'm sorry."

Sorry? She didn't understand. "You've seen the proof. How could you not choose us?" Bria's voice wavered, each word a painful stab to her own heart.

Dalton's hands, once a source of comfort to her, hung useless by his sides. "It's an impossible choice. I want you, and I want my family. Please, don't make this any harder than it already is."

She shook her head, a bitter laugh escaping her lips. "You think this is hard for you? You're not the one who keeps getting abandoned by the same person!"

"I didn't abandon you."

"You didn't choose me."

"I'm trying to do what's right. You know how much my dad means to me."

Her heart shattered a little more. She tried to keep the tears at bay. "I do, but your loyalty is misplaced, Dalton. I guess it always has been. Your mom's right. No choice is a choice in this case. I didn't want to believe it, but everything is so clear now."

His jaw jutted forward.

"Goodbye, Dalton." Somehow, she managed to move her feet and headed to the entryway. "I hope you and your family have a happy life together. Don't contact me again."

Bria turned and walked away, not stopping to see if he was following her. It wouldn't matter if he did. Nothing he said would change things.

Even with the proof he'd paid for, Deena Dwyer DeMarco had won.

Again.

Bria opened the front door and walked out. The cold night air enveloped her, its chill seeping into her bones and mirroring the ice settling in her heart.

Tears blurred her vision. She'd given Dalton her heart only to have it returned broken and battered too many times.

"Never again." Her words, a promise to herself, rang clear. There would be no more pain, no more betrayal. "Never again."

☕ chapter twelve ☕

A S THE SUN went down, making Nell's apartment darker inside, Juliet helped Charlene prepare the place for when Nell came home tomorrow. Juliet turned on a lamp even though they wouldn't be there much longer. She and Charlene had moved furniture to make it easier for Nell to get around and made a bed on the couch in case she wanted a change of scenery. They'd changed the bedding, washed the other sheets, and hung clean towels in the bathroom. Every surface sparkled. Food filled the cabinets, and a few meals that could easily be heated sat in the refrigerator.

Not that they planned to leave Nell alone. Charlene also made a schedule and stuck a copy to the refrigerator door. Someone would be either with Nell or on call and close enough to help if she needed something at any time.

Juliet washed her hands. "Anything left to do tonight?"

Charlene checked her list. "Looks like we're done. Thank you for your help."

"I'm happy to help you and Nell." That was the least Juliet could do after her friends had helped her escape from Ezra.

"Sabine's bringing Mr. Teddy back tomorrow. She has a key. I'm sure Nell will want to see him right away."

"She claims to just be fostering the cat, but I doubt anyone could pry him out of her hands." With a smile, Juliet picked up her purse. "Let me know if you need anything else. And I'll confirm everyone knows their shift."

"Thank you." Charlene tucked a stray strand of hair behind her ear. "I swear I've aged ten years this week between the accident and the engagement."

"Stop," Juliet chided as she took in Charlene's designer outfit. Not exactly what people normally wore to do housework in, but her boss never did what most expected. "You look ten years younger."

Charlene smoothed her skirt, which didn't need smoothing. "Thank you. That's sweet of you to say."

"It's the truth. In fact, you look so nice you should hit the town tonight."

"I sort of am. The girls and I are going to see Nell tonight since Gage has something work-related." Charlene removed her keys from her purse. "Do you have plans?"

"Roman texted me earlier and asked if I could spend some time with Katie tonight." He planned to have a talk with Heather, which Juliet was all for. "We're going out to eat."

"Let me guess... Lago Bacca."

"You know me well." She could never get enough of the delicious Italian food. She opened the door and stepped outside.

Charlene followed, closed the door, and locked it. "I'll see you tomorrow."

Juliet would be hosting a tea for the historical society so Charlene could drive Nell home. "Have fun with your girls tonight."

"You, too."

As Juliet walked away from Nell's place, she inhaled the crisp autumn air. The only thing missing: the scent of pumpkin spice. Juliet wanted to celebrate since Nell would be out of the hospital tomorrow and the day after Missy would be released.

On her way to the restaurant, Juliet took in the golden leaves on the trees and the ones that had fallen to the ground. A squirrel ran across the sidewalk and disappeared into a bush. A few jack-o'-lanterns remained on front porches, but those were the only reminders of October.

Soon, it would be Thanksgiving time. And this year, she would have so much to be thankful for. Most importantly, her friends and little Lulu.

When she reached Main Street, she enjoyed the autumn-themed window displays. The sidewalks weren't as crowded as on a weekend, but several were out enjoying the clear, fall evening.

Juliet loved everything about Berry Lake. Even though her marriage had failed, she blamed Ezra, not herself. She'd done everything humanly possible to be a good wife. His infidelity was on him, which showed her how far she'd come in such a short time.

She crossed the street to Lago Bacca. Even though she'd eaten this on Sunday night with leftovers the next day, Katie loved the pasta.

"Juliet!" Katie yelled.

Juliet turned toward the sound to see Katie and Roman walking her way. Katie bounced with each step, and Roman smiled at her. He wore a long-sleeved dress shirt and nice pants, something he'd worn on one of their dates last month.

Don't think about that. She forced a smile. "Are you ready to eat?"

Katie nodded. "I still haven't decided what I want for dinner, but I want that Neo ice cream for dessert."

"Neapolitan," Juliet told her. "And you can have two if you want."

"One dish." Roman shook his head. "I don't want any cavities."

Katie rolled her eyes. "I brush my teeth and floss, Uncle Roman."

"One dish is better than none." Juliet looked at him. "Should I keep Katie at my house when we're finished?"

"That would be great, unless I'm finished before you," he said.

"We'll see if there are any lights on inside." Katie sounded like they'd done this before. "If not, you can pick me up at Juliet and Bria's."

Roman stared at his niece and then shook his head. "You remind me so much of your mom."

Katie beamed brighter than the marquee at the theater across the street. "Thank you."

Juliet recognized his grief, but she hoped he knew how much that compliment meant to Katie. "We should go in so your uncle won't be late."

As Katie's smile disappeared, Roman touched her shoulder. "I'll see you in a couple hours."

Juliet had a feeling Katie was worried about what Heather might say to her uncle. "Let's get some pasta."

Katie sighed. "And garlic bread?"

"Of course." Juliet glanced at Roman, who stared at them. "Don't worry. I've got her."

He rubbed the back of his neck. "I see that. Thanks."

⁂

The warm, cozy ambiance of Lago Bacca made it easy for Juliet to pretend she'd been transported to Italy. The flicker of candlelight cast shadows on the red brick walls adorned with paintings of Venetian landscapes. Red-and-white-checkered tablecloths covered rustic wooden tables, and the scent of garlic and herbs wafted in the air, mingling with the soft notes of a mandolin playing in the background.

Juliet sat across from Katie, who twirled her fork in her spaghetti with the focus of a neurosurgeon. "Do you like your dinner?"

She glanced up. "I love it! How is yours?"

"The lasagna is amazing. It's my favorite dish here."

"My favorite is the garlic bread."

Juliet dabbed her mouth with a napkin. "That's my second favorite."

"I can see that." Katie returned to her spaghetti.

Juliet smiled, happy to see the girl enjoying herself. "Tell me about your day. Did anything interesting happen?"

Katie took a deep breath as if ready to spill the day's events. "Well, I got an A on my math test! And then during PE, we played soccer. My team didn't win, but it was fun."

"An A on your math test is amazing, Katie. You should be very proud of yourself." Juliet's smile widened; she loved seeing the bright light inside Katie shine. "I'm glad you enjoyed your day."

Katie lifted her eyebrows. "What about you, Juliet? How was your day?"

Lonely. Not really, but Juliet had been stressed about money, her impending divorce, Missy, and Nell. "I worked on a tea I'm hosting tomorrow. I made favors and packed up everything I'll need. I also helped my boss before I came here."

"I loved the tea party you did for me."

The book-themed event had been perfect. "So did I. Tomorrow's is for adults, and unfortunately, no costumes like yours."

"Bummer, but I'm sure it'll be great since you're in charge."

Warmth flowed through Juliet's veins. "Thank you."

Katie set her fork on her plate. "Do you think my uncle is going to talk to Heather about sending me to boarding school on their date tonight?"

"I'm sure he'll tell you when he does." Juliet didn't like the way Katie hunched her shoulders. "Have you been thinking about that?"

Katie lowered her gaze and nodded. "Uncle Roman told me he'd talk to Heather, but he's never mentioned it again."

"It's only been a couple of days. He might need time."

"I'd just like to know. In case I should start packing."

Juliet cringed. If Roman didn't discuss this with Heather tonight, something would need to be said. Living with the unknown couldn't be healthy for Katie given all the other changes in her life. "If he doesn't mention anything to you, I'll speak with him again. Okay?"

The corners of Katie's mouth lifted. "Okay." Not all the tension disappeared, but Katie seemed a little lighter.

That made Juliet feel better. She leaned over the table. "Ready for dessert?"

As Juliet walked home with Katie, the glow of streetlights illuminated their way. Juliet forced herself not to look at the cupcake shop. It was too painful to think of that place with Missy in the hospital. Nell, too. She focused on the coffee shop.

Katie kept walking faster. The temperature had dropped, but they both wore coats. Still Juliet didn't want her to catch a chill. "Cold?"

"No, I just want to see if Uncle Roman is home yet."

Juliet wondered if Katie had been putting on a brave face during dinner. No one could blame the girl for wanting answers. "If not, you can help me with Lulu."

Katie nodded. "Maybe Butterscotch will let me rub him."

The cat was picky about when he'd accept rubs, but he never bit or scratched anyone. "Worth a shot."

As they turned onto their street, Katie gasped. "Uncle Roman's car is in the driveway."

"Did he drive you to the restaurant?"

"Yes. I think because of where he was meeting Heather for dinner." Katie walked faster but then stopped suddenly. "Oh, she might be inside."

The quiver in her voice hurt Juliet's heart. She put her arm around Katie. "Want me to go inside with you?"

Katie's eyes widened. "Would you?"

"Of course." The answer came automatically, even though Heather was someone Juliet had avoided in school. But if she could face her bully soon-to-be-ex-husband, she could face anyone.

What has he been doing?

As Roman sat in the living room, he stared at the half-completed jigsaw puzzle on the coffee table that he'd been working on with Katie. He could make out part of the basket of puppies that she'd thought were so cute. He nearly laughed. Dogs—puppies, even—had more brains than he did.

How could I have been so foolish?

If not for Juliet speaking up, he might have made the biggest mistake of his life. No, the second one. The first was acting like a jealous idiot and making Juliet reassess their relationship. And now...

He scrubbed his face and then stared at the photograph of Katie and her parents that sat on the fireplace mantel.

Sis, I screwed up. I wish you were here. You would know how to handle this with Katie. You were such a good mom.

And he was a poor substitute for a parent.

Too bad he was all Katie had, which meant it was time to do better.

Roman straightened. A quick glance at his phone showed no texts from Juliet or Katie. Not that he expected any, but...

The house was so quiet—too quiet—without Katie. He didn't know how long her dinner would take, but he would use the time alone to think about what he would say to his niece.

I'm sorry would be a good start.

The front door opened. Katie entered followed by Juliet, who closed the door behind her.

Katie glanced around the living room. "Is Heather here?"

The hint of fear in her voice sliced into Roman like a scalpel. He stood. "No. She's not."

Juliet touched Katie's shoulder. "I'll go now."

"Stay," he and Katie said in unison.

Juliet jolted as if surprised by the request. "Okay."

"Why don't you both sit?" Roman motioned to the couch. "There's something I want to say."

Katie glanced at Juliet with a worried expression.

"It's nothing bad," he added to keep his niece from becoming upset.

The two sat, though Katie fidgeted. Roman didn't blame her, given how badly he'd handled the situation with Heather.

He blew out a breath and sat, not wanting to tower over them. "First, I want to thank both of you for coming to me with your concerns about Katie being sent to boarding school. Please don't hesitate to talk to me about anything, Katie."

She nodded. "Juliet told me I should."

"Juliet was correct." He smiled at Katie, and then his gaze went to Juliet. "I appreciate you following up with me so I took Katie's concern seriously."

She touched Katie's shoulder. "Just trying to help out."

"I know." He wished Juliet could always be there. She understood Katie and him in a way Heather didn't. That had been clear tonight. "And I'm sorry I needed you to say something. Katie's words should have been enough."

Katie straightened. "Now you know."

"I do." He took a breath. "I spoke to Heather tonight about the boarding school. You weren't mistaken, Katie. Heather wanted to send you away."

Katie's lower lip quivered, but she didn't shrink away. She lifted her chin. "Told you so."

"You did," he said firmly. "And I told Heather that would never, *ever* happen."

Katie's jaw dropped. "I get to stay in Berry Lake?"

He hated that she was so surprised, but that was on him. "Yes. You're staying with me, kiddo. Just know, you're stuck with me. Even after you graduate college, I expect you to come home for the holidays at the bare minimum."

"Yay!" Katie cheered. "Did you hear, Juliet?"

Juliet beamed. "I did."

"I also wanted you to know I'm no longer dating Heather." The breakup had been mutual once Heather learned that Katie had been the beneficiary of her parents' estate and not Roman. Heather had thought veterinarians made as much as surgeons, which wasn't true, at least not in his case. "I've decided to take a break from dating."

He had healing to do and grief to work through.

Katie leaned forward, her gaze earnest. "Are you okay, Uncle Roman? Breakups can be rough."

Juliet appeared to be hiding a smile.

He loved Katie so much. "They can, but this is what's best for me." And one hundred percent what was best for her. "I made a mistake by trying to rush things. I thought you needed a family."

Katie's face scrunched. "I have a family. You and Juliet."

Juliet's wide eyes met his. She swallowed and put her arm around Katie's shoulders. "You do have your uncle and me."

If only they could be a family, and twice now, his rushing things had messed things up. "The problem was I didn't understand that 'family' had different meanings. I was thinking more along the lines of you having a mother-figure and sister."

"Oh, no. I don't need those." Katie bit her lip. "But I know you might want that. And that's okay, but don't do it for me."

"You're very smart for a twelve-year-old," Juliet said.

Roman nodded. "Takes after her parents."

Katie gazed up at him with an expression full of love. "And my uncle."

He had to force the words out of his tight throat. "Thank you. And I promise to do better."

Katie jumped to her feet and held out her arms. "Group hug."

Roman went over to her and hugged her.

"Come on, Juliet," Katie urged.

Juliet stood and joined in, and he wrapped his other arm around her. Her light floral fragrance brought back memories of their embraces and kisses. He understood why she needed time and didn't want a romantic relationship with him, but he would cherish that time they'd had.

"This is all the family I need," Katie announced.

Even if this didn't match what Roman thought Katie needed, it was more than enough.

For now.

chapter thirteen

C UPCAKE POSSE GROUP Chat…

JULIET: *Jenny says there's still no word from Missy, but she's out on Thursday. And Nell gets sprung tomorrow!*

NELL: *Thanks for helping my mom get my apartment ready, Juliet.*

SELENA: *I wish I'd been there to help.*

JULIET: *It didn't take long.*

NELL: *I'm so excited to go home, but I feel so guilty about Welles.*

SELENA: *What's going on with him?*

NELL: *There's no one to care for him, so he'll have to go to a facility until he's better.*

JULIET: *That's too bad.*

NELL: *I asked my mom if she could help him, but she has to work. That's Buddy's problem.*

SELENA: *Wait. You're neighbors, right?*

NELL: *Yes. He lives next door to me.*

SELENA: *You and Welles can recover together. We've already worked out a schedule for you.*

NELL: *Yes, that makes sense, and I'd feel better. But I don't have a guest room. I could give him my room and sleep on the couch.*

SELENA: *No couch.*

JULIET: *Charlene bought an inflatable mattress for whoever was staying with you, but that wouldn't be good for someone trying to heal.*

SELENA: *Why don't we get walkie talkies?*

JULIET: *What if he falls and wasn't near the device to press the button? A baby monitor system might work better. Welles can spend the day with you and sleep at home. If he needs something, he just calls out and whoever's with Nell can go over to his place.*

SELENA: *Yes! That would work!*

JULIET: *What do you think, Nell?*

NELL: *I like the idea. I've been feeling guilty about everything that's happened.*

SELENA: *Don't!*

JULIET: *Listen to Selena T.*

SELENA: *Always. Wait. Where's Bria?*

JULIET: *In bed. She said I could tell you guys what happened earlier.*

NELL: *What? Is it her dad or Molly?*

SELENA: *Spill now.*

JULIET: *Dalton hired a PI, who proved that Brian has been telling the truth about Molly's accident.*

SELENA: *That's great. Now they can be together.*

NELL: *Finally!*

JULIET: *That's what she thought, but then Deena said the evidence was fake, told him to choose between his family or Bria, and asked what his dad would do in this situation.*

SELENA: *I can't believe he would choose his family over Bria.*

NELL: *No way. Even if he's been a jerk lately, he seemed to really care about her.*

JULIET: *He didn't choose his family.*

NELL: *Thank goodness.*

JULIET: *Dalton said he couldn't make a choice. Which Deena took as a win and kicked Bria out of the house.*

SELENA: *Ugh! So he still made a choice by not choosing.*

JULIET: *Yep. And Bria said this was the last time. She's heartbroken, and she's adamant she won't put herself through this again.*

NELL: *I don't blame her.*

SELENA: *Anything we can do?*

JULIET: *She needs time. I'm going to try making her some cupcakes, but they won't be as good as Missy's.*

NELL: *Any cupcake will help. But I'm truly surprised. I really thought Dalton had come around after he showed up at Elias's office.*

SELENA: *Me, too. I never knew his family meant that much to him.*

JULIET: *Bria says it's new. And he was so sweet to us that night of Missy's arrest. Got us dinner. Tucked her in.*

NELL: *Loser. And now I can't wait to get out of here so I can cheer her up.*

SELENA: *Same. I'll be there in a couple days. I want to cheer up you and Missy, too.*

JULIET: *Speaking of which, you know what Missy would say right about now…*

NELL: *Cupcake Posse Forever!*

SELENA: *Cupcake Posse Forever!*

JULIET: *Cupcake Posse Forever!*

The next morning, Welles tried to keep a smile on his face as he spoke to Nell, who'd come to say goodbye. He was happy about Nell getting out of the hospital, but that meant she wouldn't be coming to his room anymore to visit. He enjoyed spending time with her when they weren't working or with…Gage.

"What time will you be discharged?" he asked.

"They think around eleven."

"That's great." But he was green with envy. "Is your mom picking you up?"

She nodded. "I'm not sure if anyone else will be here."

Someone else *should* be there. "What about Gage?"

Nell shook her head. "He has a work thing."

If it was Welles, he would have canceled the work thing or taken the day off if his fiancée was getting out of the hospital.

Who was he kidding? He wouldn't have thought twice about doing that for Nell.

"So…" She blew out a breath.

He glanced at her left hand. The stupid ring was still there. "Something wrong?"

"Not wrong. But remember how we agreed to help each other out on Monday?"

Welles nodded. "I'll always do what I can for you, Nell. I hope you know that."

"I do." She didn't hesitate to answer. "And I want to do the same for you."

He tried to understand what she meant. Tried and failed. "What do you mean?"

"Don't go to an SNF to recover. Come home. You can stay with me during the day. My friends and family already have signed up for spots to help me out, and none will mind having two patients."

His mouth gaped. "Are you serious?"

"One hundred percent," she said without hesitating. "It was Selena's idea and a good one."

The idea of not being stuck at another facility appealed to him, but being able to spend that much time with Nell was the best part. Except… His shoulders sagged. "That's during the day. I might need help at night."

"Someone will be staying at my place each night, too. They can help you get in bed at your apartment until I'm able to do that myself, and we can use a monitor in case you need something in the middle of the night. Our places are closer than some nurse stations are to rooms."

Everything she said was true, and he was grateful for her thinking of this, but… "What about Gage?"

"What about him?"

Oh, sweet Nell. Welles would have to spell it out. "Do you think he'll mind us spending the days together?"

"Why would he mind?"

Because if you were mine, I wouldn't want someone like me hanging around you all day. "You're engaged now. Gage might be the jealous type."

She shook her head. "We've known each other our entire lives. And he likes you, or he wouldn't have invited you out with us. It won't be a problem."

Welles wasn't as confident as she sounded, but hey, her plan made sense. "Then yes. That'll be great. Thank you!"

Nell's smile brightened her face. "Talk to your care team and let me know if there's anything special that needs to be done for your recovery."

Her words filled his stomach with butterflies. Two could play that game. He flashed her his most charming smile. "Why, Nurse Nell, you sound like you care."

"Maybe I do, Paramedic Welles. After all, you not only saved my life, but you gave me M&Ms."

Hmm. He would need to ask Dad to buy him a lot more packets. Anything for Nell. And something told Welles her fiancé would never think to bring her candy.

At her apartment, Nell inhaled deeply. She understood what Dorothy meant in *The Wizard of Oz*. There was no place like home.

Mom hovered next to her, holding a blanket. "You need to sit."

"I'm fine." Still, Nell slowly lowered herself onto the couch. Her abdomen was still tender from the surgery, but she was healing. That was the most important thing.

Mom covered Nell with the blanket. "You need to stay warm. The last thing you need is to catch a chill and get sick."

She'd been this way since the accident, which Nell understood, but Charlene Culpepper was already a meddlesome mom.

Nell needed to set some boundaries or this could get out of control fast. "Thanks, Mom. I appreciate all your help, but don't forget, I'm thirty-seven, not seven, and an RN."

"I know, but you'll always be my baby. No matter how old you are."

Of course she would say that. Nell blew out a breath.

"As soon as you feel better, we'll discuss my ideas for your wedding." Mom handed her a water with a straw sticking out. "Now drink so you stay hydrated."

Nell did. She knew following orders was better than arguing with Charlene Culpepper. And maybe once Nell felt better, she'd be up for discussing the wedding. Even with the ring on her finger, she didn't feel engaged. It was odd and unsettling how not excited she was.

Must be because of the accident.

Mom fluffed a throw pillow and placed it behind Nell's head. "I'll make you a cup of tea. The warm liquid will be good for your stomach."

"Thanks." Just getting dressed and the drive home exhausted Nell. Maybe she would grab a nap later. "Is today your shift here?"

"For a little while. Juliet has everything under control for our event today." Mom touched Nell's forehead as if checking her temperature. "You're tired."

"I am, but I'm happy to be home." The only problem was she thought Mr. Teddy would be there to greet her, but she didn't want to complain when so many were doing so much for her. "It's weird not taking care of patients. It's only been a few days, but now I'm not used to doing more than a few laps around the surgical floor."

"You'll be good as new soon. I also bought you some clothes that might be more comfortable with your stomach than the leggings and yoga pants you usually wear around here."

Of course she would have thought of that. For all her meddling and gossiping, Mom cared so much for her family.

"I love you, Mom."

"I know. And I love you."

A knock sounded. Mom headed to the door. "It's about time." She opened the door.

Sabine entered with a cat carrier. "Someone misses you, Nell. He meowed the entire drive here. I think he knew you'd be home."

Familiar whiskers stuck out of the grated gate. Nell's heart thudded. "Mr. Teddy."

"Remember what the doctor said," Charlene warned. "You can't lift anything. That includes the cat."

"Mr. Teddy doesn't need to be held." Sabine opened the pet carrier door. The cat ran straight to Nell and rubbed against her. "Guess we know who his person is."

The cat's purrs soothed Nell's soul. She rubbed him. "I missed you, too."

Sabine smiled. "Mr. Teddy was very interested in Missy's kittens and tried to get into their room."

Nell wouldn't have expected that. The cat reminded her more of an old man in a fur coat than a fun-loving feline interested in kitties. "Was he any trouble?"

"None," Sabine said sincerely. "And you know, we're running a special on foster adoptions."

"Not now." Mom shook her head. "Nell has to heal and a wedding to plan."

Sabine came closer and studied Nell's hand. "That's some ring."

"Yes." Nell glanced at it. The ring was big and showy—a lot like Gage, she realized. "Gage picked it out."

Sabine scratched behind Mr. Teddy's ears. "Gage must love you a lot to spend that much. You're a lucky woman."

"And Gage is a lucky man to be marrying my Nell." Mom practically beamed. "It'll be the wedding of the year in Berry Lake."

Wait. What? That didn't make sense to Nell. "I thought that would be Sheridan and Michael's wedding."

Mom wagged her finger. "They're getting married next month, which is this year. Your wedding will happen next year."

Nell's stomach ached. From the surgery or from something else, she couldn't tell.

Another knock sounded and the door cracked open. Gage entered with bags of fragrant takeout food. He wore nice slacks and a button-down shirt. She enjoyed seeing him dressed for work. It wasn't the first time, but he usually dressed more casually when they were together.

He smiled at her. "I know you didn't like the hospital food, so I thought I'd bring you something tastier."

Mom rubbed her hands together. "Isn't that sweet? A handsome man bringing food to his future wife."

"It is," Sabine agreed.

Nell's cheeks heated. "Well, you know how I love to eat. Thanks, but I thought you had a work thing."

"I did, but it ended early, so I came right over. I'm sorry I couldn't be at the hospital this morning." As he came closer, his eyes were filled with concern. "How do you feel?"

"Better," she admitted. "Especially now that you and Mr. Teddy are here."

"That's what I want to hear." Gage placed the bags on the coffee table. "Oh, hey, cat."

Mr. Teddy's emerald eyes narrowed. He hissed, baring his teeth, and arched his back.

"Be nice." Nell touched the cat and glanced at Gage. "I'm sorry."

"Mr. Teddy has had his routine completely upended," Sabine said. "He didn't hiss once at our house. I'm sure he'll settle down."

Gage nodded, his gaze softening. "He's upset because I didn't bring him a treat. But only my girl was on my mind. Next time."

Still, Mr. Teddy eyed Gage warily. It wasn't the first time the cat had done that, but she hoped the two could get along or at least tolerate each other.

"There's enough for all of us," Gage announced.

"Thanks. I have to get back to the animal rescue." Sabine smiled at Nell. "You take care. I'm on your schedule, so if you need anything for Mr. Teddy or Welles, please let me know."

With that, Sabine headed out the door.

"Has Welles been released?" Gage asked.

"Not yet, but soon."

Mom rolled her eyes. "I still can't believe you're going to let Welles recuperate here."

Gage's eyes narrowed. "What do you mean here?"

Nell didn't know why Mom didn't like Buddy or Welles or why Gage's tone had become harsher. "He doesn't want to go to a skilled nursing facility. There's no reason when I'll be off work while I heal and everyone will be here to help me."

"Can't his dad help him?" Gage asked.

Mom nodded. "I said the same thing."

"Buddy has a business to run." Nell shouldn't have had to explain common courtesy to friends in need to either of them. "And if Welles hadn't shielded me, I could have died."

Mom sighed. "That's true, but I'm sure his firefighter training played a role in that."

Nell wished these two would understand. Welles had saved Missy and her. She should have thought of this herself. "It doesn't matter why he did it, I'm grateful, and I want to do the right thing here."

"My Nell always does the right thing," Mom said.

"She does, but I have one question." Gage rubbed the back of his neck. "Where is Welles going to sleep?"

Really? That was what he wanted to know?

Nell took one breath and then another. "In his apartment. Selena ordered a baby monitor system, so it should arrive tomorrow." She pinned Gage with a stare. "Anything else you want to know?"

His jaw jutted forward. "Exactly how long will this arrangement with Welles last?"

She couldn't believe Gage was upset over Welles. "As long as he needs help."

chapter fourteen

O N THURSDAY AFTERNOON, a county deputy escorted Missy out of the Berry Lake Regional Hospital's psych ward. She carried a plastic bag with the few things she'd had with her when she'd been arrested—her dead cell phone, a necklace, earrings, and a watch. She hoped someone at the law office or Bria had her purse, but that was something Missy wouldn't worry about now.

She stepped outside, breathing fresh air for the first time in three days. Even though the sky was overcast, the natural light made her blink. But she took another breath, letting her lungs fill.

Free!

Not totally, but she would call this freedom for now.

Getting out of the hospital was the most important thing. The seventy-two-hour court-mandated stay had left her feeling weak and vulnerable, like a butterfly with tattered wings. The heavy monitor around her ankle reminded her the nightmare wasn't over yet.

As a cameraman filmed, a reporter stood nearby, but neither said a word to her.

"Missy!" Jenny yelled. Dare stood next to her and waved at Missy.

"I'm driving her home," the deputy said to them.

Dare nodded. "We know the procedure, but we're family and wanted to see her as soon as possible."

Missy's gaze fell to the ground. She didn't see Sam or Briley and should have asked where they were except she felt too raw and exposed. "Thanks."

Jenny gave her a comforting hug. "We'll see you at home, okay?"

She nodded, unsure if anything would ever be okay.

Once again, she found herself in the back seat of a police car. No handcuffs, however. As the officer navigated through the quiet streets, she glanced out the rear window to see Dare and Jenny in their SUV.

Missy hated dragging them into this, but she had nowhere else to go. Besides, the guest cottage was her home. But that gave her even more motivation to clear her name.

Somehow.

The police officer glanced in the rearview mirror. "You know the rules."

It wasn't a question. She glanced at the ankle monitor. "Yes, they reviewed them at the courthouse, on the way to the hospital, and at the hospital." She wasn't allowed to leave the property unless it was for a meeting with Elias or a medical appointment.

When they pulled up to the house, a few extra cars were parked out front. She recognized a couple of them. Sam and her friends were there to greet her. Someone had hung a large banner that read *Welcome Home* across the garage.

As the corners of her eyes stung, she waited for the officer to open the back door since there wasn't a handle for her to use. She hoped this would be her home for a long time. The last place she wanted to return to was jail.

Don't think about that.

Missy did a breathing exercise she'd learned in the hospital to keep herself from spiraling. Having a panic attack in front of the deputy wouldn't do her any favors. She inhaled again for good measure, counted to five, and exhaled.

The back door opened, and the deputy motioned her to exit the car. "Do you have everything?"

She showed him the plastic bag. "This is all I had."

"I'll escort you inside."

"I live in the guest cottage in the back." Missy motioned to the gate. "It's through there."

He followed her to the door. Before she could knock, the door opened.

Sabine held Briley in her arms. Her gentle smile was full of warmth. "Welcome home, Missy."

As soon as Briley saw Missy, the little girl put her arms out. Missy took her and held her close, soaking up her baby scent. The tears she'd been trying to hold back slipped out. "Auntie missed you so much."

"Looks like the feeling is mutual," Jenny said behind her.

Missy glanced over her shoulder to see Jenny and Dare. The guard was nowhere in sight, and she breathed a sigh of relief.

"Go on in," Jenny encouraged. "And let me take her."

Missy handed over the baby. "I'll want her back soon."

Jenny smiled at her. "Of course."

"Mama cat and the kittens are with another foster. They're doing great thanks to the start you gave them," Sabine said. "I figured I'd let you get settled and see if you want me to bring them back. You've been through a lot."

Missy's gut instinct screamed to bring them back today, but that wouldn't be the best for any of them. She hadn't been home in more than a week and her life was in flux. "Thanks. I'll let you know."

As she went farther into her living room, she noticed Sam leaning against the wall, his gaze brimming with concern and love. Her heart fluttered.

Sam straightened and went to her. He kissed her lightly on the lips. "I've missed you."

She touched his chest to reassure herself that he was real, that she was where she belonged. "Missed you so much."

Sam hugged her, and she rested her head against his chest, hoping she could soak up some of his strength. "I'm so glad you're home."

"Thank you." She didn't want to let go, but she heard a familiar sound—two of them—and let go of Sam. "Peach and Mario." Missy dropped to her knees.

Her cats meowed and climbed onto her, rubbing against her.

She kissed the tops of each of their heads. Tears fell and she didn't care. "I missed you both so much. I'm sorry I just disappeared, but I'm home now. I'm home."

A hand touched her shoulder. She didn't have to look up to know it was Sam, but she glanced his way.

His eyes gleamed. "Everyone is so happy to see you."

Bria and Juliet came out of the kitchen. Each carried a plate of cupcakes. "Surprise!"

Juliet grinned. "These aren't nearly as good as yours, but you know what Elise always said…"

"There are no guarantees in life, but a cupcake always helps," the three of them said in unison.

As they laughed, Missy stood. Her cats stayed attached to her legs. "Thank you."

Bria raised her plate. She was smiling, but the circles under her eyes suggested she hadn't slept much last night. "This one has vanilla."

"But before the sweets, we have something else for you," Juliet announced.

Selena came out of the kitchen with a plate containing a burger in a Burger Barn wrapper, French fries, onion rings, and Missy's favorite dipping sauce. "Surprise number two."

Missy couldn't believe it. "You're here! I mean, you brought my favorite food, but…"

Her voice trailed off. She couldn't quite find the words to thank her friend who had put up her bail money. Sheridan's fiancé, Michael, had offered to help Jenny cover Missy's legal expenses.

"I'm here." Selena handed the plate to Sam and hugged Missy. "It's so good to see you. And we're all here to help you."

"Whatever it takes," Sam said.

His and her friends' unwavering belief in her stirred a feeling deep within Missy—a feeling of hope. "Thanks. And would you mind if I ate? I'm starving."

Laughing, Sam handed her the plate. "Go for it. Selena got enough for all of us."

"You can start with a cupcake if you want," Bria offered. "No one will tell."

Missy grabbed a vanilla one. "This one is in honor of Elise."

The daylight pouring through the windows cast a warm, homey glow around the cozy living room. As they enjoyed the food, Missy popped another French fry in her mouth. Her ankle monitor, an unwelcome reminder of her impending court date, chafed against her skin.

She glanced around at the people who'd come to welcome her home: Sam, Bria, Juliet, Selena, Sabine, Jenny, Dare, and Briley. Some sat on the couch, others on chairs brought in from the kitchen table, a couple were on the floor.

The only person missing was Nell, who was at home recovering. "I wish I could see Nell. Someone at the hospital mentioned she's engaged."

"She is, and she's getting better each day," Sabine said. "Welles is going to be released tomorrow."

Relief flowed through her. The guy had saved Missy's life and now Nell's. "That's wonderful news. I'll have to make him cupcakes."

"Do!" Sabine grinned. "Because he'll be recovering during the day at Nell's place, and I'm sure she'd love some, too."

"And all of us who'll be helping them out would love some, too," Juliet teased.

Missy couldn't wait to bake again, but she motioned to what remained of the cupcakes. "The ones you made were delicious."

"But they weren't Berry Lake Cupcake Shop worthy, even though we used the same recipe," Bria admitted. "I'm not sure what secret Elise taught you, but something seems to be missing in ours."

Selena leaned forward. "Oh, is there a special ingredient?"

Missy thought back to that summer fifteen years ago when they'd all met and the training they'd received for their jobs.

They'd all learned the same things to make it through the busy tourist season. It wasn't until the other four left to go to college that Missy's real training with Elise began, and not really until she went to work full-time there.

"It's not a secret ingredient, per se." Missy could almost hear Elise teasing her for loving vanilla cupcakes. "But one day, after Rob had left for bootcamp, I was missing him so bad. I was doing what I needed to do, and the cupcakes were fine. No complaints from customers, but they didn't taste exactly like Elise's, so I asked her that same question."

The living room went pin-drop quiet.

Bria bit her lip. "What did my aunt say?"

A pang hit Missy's heart, but the pang was better than a tsunami of grief. "Elise said to imagine the people you love and that each cupcake you make is for them." Missy once again looked at everyone. Each had inspired her baking as had Elise and Rob. "So that's what I do whenever I bake."

Sam, who sat next to her, brushed his lips over her hair. "That is one extra-special ingredient."

"So beautiful," Selena said.

Juliet nodded. "I can almost hear Elise say that."

"Same." Bria sniffled. "Aunt Elise knew you'd be able to do that, Missy. You're as much the cupcake shop as she was."

Jenny shifted Briley to her other arm. "I've told Missy as much, so it's good others agree."

As a lump formed in Missy's throat, her heart swelled. "You guys. I'm going to ugly cry in a minute."

Sam wrapped his arms around her. "That's okay. We're all here to wipe the tears."

She leaned back against him, his warmth making her heart flutter. "I don't know what I'd do without all of you. Thank you."

"And we'll do whatever we can to prove your innocence," Dare added, his voice steady like a protective big brother even though she was older.

Everyone nodded.

Missy glanced at Rob's photo on the mantel. If there was ever a time for miracles or divine intervention, it was now.

Please help us, Rob.

She had a feeling that might be the only way to prove her innocence.

After everyone had left except Sam, Missy leaned against the windowsill, staring out the front window. Peach and Mario sat nearby. They hadn't left her side since she arrived home. Her being away must have been as hard on them as it was on her.

Poor fur babies.

In the backyard, the wind stirred through the trees, carrying golden leaves from branches. She'd taken the outdoors for granted, but never again. She couldn't wait to spend time working in Jenny's garden, though her feet would need more time to heal before she was up for a walk around the inner perimeter.

Sam came up behind her and wrapped his arms around her. "You must be exhausted."

"I'm tired, but it was nice of everyone to come over."

He gave her a squeeze. "Jenny was worried it would be too much, but Dare and Sabine convinced her it would be okay, that people would be able to tell when you'd had enough."

"Hey, if people want to bring me burgers and cupcakes, I'm not going to say no," Missy joked.

"That was Selena's idea."

Missy laughed. "She loves the Burger Barn as much as I do."

"Is there anything you want to do?"

"I wish we could go out"—she wiggled her leg with the ankle monitor—"but that's not possible."

"A movie, nap, quiet time, just name it."

How had she gotten so lucky to find a special kind of love twice? This man, who loved, supported, and believed in her, had come into her life at exactly the right time. "There is something."

"What?"

She glanced over her shoulder at him, only able to see his profile, but that was enough to quicken her pulse. "Want to help me bake cupcakes?"

"I would love to, but you'll have to tell me what to do. I've never really baked except when I was younger and helping my mom."

After days of feeling helpless and trapped, she needed to fill her home with the warm, comforting aroma of cupcakes as a way of reclaiming her life, one sweet treat at a time.

"It's easy-peasy."

He laughed. "Says the baker who makes the best cupcakes in Washington."

She feigned a pout. "Only Washington?"

"Oops. The best cupcakes in the world." He winked. "Better?"

"Yes, though 'best in the galaxy' might've been nice." She took his hand and led him into the kitchen, a place she hadn't been since arriving home. Mario and Peach followed along. "Come on."

The quiet hum of the refrigerator offered a comforting backdrop. The counter sparkled and not one dirty glass or cup was in the sink. She appreciated whoever had cleaned up after they'd eaten.

"What do you need me to do?" Sam asked.

She opened a cabinet. "This is where I keep my baking supplies."

He motioned to the stainless-steel shelving unit on wheels. "What's that for?"

"That's if we get the cottage food permit. I have to keep the shop's supplies separate from mine."

"Well, once you get a permit, if you need an assistant, I volunteer."

"That will be great, but…" Missy studied him. "What about looking for another job?"

"My parents told me I can stay with them for as long as I need to. I want to make sure I'm available for you until we clear your name. And I can do gig-type stuff until then."

Love overflowed, filling every part of her. Sam gave her without her even needing to ask for anything, but… "You still need to watch out for your future, if—"

"No ifs." He leaned his forehead against hers. "You're not guilty. If the police and fire investigator won't look for proof, then I will. Trust me."

"I do. I trust you completely."

"Good, now show me how you make cupcakes."

She removed the flour, sugar, powdered sugar, baking soda, vanilla extract, and oil from the cabinet. "Grab the eggs and milk. Jenny said she restocked the fridge before I got home."

He did. "My mom always used a mix from a box."

"Nothing wrong with that." She grabbed a bowl, a mixer, and a whisk. "I've just done this so many times it's as easy as a mix now."

"What do we do first?"

She grabbed two aprons off a hook. "Put this on. Even the best bakers get dirty sometimes."

Sam did and looked cute in the cupcake print apron. Hers was covered with cats. Both had been gifts from Selena. "I'm going to preheat the oven while you crack two eggs into the bowl. Then you'll use the mixer and add in the sugar. You'll need to whip until the mixture changes. You want it to be white and fluffy."

"White and fluffy. Got it." He did exactly as told. His brow furrowing, he glanced over at her. "Like this?"

"You're already a pro."

His grin sent tingles erupting through her. She showed him how she was adding the flour, baking powder, and salt together. After about six minutes, the mixture was white.

She whisked the dry ingredients. The familiar scents of flour and sugar enveloped her, bringing back good memories of working in the cupcake shop and baking here at home. "Now we fold this in."

"Fold?"

"We'll add about a third and only use the mixer in a burst. Then add in the next third."

"Got it." He poured in some and mixed it. "This isn't too hard."

"Nope." She put the milk and butter into a glass measuring cup. "I'm going to heat this in the microwave."

"Does it have to be hot?"

"No, but having it warmer helps the cupcakes rise better." The cup went into the microwave, and at the beep, she pulled it out. "Now we're going to add the oil and vanilla to this, then a little of the egg batter to the milk and butter. This is called tempering to bring down the temperature of the milk mixture. You'll want to whisk it, and you don't have to go easy."

He did it. "Enough?"

As she reached for the bowl, her hand brushed his and a spark jolted her. She pulled her arm away. "A tad more."

Sam poured with such precision he looked more like he was conducting an experiment with reactive chemicals rather than baking cupcakes. "What's next?"

At his eagerness, her stomach filled with butterflies. He was so sweet to be baking cupcakes with her. "The milk and butter mixture goes into the whipped eggs. You don't want to beat it too much though."

While Sam did that, she prepped the cupcake pan by adding liners. "That looks good. Now fill these up about two-thirds of the way full."

He did and grinned. "Now what?"

"We put the tray in the oven, and in about twenty minutes or so, we'll have cupcakes. Once they cool, we can frost them."

Sam placed the pan in the oven. "This was much easier than I thought it would be. We make a good team."

"We do." Missy leaned back against the counter, suddenly aware they were close enough to one another that she could feel the heat radiating from him. Who needed an oven when she had him around? She stared up at him, feeling lighter than she had in a week. "But we're not finished yet. We have to make the buttercream frosting, which is my favorite part. So sweet."

"You are the sweetest thing ever." He reached out, tucking a stray lock of hair behind her ear. His hand lingered, cupping her cheek, and then he dipped his head. His lips brushed against hers, teasing and tempting her. "And I don't think I'll ever get enough of you, Missy Hanford."

Missy rose onto her tiptoes and kissed him on the lips. The kiss was soft and sweet, filled with tenderness. She melted into him, her hands sliding around his neck to pull him closer. It felt so right, like coming home after a long journey. She would never get enough of Sam. And that was okay as long as she remained out of jail. If she didn't...

She would do what she had to do no matter how much it hurt. That would be the best thing for Sam even if it wouldn't be the best thing for her.

chapter fifteen

A FTER THE VISIT at Missy's cottage, Selena drove to Nell's apartment with Bria and Juliet. Could the visit wait until tomorrow? Yes, but Selena had only gotten into town a few hours ago and wanted to see for herself how her other friend was doing. Bria, however, appeared to be struggling to hold herself together. Juliet had said Bria cried all night, but no tears had fallen today.

Selena glanced in the rearview mirror at Bria in the back seat. "I don't mind swinging by the house if you're not up for another visit tonight."

"Thanks, but I want to see Nell." Bria attempted a smile, though she was only half successful. Dalton had really done a number on her—again. "I'm also trying to be positive rather than throw myself another pity party. Poor Juliet must be getting tired of them."

"Hey, I'm happy to be a card-carrying member of the man-haters club right now," Juliet joked.

That brought a genuine smile to Bria's lips. "Same. And the last thing I want to do is be anywhere where I have too much time to think and wallow."

Juliet glanced Selena's way with a concerned expression. "You want to take this?"

Selena nodded. "Being positive is great, Bria, but ignoring anything negative causes future problems because those feelings can get stuck inside a person. Acknowledging all the emotions, even the dark ones that hit right in the solar plexus, releases them. That might mean crying, punching your pillow, throwing eggs, breathing exercises, meditating, or taking lots of hot showers. Draining? At times, yes, but then a person can move on and get back to the more positive feelings."

As both women nodded along, she naturally shifted into her Selena T persona. Yes, they were both her, but Selena T had a specific way of talking and even her mannerisms changed. It reminded her of Norma Jean becoming Marilyn Monroe. Talk about a perfect illustration of the law of assumption—assuming whatever you wanted was already on its way, be it confidence, becoming a star, wealth. The options were endless.

"After you do that, you'll be able to move on," Selena continued. "But if you ignore them or pretend that they don't exist, they stay with you. Sometimes they get stuck and are even harder to release."

"Oh, I remember you telling me that after I lost my job. You had me buy a carton of eggs," Bria said.

"Did it help?" Selena asked.

"Yes." Bria laughed. "I forgot how well. I've just been telling myself I should be strong."

Bria wasn't the only one. Selena felt that in her core. "Forget about any *should*. And trust me, dealing with your emotions will only make you stronger."

"She's right," Juliet chimed in. "I'm still taking baby steps, but once I started letting myself feel everything, it was easier to let it all go."

"Baby steps are all it takes!" Staying in Seattle with Logan had been the right decision since Nell had been in the hospital and Missy couldn't see anyone. Selena knew that in her gut, but now her friends needed her, and she wanted to do all she could for them.

She loved using what she was good at to help her friends.

Juliet was doing better, given where she'd been after her marriage had fallen apart in September, but Selena wanted to see how she was feeling as the divorce was being drawn out. Nell had plenty of family in town to help her, but this engagement of hers sounded rushed. The last time Selena spoke to Nell about Gage, she was only dating him to keep Charlene off her back. So a huge diamond and proposal seemed…off.

Sweet Missy was putting on a brave face. She'd lost weight though, and her sunken eyes suggested she hadn't slept much. At least she had Sam. He acted as if she was the sun and his world revolved around Missy, and Selena couldn't be happier for her friend. She and Logan used to be like at the beginning of their marriage. She hoped they would be like that again after his retirement.

But Bria worried her the most. Bria, the most practical of them, normally said what was on her mind, but she hadn't mentioned Dalton all day, so Selena hoped some of what she'd said would help Bria not to hold everything inside her.

"Here we are." Selena parked in the lot. They each grabbed something from the trunk—flowers, candy, groceries—and headed to Nell's place. "Something I didn't think of was the stairs. Those might be difficult for Welles to maneuver."

"There's an elevator." Juliet pointed at the hallway. "Nell's place is closer to the stairs, so no one ever uses it when they visit her."

"Good point." Selena knocked on the door, eager to see her friend.

Evie opened the door and hugged her. "Oh, Selena. I'm so glad you're here."

She and Nell used to babysit her two younger sisters. "Me, too. How is our favorite patient?"

Evie leaned closer. "The worst. She's a much better nurse."

"I heard that!" Nell yelled. "Excuse my sister's lack of manners and come in."

Evie grabbed her purse. "While you're all here, I'm going to run a couple errands. I'll be back soon."

Selena entered the apartment that was Nell's safe haven. The place exuded comfort and warmth, something her nurturing friend was known for, but her attention was on Nell, who didn't look quite like herself. Nell's complexion was pale. Her rosy cheeks and glowing skin were missing.

That was understandable. The rockslide must have been a terrifying ordeal. Thank goodness Welles had protected her.

"Hey, you. How are you feeling?"

"Better." Nell smiled, but it didn't reach her eyes. "We've got four-fifths of the Posse together, which makes my day. How's Missy?"

As Selena handed Nell the flowers, Juliet and Bria carried the other items into the kitchen. "She's happy to be home."

"That's good," Nell said. "As soon as I'm a little better, I'll visit her. Short walks are all I'm up for right now. Other than lying on the couch."

"You went through a lot." Thinking about it sent a shiver along Selena's spine. "You need to rest and recover."

Nell rubbed her neck. "Something happened when I went climbing. I think… I mean I don't know…"

Selena sat next to her on a chair. Nell needed answers. That much was clear from the tremble in her voice. "Tell me what happened."

"The entire time I was climbing, I kept getting this feeling I should stop and go home." Nell's words came out in a rush. "Sometimes it was a little flutter almost. Other times it felt like my gut was twisted into knots. I thought I heard a voice even."

Selena relaxed. She knew exactly what had happened out there. "Did you want to follow what you were feeling or hearing?"

"Yes, but at the same time, I'd committed to the climb, so I kept going."

"You felt torn."

Nell nodded. "But I think it was easy to justify continuing. I don't know that in the moment I thought of myself as no-nonsense, but I ignored the weird feelings. I was certain logic would prevail. I mean it was a well-worn climbing path. Statistically, we should've been safe, especially with two other skilled climbers with me. But then the rockfall…"

Selena touched Nell's arm, hoping to ground her as she recalled what happened. "It's okay. You let that logical part of you ignore your intuition. It happens, but my guess is your gut instinct was trying to keep you safe."

"I wish I would have listened. Then maybe none of this would have happened."

"We can't know what would have happened or not, but when you're not used to being in a situation like that, or trusting yourself, you might think you're overreacting."

"I did think I would be overreacting if I said I wanted to leave."

"Totally normal," Selena admitted. "But if it happens again, and it will, trust the feeling. That's stopped people from flying or driving or made them move from where they were standing. The human body is an amazing creation. We've barely tapped into the potential."

Nell stared off, a faraway look in her eyes. "I'll do something about it if it happens again."

"Not if, when."

She shivered. "That kind of scares me."

Selena squeezed Nell's arm. "Don't be afraid. Intuition is a gift."

Nell shook her head slowly as if she wasn't convinced.

"We have a surprise for you," Juliet said, walking in front of Bria.

Bria stepped to the side and showed off a plate of cupcakes. "We made these. And they're not as good as Missy's, but they're still tasty."

Nell perked up. "I won't ever turn down a cupcake. Thank you."

Juliet and Bria joined them in the living room. Each took a cupcake. An extra one sat on the plate. Selena assumed it was in honor of Missy, who couldn't be there.

As Nell took a bite from hers, her diamond ring shot prisms around the room.

That reminded Selena... "Congratulations on your engagement."

Nell nearly choked. She swallowed. "Thanks."

That wasn't the reaction Selena had expected. She studied her friend. "Everything okay?"

Nell's nod quickly turned to her shaking her head. "I-I..."

Juliet handed Nell her water bottle. "Take a sip."

Nell did. "Thanks."

"So, what's up?" Bria asked.

Nell stared at her ring. "It's beautiful. And Gage is smokin' hot."

Uh-oh. Selena didn't want to react without more info. "Why do I hear a but coming?"

"But I never said yes to his proposal. My mom did."

Bria snorted. "Typical Charlene."

"Right?" Nell half laughed. "I like Gage. And you all know how much I want to get married, but this just feels..."

"Trust your instinct," Selena urged.

Nell tilted her head as if thinking. "Too much, too fast."

"There's nothing that says you have to have a short engagement," Bria suggested. "Maybe you just need more time."

Juliet nodded. "The wedding your mom imagines is going to take some planning. It's not something we can throw together in a couple of months."

"More time," Nell echoed. She smiled. "You're right. There's no rush at all to get married."

Juliet finished her cupcake. "I'm going to put you on the spot. Do you love Gage?"

Nell shifted on the couch. "I... Maybe. We haven't known each other long, and the last person I loved..."

"Andrew the jerk," they said in unison.

"Yes, but this doesn't feel like that. I was crazy in love with Andrew."

Bria shrugged. "That was also more than five years ago."

"And Selena T mentioned on the podcast that sometimes we rewrite our histories to make them more palatable," Juliet said.

The way Juliet remembered things from the podcast pleased Selena. "That's true. But Gage isn't Andrew, so I wouldn't compare them."

Nell snickered. "Andrew would never try a quarter of the stuff Gage has done."

"And you, too!" Bria grinned. "You surprised us all by becoming an outdoorsy woman."

Nell pointed at her stomach. "Only that didn't work out well."

"Rookie mistake." Selena winked, and they all laughed. "Not that Welles is a rookie, but I still see him as that bothersome kid who used to follow Nell around like a lost puppy. When does he arrive?"

"Tomorrow, if everything goes as planned. Max and Buddy moved some of my furniture around since Welles will be in a wheelchair and then a knee scooter."

Juliet shook her head. "He's going to hate both of those."

"For sure." Nell sighed. "He was not a happy patient."

"Well, if anyone can turn his frown upside down, it's you," Selena teased. "And now that you're engaged, he won't keep asking you out."

A thoughtful expression crossed Nell's face. She opened her mouth to speak but then closed it.

"What?" Selena asked.

"You know how I always thought Welles was joking when he asked me out?" Nell stared at her engagement ring. "Well, Buddy told me he was serious."

"Of course Welles was serious." Juliet sounded dumbfounded. "You, Nell Culpepper, are a catch."

Nell shrugged. "Thanks, but Welles is out of my league. Gage is, too."

"Tell that to the gigantic rock on your finger." Selena pointed at the diamond. "Either man would be lucky to have you love them."

"I just…" Nell wet her lips. "I just don't know how I can ever repay Welles. He saved Missy and then me."

"The guy's a true hero," Bria announced. "That's hard to find these days."

"They are, but Sam fits the bill," Selena added.

"Logan, too," Juliet said.

Selena nodded. Maybe this was the segue to get Bria to talk about Dalton.

"And now Nell has Gage," Bria added before Selena could say anything.

She guessed the talk would have to wait. Unfortunately.

Selena glanced at Nell. "So tell us about the proposal you didn't say yes to…"

Later that night, Selena sat with Juliet and Bria in the living room at Elise's old house, which she knew was Bria's now, but old habits died hard. They'd all changed into their pajamas, and Juliet had made each of them a cup of herbal tea. The coziness warmed Selena's heart, reminding her of when they'd had sleepovers with Elise more than fifteen years ago. Elise would be happy to see her house full this way. Well, minus Nell and Missy.

I'm never lonely in Berry Lake.

Selena sipped her tea. Once the lake house and the season were both finished, she couldn't wait to move here and be closer to her friends.

Lulu stretched out at Juliet's feet. Her tail didn't wag much, but she seemed happy, which was all that mattered.

"Lulu looks good," Selena said.

Juliet reached down and petted Lulu. "She keeps improving, but she no longer jumps up on the furniture. She must remember what happened that last time."

"Butterscotch has been better with her, too." The cat was curled up on Bria's lap. "Especially since the couch is all his now."

Bria appeared more relaxed. That pleased Selena.

They'd stopped by the grocery store on the way home from Nell's and bought three dozen eggs. They'd tossed them into the kitchen sink, laughing and crying. Bria named her eggs Dalton and Deena. Juliet got into the spirit of it with her eggs named Ezra, Remy, and Mrs. Jones. Selena tossed a couple which she called Ted.

"So how did tossing eggs work for you?"

"I feel better. That knot inside my stomach isn't completely gone, but it's lessened. Thanks." Bria stared at Butterscotch, purring like an idling engine. "I think part of my problem is I feel stupid."

Juliet shook her head. "You're not stupid, Bria. You're one of the smartest people I know, but the heart isn't logical."

"Mine sure isn't. I might be good with numbers, but when it comes to men…" Bria sighed. "I have no idea why I date the most horrible guys. First, Fritz and now Dalton. I even went back for a second and third helping of his idiocy. Maybe it'll be better if I stay single like Aunt Elise did because something is wrong with me."

"Nothing is wrong with you. It's easy to want to take responsibility for this. And if you choose to be single, that's okay." Selena understood wanting to make the right choices and choose a good man, to not fall in love with a jerk. "Just know the problem isn't you."

Juliet nodded. "For sure not you. But I totally know what you mean. I'm embracing my singlehood, and it feels so good right now. I won't put a timeline on it though. I'm still healing from Ezra's affair and all his abuse. So who knows how I'll feel in the future."

"It can be hard not knowing," Selena advised. "But you don't need to, either. That can be hard for those who are planners."

Bria raised her hand. "I do love my plans."

"Nothing wrong with planning, but romance is hard to do that with because there's another person involved." Selena tilted her head, thinking for a moment. "Maybe you can plan a vacation somewhere or do something you've always wanted to do."

"That might be fun." Bria sighed. "Though I'll be doing whatever I plan alone."

"And that's okay. Not everyone who enters our lives is meant to stay there forever. Sometimes we have something to learn or experience that we can only get from them." Selena wished she could wipe away Bria's heartbreak. "You didn't expect to see Dalton again let alone reunite. And you never expected to move back to Berry Lake when you left. Yet here you are. Nothing is absolute, even if it feels that way. But now isn't the time to make any big decisions. It's time to heal."

Bria's gaze went from Selena to Juliet. "I'm so glad I have you to help me do that."

"We might need more eggs for tomorrow," Juliet said lightheartedly.

That brought a laugh from Bria. "Yes, we will."

Selena's phone rang. She glanced at her screen and saw Missy's name and number. "It's Missy."

"I hope everything's okay," Juliet said.

Selena took the call. "Hello, are you okay?"

"Yes. No. I don't know." Missy's words rushed together.

"I'm with Juliet and Bria. Is it okay to put you on speaker phone?"

"That's fine." Missy's voice wavered.

Selena hit the speaker button. "We're all here. What's up?"

"Sam's planning to stay the night. I don't want to be alone, but I'm not ready for…more." Missy sighed. "I love him, and I want to make him happy, but Rob and I waited until we were married to make love. And…" Missy sped up as she spoke. "I don't want to lose Sam."

Selena looked at the other two women, who shared her concerns. "Did Sam say he wanted to take the relationship to the next level?"

"No, but he said he wanted to stay and I said yes because I didn't want to be alone, which he knew, but then I started thinking when he went to get his bag from the car. I mean, why else would he want to stay the night?" Missy asked.

"Because he loves you," Bria answered before Selena could. "I don't know Sam that well, but he won't push you into anything you're not ready for."

"Just talk to him. Tell him how you feel." Each of Juliet's words was full of concern. "That's something I didn't do, and I should've from the beginning."

"I know, but I'm afraid I'll mess everything up. I just never thought I'd feel this way again, and I don't want to lose him. I love Sam, but I guess I'm old-fashioned and still don't want to have sex unless we're married."

"Hey, babe, I'm happy to wait until then." Sam's soft, gentle voice could be heard in the background. "I just want to hold you tonight so you're not alone. Okay?"

"I've got to go," Missy said quickly. "Thanks."

The line disconnected.

A genuine smile raised the corners of Bria's mouth. "At least Missy found a good one. I'm so happy for her."

"Me, too." Juliet touched Lulu. "Even though I'm not ready to date yet, Missy and Sam give me hope."

Selena nodded. "Hope is all we need. That hope can lead us to great joy."

She only hoped all five of them experienced that joy sooner rather than later.

chapter sixteen

"**Y**OU DIDN'T GET enough sleep last night." Mom carried a cup of tea over and set it on the coffee table in front of Nell. "I heard you groan, which tells me you were in pain, and the grimace on your face right now tells me you still are. Do I need to call your doctor?"

"No." Nell struggled not to yawn. That would only prove Mom right. Nell chalked her soreness up to overdoing during the visit with her friends, but she had no regrets. Spending a few hours with Selena, Bria, and Juliet was worth it. Nell hadn't felt so content in days.

"Are you sure?" Mom asked.

"Yes, and I'm nice and comfy in my new spot." Mom had made up the couch for when Welles arrived later today, so this was Nell's first day using the chair and ottoman. Her abdomen was sore, but she was healing and beginning to feel like her old self again. Even Mr. Teddy, who lay next to her, seemed more at ease. "You know there can be good days and bad days."

"Yes, but this seems worse than before. Or is it a combination of things?"

Mr. Teddy rolled onto his side so he could get belly rubs. Nell happily obliged. She'd also had nightmares, but she didn't want Mom to know that either. She'd worried enough about Nell. The nightmares had happened for the past two nights. Between the bad dreams and pain, she was exhausted. "Do you mean tired and hurting?"

"That and being more emotional."

Huh? Nell still wasn't getting it. "After seeing my friends yesterday?"

"No, after not seeing Gage since he couldn't come over last night." Mom's gaze softened. "It must be hard to be apart when you're so in love."

Umm. Nell didn't have a clue how to reply. She'd discussed Gage with her friends and showed off her ring, but she hadn't missed him. Other than talking about the proposal, she hadn't really thought about him.

Was that bad?

Her anxiety ramped up. *Oh, man.* He was her fiancé and future husband. She should have been thinking about him at some point when he wasn't around, right?

"Don't worry." Mom grinned as if she were picturing bridal fittings and grandbabies all at the same time. "Once Gage finishes his project, we can discuss the wedding."

A chill shot down Nell's spine. Her gaze shot to the ring on her finger. "There's no rush. We just got engaged. I'm still recovering."

"Weddings take time. We have more than a ceremony and a reception to figure out." In a flash, Mom turned into Charlene the event planner. The only thing missing was her tablet. "There's the engagement party, the bridal shower, and the bachelorette party."

Just stop!

The feeling she'd had on the climb returned like a punch to the gut. Selena had told Nell to listen to her intuition the next time. She wanted to, if only for her own peace of mind. "Can we wait until I feel better, please? Gage and I haven't discussed anything. I don't want to force him into making plans before he's ready."

"He's ready."

"You mean *you're* ready." Nell had been here before. Mom had believed Andrew would propose and had begun making tentative plans for their nuptials. Nell had gotten swept up in that, which only added to her heartbreak when he married someone else.

Mom's lips twitched. "I only want what's best for you. Gage is perfect."

Except for his adrenaline addiction, maybe. But thrill seeking was a huge part of who he was. No matter his attempts to reassure her, she didn't see that changing. Not that she would ask him to do that. She was the one who hadn't been honest about being more of a couch potato than an outdoor adventurer.

A knock sounded at the door, startling both Nell and Mr. Teddy.

Mom opened the door. "Oh, Welles. Buddy. I wasn't expecting you this early."

"The nursing staff wanted me out of there," Welles said. "They got through all the discharge paperwork quickly."

Nell turned, but she could only see Mom in the doorway. "That reputation will follow you, Paramedic Welles," she said.

He laughed. The sound was warm, like her favorite hot cider. "It only adds to the one I already had, Nurse Nell."

"Well, come in." Mom didn't sound happy, but then again, she'd never been a fan of the Riggs family for some reason. She stepped away from the doorway.

Buddy pushed Welles into the apartment in a wheelchair, and a vise tightened around Nell's heart. No matter what anyone said, she blamed herself for getting him involved with Gage. Welles should have been bouncing around on his feet, not stuck sitting with his leg extended out in front of him.

"It'll take me a couple of trips to get everything," Buddy said.

Welles nodded. He wore a sling that supported his broken arm. The poor guy. He didn't even look like the same Welles she'd known most of her life. His scruff had become a beard. His usually-sparkling-with-amusement-or-mischief eyes appeared duller. His complexion was paler. He looked more tired than the last time Nell had seen him. That wasn't surprising given the vitals checks throughout the night. His broken bones would hurt, too. So, logically, she could explain everything she saw. But something still bothered her, and she hoped that was all it was.

"I should be able to get next door by myself," he said.

"Nope." Nell didn't hesitate to answer. She used her nurse's voice, which came in handy when patients wanted to be difficult. No way would Welles get away with that. Not on her watch. He might not think so, but she owed him and payback started now. "Whoever's here at night will make sure you're settled in at your place for the evening," she said in a matter-of-fact tone.

Welles opened his mouth.

"Not up for discussion." She cut him off.

With a chuckle, Buddy closed the door behind him. "You're not going to be able to sweet-talk yourself out of this one, son."

Welles sighed dramatically for maximum effect, but he was quite the charmer when he wanted to be—which was most of the time. "Unfortunately, she's immune to my charms."

"Always said my daughter was a smart woman," Charlene muttered.

Buddy rolled his eyes. "Takes after her father. Max is a good man."

The tension in the apartment thickened as if a fog had settled over all of Berry Lake. Not good.

Nell wanted to help Welles, not agitate him. "I'm glad you're here, Welles. Put your stuff on the kitchen table and we'll figure out what goes where once you're settled. Bet you want out of that chair."

As Welles did as he was told, lines formed around Mom's mouth, but she didn't say anything.

Buddy pushed Welles closer to the couch. "I'll move the coffee table."

Mom huffed. "Don't do that on your own. You'll hurt yourself. I'll help. We can put the coffee table against the wall in the dining area. I brought over TV trays they can use instead."

"Thanks, Charlene," Welles said, and Nell thought he'd done that to preempt whatever Buddy might reply with.

"Well, let's get it done." Buddy headed to the table. "Don't break one of those fancy fake nails of yours, Charlene."

"These nails are all mine minus the gel polish." Mom went to the other side of the table. "Be sure you don't hurt yourself. Men your age can easily overdo it and strain a muscle."

Buddy's jaw jutted forward. "What does that say about you since we're the same age?"

The two were acting so strangely. Nell didn't understand it. Welles glanced at her, and she shrugged. She had no idea what had gotten into their parents.

Mom and Buddy picked up the table and carried it into the dining room, leaning it vertically against the wall to take up less space.

"At least we didn't have to put them in time-out," Welles whispered.

Nell laughed, feeling conspiratorial with him. "I would have liked to see that."

"See what?" Mom asked.

"Me lining up dates while I was in the hospital." Welles grinned. "Now that Nell's engaged, I can't ask her out anymore, so I made sure my dance card—or in this case, my date card—is full once I'm on my feet again."

Buddy laughed. "That's my boy. Nothing keeps him down for long."

Lots of nurses dated firefighters, paramedics, and police officers. It had almost become a joke. Nell used to get annoyed with Welles asking her out each time he came into the Emergency Department, so a part of her was relieved that would be over. But surprisingly, she also felt a twinge of disappointment.

Nell shook away that thought immediately. She was engaged now. What Welles did or didn't do shouldn't have even been a blip on her radar. And it wasn't. No matter what Buddy had told her, Welles just liked to joke around with her and yank her chain. That was all it had ever been.

Of course it was. And she would prove it.

"I'm sure Welles has plenty of women who want to make sure he recovers properly." *See, not an issue.* But Nell hoped they kept quiet since their apartments shared a wall. Seeing women going in and out of his place happened, but she didn't want to hear him on his dates.

Buddy pushed the wheelchair closer to the couch. "Let's get you settled, son."

As Buddy tried to help Welles, Mom made her way over there. She locked the brake on the wheelchair. "Stop. You're going to hurt him."

"Out of my way." Buddy's lips curled. "I've got this."

"The only thing in the way is your male ego." Mom stood on the other side of the wheelchair. "Welles, hold on to us and pretend we're crutches."

Nell was impressed. Mom's idea was a good one.

Welles did as told, using his good leg, and the transfer from wheelchair to couch went easy-peasy.

Nell released the breath she'd been holding. The last thing she wanted was for him to injure himself more at her place. "Nice work."

Buddy grumbled. Surprisingly, Mom didn't rub it in, which must have been a first.

"I'm going to get the rest of the stuff." Buddy headed to the front door. "Be right back."

"Need help?" Mom asked, her tone as sweet as artificial sugar.

A muscle ticked at his jawline. "Yes, it'll save me a trip."

Mom did a double take as if shocked he'd accepted her offer. She smoothed her skirt. "We'll be right back."

The two left, and the door slammed shut.

Welles let out a whistle. "I'm not sure if they've telepathically called a truce or if they're just stocking ammo for the future."

Nell glanced at the front door. "The latter."

They burst out laughing.

"Thanks for making me a cozy spot," Welles said.

"My mom did all the work." Even though Mom didn't think having Welles there during the day was a good idea, Nell had ignored her protests because she had no concrete reasons. Something told her that Buddy Riggs played more into her reasoning than his son. "I just supervised, which I'm excellent at."

"You've always enjoyed telling people what to do. I still appreciate you letting me hang out here," he said. "I hope you don't hate being stuck with me."

"I won't mind at all unless you eat my candy." Nell winked. She'd gotten to know him even better during the outings with Gage, and she liked Welles. He was so much more than the flirty paramedic who showed up at the hospital. "Seriously, having you here is the least I can do after all you've done for me. And neither of us will be lonely this way."

Welles studied her, but he didn't say a word. His expression was...inquisitive.

She waited for him to say something, but he didn't. "What?"

He shrugged.

"Tell me," Nell pressed because this wasn't a side of him she'd seen before.

"Just wondering why you of all people would be lonely when you have your friends, family, and fiancé. You hit the trifecta with all of them."

True, and Nell struggled to keep her expression neutral. "Yes, but we all have our moments."

She hoped that was vague enough that he wouldn't ask questions.

It was his turn to wink, and the gesture looked much sexier and less cheesy on him. "I'll make sure there aren't any of those moments while I'm here. How does that sound?"

"Wonderful."

"I'll do whatever it takes to keep a smile on your face. If not for you, I'd be in an SNF and hating life." Despite Welles's light-hearted tone, his shoulders tensed as if something was bothering him. "I much prefer this."

A meow sounded from the hallway to her bedroom.

"Come here, Mr. Teddy," Welles called to her cat. The cat sauntered over to the couch and jumped up. He circled until he plopped next to Welles, who laughed. "Nice to see you, too."

The cat purred so loudly she could hear it from where she sat. She smiled. "He likes you."

"The feeling's mutual." Welles scratched behind Mr. Teddy's ear with his good hand. "Is he getting along better with Gage?"

"They're...working on it."

His gaze met hers. "I'll take that as a no."

Complaining about Gage would have been so easy to do, but it wouldn't have been right. She'd learned from watching her parents and Sabine navigate life after divorce and then during a second marriage—never talk bad about your spouse, whether current or an ex. "As I said, they're working on it."

"Hey, just teasing." Welles held up his unfractured arm as if surrendering. "Didn't realize it was a sore spot. I won't ask again."

Heat pooled in her cheeks. "I'm sorry. It's not you. I..."

His gaze darkened, matching his serious expression. "What's going on?"

She didn't even know how to vocalize what she was feeling. "It's just... The engagement feels like a lot."

"You're still healing. That's what you should be focusing on right now."

Nell hoped that was it, but she wasn't sure of anything. "Yes, but my mom is all into the wedding planning already, and I'm still getting used to the ring on my finger. Everything feels so... rushed."

"Slow it down."

"A part of me just wants to stop it." The words flew out of her mouth before she could stop them. "I...I shouldn't have said that. I'm just..."

"Confused," Welles offered.

She nodded. "Among other things."

"There's no reason to fast-track the wedding. You need to heal, and I've been told by many of your colleagues at the hospital that speaking to a professional about the accident would be beneficial. You might want to consider doing that, too."

Nell had seen a therapist when she'd returned to Berry Lake five years ago. The sessions had helped her come to terms with a situation that made no sense to her and destroyed her self-confidence. Selena was a proponent of therapy, so she would likely agree with what Welles had said. "Yeah, that sounds like a really good idea. I've been having nightmares."

He reached out to her but then seemed to remember he was too far away to touch her and lowered his arm. "About the climb."

She shivered, remembering what she'd felt last night. "Yes. I wake up terrified and feeling as if I'll never be safe again."

"I'm sorry."

Her gaze narrowed. "Don't be. If not for you, things would have been much worse. I owe you."

"No, you don't."

She did, but he would never accept that. Still, she would try to do what she could to repay him, and there was one thing she could give him. "I'll call someone later today and see if I can make an appointment."

Welles beamed. "Great. And I'll do something in return. Since everyone's already putting so much pressure on you about it, I promise not to mention the W-word to you."

"W-word?"

"W-E-D-D-I-N-G."

She laughed. "You're on. And I know we joke around a lot, but I'm happy you're here, Welles."

His grin spread all the way to his eyes, crinkling the corners and making him look even more handsome than usual. "I can honestly say there's no place I'd rather be than with you, Nurse Nell."

That afternoon, Welles stared at Nell while she slept in her chair with her feet up on the ottoman. He'd been worried when she'd mentioned having nightmares and not feeling safe, but she seemed to be okay right now. That pleased him. He only wanted her to feel safe around him.

Mr. Teddy slept on her lap. He'd moved from his side to her lap about an hour ago as if anticipating her nap. Welles never thought he'd be jealous of a cat, but he would have loved to use Nell's lap as his pillow. No doubt his blue eyes were green right now.

He should have felt like a creep, watching her sleep.

Though it's not like there's anything I can do about it.

He was facing her direction. Sure, he could have napped himself, but he enjoyed watching the gentle rise and fall of her chest with each breath and the slight smile curving her lips that made him wonder what she dreamed about. If only it was him…

Stop, Riggs.

You missed your chance.

Not that he hadn't tried to shoot his shot each time he'd seen her, but she'd friend-zoned him when he was just a kid and he'd been parked there ever since.

So not fair.

But then again, life wasn't.

Look at Nell getting engaged or Missy being blamed for the arson or Juliet's husband cheating on her or Bria not being chosen by Dalton. Speaking of Bria, she was in the kitchen, making them hot cocoa.

Still, Nell seemed more torn than he'd ever seen her. She'd been devastated, nearly lifeless when she returned to Berry Lake after being dumped by that loser doctor. Welles had done everything he could to cheer her up, including moving in next door when the unit became available.

Not to creep on her, but to be a friend if she needed one.

And until the rockfall, he'd believed friends-to-lovers would happen for them. It didn't matter that she was four years older than him or still treated him like the kid she'd once babysat whenever Dad was in a jam. Nell was special. He didn't understand why she always mentioned needing to lose weight when she was perfect in his eyes. Nothing was wrong with a sweet tooth or curves. Man, he loved hers.

Her lips parted, and he wondered what her kiss would taste like.

Dial it back, Riggs.

Welles reached for his water bottle and took a long swig. Still, something about Nell had always made him think of slow, hot kisses and living happily ever after. One thing was clear—she would be a beautiful bride. Though he would need to plan a vacation, so he was away on her wedding date. Friends or not, watching her say "I do" to another man was not going to happen.

Bria carried out three mugs and placed one on the TV tray near him and another on the end table by Nell, who hadn't even stirred. The third she held on to while she settled herself on the floor. "I thought you might've fallen asleep, too."

"Nell made me sleep earlier. If I rest more, I won't sleep tonight." His gaze kept straying back to Nell, and he forced himself to stare into his drink. Miniature marshmallows floated on top of the hot chocolate. He took a sip—sweet and warm. "This hits the spot. Thanks."

"You're welcome." Bria took a sip and lowered her mug. "And you're right, this is just what I needed."

He'd gone to school with Bria and Dalton. They hadn't been in the same friend group back then, so they hadn't hung out together, but in a small town like Berry Lake, he knew them. He'd had classes with Bria and played on sports teams with Dalton over the years.

Bria had always been the smart girl at school. She'd been nice and never one to get in trouble—a rule follower. Dalton had been the star quarterback and one of the rich kids. He'd hung out with other kids like that. But until Dalton broke up with Bria so publicly and harshly before prom, Welles had thought Dalton was a decent guy.

Nope.

And the way Dalton had been acting with Bria since returning to Berry Lake in September kept proving he wasn't a good guy at all. But that didn't lessen what Bria was feeling. "Are you feeling okay?"

Bria half laughed. "I should be asking you that."

"You have. Many times since you took over for Charlene." He took another drink. "Now answer my question."

"Pushy."

"A concerned friend." He wanted to clarify. "We've known each other since you moved in with your aunt."

"True." Bria rubbed the back of her neck. "So you heard what happened?"

"The gossip version."

"Which is?"

"Dalton wouldn't choose between you and his family and Deena kicked you out, but he didn't stand up for you, so he made his choice then."

Bria formed a perfect O. "Spot-on. Which is kind of scary."

"Small town."

"You were in the hospital."

"Dude, first responders and hospital staff help propel the rumor mill."

"I suppose." She shook her head. "It's going to take some time. I mean, things were already rocky, but I thought he wanted the same thing as me. I just don't understand men."

"What about men?"

She tilted her head. "Why would a guy say he wants to be with you, go out of his way to get proof so he can show his mom what she thought wasn't true, only to backtrack when she discounts every piece of evidence that he's brought to her?"

"Maybe he loves his mom so much he can't see past that. My mom died. For so long, it's been Dad and me. Right or wrong, I can't imagine letting anyone come between us." He glanced at Nell. Despite Dad not getting along with Charlene, he liked and respected Nell. They wouldn't have had those kinds of issues. "Maybe since Dalton's dad died, he doesn't want to lose his mom, even if she's super sketchy with a back catalog of ex-husbands."

"Maybe, but you're right. Deena DeMarco is the definition of sketchy." Bria sighed. "I can't remember who said it, maybe Nell, but they asked me if I'd want Deena as a mother-in-law."

"I know what my answer would be."

Bria nodded. "Now I just have to get through all the tears and hope the lonely spot in my chest doesn't keep growing. Logically, what happened probably saved me lots of heartache in the future, but my heart hasn't gotten the memo just yet. A long-winded way of saying I'm still working through things, but I'll be okay."

Her words looped through his head.

Logically, what happened probably saved me lots of heartache in the future, but my heart hasn't caught up just yet.

He stared at Nell, who looked like an angel while sleeping. Maybe he needed to take Bria's words to heart regarding Nell's engagement to Gage. For all Welles knew, she would have never agreed to go out with him, and he would have kept trying until she met someone else.

His gaze dropped to the engagement ring on her finger.

Like Bria, all he needed was for his heart to catch up, too. And then he could leave his decades-long crush behind and finally move on.

chapter seventeen

THE SCENT OF bacon woke Missy. She blinked, letting her eyes adjust to the light filtering around the blinds, and then yawned. *Wait.* She glanced around, trying to figure out where she was…

And then it hit her.

Home.

Her breath caught in her throat.

In her bedroom.

Her eyes stung.

In her own bed.

She wrapped her arms around herself.

Missy must have slept through the night, which was a first since Wednesday. That reminded her…

She glanced at the spot next to her. Empty, but an indentation on the pillow remained.

Sam.

Heat rushed up her neck and pooled on her cheeks. Talk about embarrassing. When Sam had mentioned having a bag in the car if she wanted him to spend the night, Missy hadn't known what to say and nodded. And then her mind had gone every which way until she'd been on the verge of a panic attack.

Cue calling Selena in a panic.

But then Sam had overheard her. He'd been even sweeter than usual, telling her he only wanted to hold her so she wouldn't be alone. He'd added that he would never push her to take things to the next level.

She'd been so grateful for his understanding and for not having to bring up the topic on her own, but she'd still been nervous, given she'd slept with only one man—Rob.

Sam had acted like a gentleman. He'd held her, even sleeping above the sheet to make her feel more comfortable with him. And she was comfortable. Having him next to her had made falling asleep easier than she'd thought possible. She'd never been so comfortable. It was disturbing and wonderful at the same time. Seriously, how had she gotten so lucky to find Sam Cooper?

She got up, made the bed, and went to the kitchen, where the table was set. Sam stood at the stove. Her stomach grumbled in anticipation. "I can't remember the last time someone made me breakfast."

As he turned to face her, he smiled. "Then it's long overdue. How'd you sleep?"

"Wonderfully. It's good to be home and not alone. Thanks."

"I slept well, too. It's the first time since last Wednesday. I needed last night."

Missy needed him. She took a breath, but panic didn't hit. Not the way it had yesterday. This felt cozy and right. The only other person who'd made her feel this way was Rob, but Sam wasn't him. He was the best parts of Rob, but dare she admit… more. Sam put her wants and needs ahead of his own in a way she'd only dreamed about.

"Me, too," she admitted.

"Now sit and eat."

As she sat at the table, Missy smiled at the orange juice, toast, scrambled eggs, bacon, and fruit. "Everything looks amazing."

"I hope it tastes good."

"I'm sure it will." The effort he'd put into making breakfast would amplify the taste in only the best possible way.

He sat next to her, and they passed the dishes to each other.

She took a bite of the eggs. "Delicious."

Sam blew out a breath and smiled as if he'd been waiting to hear what she thought. "Now I can eat."

They both laughed and enjoyed their breakfast as if they'd done this a million times. She reached for the salt and so did he. Their fingers brushed, and a tingle shot up her arm.

He laughed and pulled his hand away. "You go first."

"Thanks." She sprinkled some onto her plate and then handed him the saltshaker. "Your turn."

He added some over his eggs and then bit into a slice of bacon. "Do you need any errands run today? I'm happy to do whatever you need."

"I'm okay, but I do want to go through my mail and pay a couple bills. Boring life stuff I'm thrilled to be able to do."

He raised his orange juice in a toast. "Here's to doing boring life stuff."

Missy tapped her glass against his and then drank. "I realize now boring is good."

"That can be our new goal—boring days."

They continued eating.

A notification sounded. It wasn't her phone. Sam glanced at his. His face paled.

She leaned toward him. "Is everything okay?"

He tapped on his screen and sighed. "I can't believe this."

The sadness in his tone made her lean forward. "What?"

"I…" Sam turned his phone to her. "I'm so sorry, Missy."

On the screen showed the local newspaper's website. The headline read *Local Baker May Have Set Cupcake Shop on Fire in Suicide Attempt.*

She blinked as if her eyes were playing tricks on her, but when she opened her eyes, the words hadn't changed. If anything, they'd become bolder.

Her stomach did a backflip. Her palms turned clammy.

With a trembling hand, she took his phone and read the article. Each sentence sent her heart sinking more and then…

No, this can't be happening.

The paper had included actual pages from her journal. The first photo displayed a tear-stained page, filled with her deepest grief, detailing the pain of losing Rob and how the darkness inside her had become all-consuming. The second photo showed a journal entry where she admitted to feeling hopeless, questioning her purpose in life. The third photo was a sketch of a phoenix rising from the ashes, symbolizing rebirth and starting anew, but then the reporter had twisted the drawing and her words to imply Missy's guilt.

Her most private thoughts after the most difficult time in her life were there in black and white for all to read. It was bad enough she'd been accused in this way, but for someone to do this…

The weight of the accusations crushed her spirit. Her heart pounded in her chest, and she fought back the tears threatening to spill over. Berry Lake now knew her darkest secrets, and if they didn't think she was capable of something so heinous as arson before, they probably did now.

Missy's stomach churned. She thought she might be sick. "They have excerpts from my journals."

"What?" Sam jumped to his feet. He stood behind her. "That's evidence. How did the newspaper get ahold of those passages?"

She could barely breathe. Her chest felt so tight. "I…"

"Hey, babe." Sam put his hands on her shoulders. "I need you to breathe."

"C-can't." A lump in her throat burned, and her eyes stung. She still couldn't force air into her lungs, and she nearly gasped in an attempt to breathe.

Sam spun her chair around as if she weighed nothing. "Look at me."

Missy could manage that.

"I want you to breathe with me." He stared into her eyes. "Inhale and hold it."

She tried and failed.

"Again," he encouraged and then inhaled.

That time she somewhat succeeded.

"Great job." He kept hold of her shoulders. "Let's do it again."

Missy did, and slowly her breathing went from quick huffs to longer breaths.

"Better?" Sam asked.

She nodded, but… "What am I going to do?"

"First, we're going to call Elias." He kissed the top of her head. "This is a huge invasion of your privacy. What you wrote is how you felt after your husband died tragically. No one can blame you for anything you said while grieving years ago. And whoever did this needs to pay."

As she gave him the phone, Missy's fingers shook. Her appetite had vanished, too.

Sam tapped on the screen and put the phone to his ear. "Hey, Elias… We saw it… Not great, but this is illegal, right? … Okay, just wanted to confirm. We'll be here. Thanks." Sam hung up. "Elias is heading over here."

Not trusting her voice, she nodded.

Sam hugged her. "Someone is trying to use your own words against you and make you suffer. We won't let them win. The truth will prevail. We'll find out who did this to you and bring them to justice."

The determination in Sam's voice comforted Missy, giving her the smallest spark of hope that there might be a way through this. But she had no idea how that might happen.

"I'll file a motion with the court to stop this from happening in the future. I'm meeting with my dad and grandfather to discuss which would be the best course of action."

Sam kept his arm around Missy, doing what little he could to comfort her. She hadn't said much since Elias arrived. Not that Sam blamed her. He'd spoken to Jenny and Dare and called Hope, asking her to reach out to Missy's friends. She would need all the support she could get. "Do you mean a gag order?"

"That's one option, and if violated there are penalties. We can also request a protective order or to have the records sealed.

I'm sorry I didn't do this preemptively, but I've had cases with the DA and never thought this would happen." Elias sighed. "I'm so sorry, Missy."

"It's not your fault." Her voice held no judgment, but she sounded so tired—and worse, resigned. "But if anything, this proves someone has it in for me."

"None of what's happening with this case makes sense." Sam had been trying to piece together the case from what the DA had presented at the bail hearing. "I'm completely biased. I admit that, but it seems like someone is trying too hard to make Missy look guilty."

She leaned against him, and Sam pulled her closer.

"A PI is working on this, but those images being released in the paper tells me we need to figure this out sooner rather than later. Someone wants to convince everyone that Missy did this."

"Is there any chance they'll let us into the cupcake shop?" Sam asked. "This feels like an inside job, and for all we know, someone found those other keys and got rid of them."

"I'll see where the investigation is." Elias jotted notes on a notepad. "Reggie has had plenty of time to gather their evidence. But safety will be a priority on the site. We don't want anyone to get hurt."

Missy shivered. "I don't want that."

"I know, sweetheart." Sam rubbed her arm, only to feel goose bumps under his palms. "What if we use a drone?"

"A drone?" Elias asked.

"Bentley is into robotics and drones," Sam explained. "He's the one who suggested it, but I told him as long as the bakery was considered a crime scene it wasn't worth the risk."

"Bentley's really into science stuff," Missy added. She always seemed to have a soft spot for her employee and vice versa. "He's so smart. If anyone could figure out how to fly a drone in to search the cupcake shop for the keys, Bentley could."

Elias tapped his pen against his notepad. "Having a secondary option to traipsing through the rubble might work in our favor. I'll see what I can do. Can you reach out to Bentley?"

Sam nodded. "I'll do it today."

"Good." Elias stared off as if he were deep in thought. "I'll play nice until it's time to play hardball so we get access to the cupcake shop."

"It's about time something finally worked in our favor." Missy rubbed her face, and Sam wished he could wipe away all her worry. He kissed the side of her head instead.

"Do you have any other questions for me?" Elias asked.

"No," Missy said. "I just wish this wasn't happening."

Elias put his pen and notepad in his briefcase. "Just have faith that justice will prevail."

"I'm trying." She attempted to sound strong, but her voice wavered.

"You're doing an amazing job." The more Sam watched Missy deal with this situation, the more his respect for her grew. He'd fallen in love with a girl back in high school. That had been nothing more than a crush because he hadn't known her well enough for love to develop. But the woman sitting next to him captured his heart in a way he'd never imagined. It was better than any dream.

Elias stood. "Hang in there. Both of you. I'll call you as soon as I know the plan."

Missy went over and hugged Elias. "Thank you."

Sam rose and shook Elias's hand. "If you need any help…"

"I'll let you know, but please don't go rogue. I know you want to help her. So do I, but we need to do it the right way."

Sam's collar tightened. He'd wondered if he and Bentley could get the drone inside the cupcake shop with no one noticing. "I just want to support Missy."

And he would do that in whatever way it took.

Another knock on the door didn't surprise Missy. Her little cottage was more like Grand Central Station today. Jenny had been there twice already. Bentley had delivered coffee and muffins from Brew and Steep. And, of course, there was Elias.

"I'll get it." Sam had been fidgety all morning. The article, no doubt. That sucked. She never wanted to hurt Sam, but these false charges against her were changing his life as much as hers.

Sam opened the door. In streamed her favorite friends in the world—the Cupcake Posse. This time Nell was with them.

Missy gasped. "Nell, what are you doing here? You should be at home recovering."

"I needed to see you." Nell hugged her gently, but Missy was afraid of hurting her, so she just squeezed Nell's shoulder. "Cami is with Welles today. If anyone can keep that man in line, it's the mother of twins."

Missy motioned to the couch. "Sit. Now."

"You don't have to tell me twice." Nell moved slowly but made her way over there.

"Hope said she and Josh were going to be at your folks' house," Bria said. "We'll be here with Missy if you want to go see them."

Sam laughed. "I can take a hint."

"You'll be back?" The question sprang out of Missy's mouth full of the same anxiety twisting her insides. "I mean, it doesn't have to be later today or—"

Sam kissed her hard on the lips, a possessive kiss she would want to continue if her four best friends weren't watching. "I'll be back in a couple of hours. Promise."

She released the breath she hadn't realized she was holding. "Thanks."

"See you soon." Another kiss, and then Sam left.

The door closed behind him, and Missy realized he hadn't taken his bag with him. That made her smile.

Selena sat next to Nell on the couch. Bria carried over two chairs from the kitchen table while Juliet made tea. It was like old times, but one thing was different for Missy—the stupid monitor on her leg.

She sat in her chair. "You all were here yesterday."

"Not me," Nell piped up.

Selena shook her head. "You were here in spirit. But I'm so happy you could come this morning. I can't stop seeing that headline."

"I'm so sorry about the article," Juliet said.

Bria shook her head. "It all just seems so sketchy."

"It does," Missy admitted, trying to hold back tears. It was so good to have her friends all together again. "But Elias is on it. I just wish the police hadn't stopped looking for the real arsonist."

"Well, between Sam and Elias, they'll figure something out," Bria said. "Both seem determined."

Missy nodded. She had something difficult she needed to bring up to them. Her hands trembled. "They are determined, but I've got to be honest. I feel like someone wants me to go to jail for this. And we need to talk about what that means for the future of the cupcake shop."

"Nothing has changed." Juliet's voice rose an octave. "The cupcake shop wouldn't exist without you. And we're not going to let some false accusations ruin everything we've worked so hard for."

"That's right," Selena said a beat later. "The five of us are the Cupcake Posse. Note the number five."

Nell nodded. "Yep. All for one."

"The Berry Lake Cupcake Shop is more than just a business," Selena added. "It's a symbol of our friendship, and nothing—not even these lies—can tear us apart."

"One hundred percent. We're the Cupcake Posse. We stick together, through thick and thin," Bria said. "Though I understand your concern from a business perspective."

Leave it to Bria to talk about the bottom line, but then again, she was the CPA.

"But people have very short memories," she continued. "Another incident will be on their minds by the time this is over with, and you're the heart of the cupcake shop. We need you."

Their words filled Missy with warmth, but she needed to be realistic. "If I'm found guilty—"

"You won't be," they said in unison.

She wasn't as sure as them. "Fine, we can discuss that if it happens. But I don't want everything that's happening to affect the bottom line. People have been so quick to say I'm guilty. Even for cupcakes, I'm not sure they'll change their minds."

Selena tapped on her chin. "For your cupcakes, they will. But this might be a good time to expand. Internet, other businesses, even a mail-order cupcake club."

Nell grinned. "This is why they call Selena T the queen."

Selena bowed. "Even without the stupid charges against Missy, expanding makes sense long term."

"It does," Bria said. "I'll do some analysis for us to discuss."

Missy was dumbfounded. "You really don't care if I ruin the bakery's reputation?"

"You won't." Selena smiled at her. "If some people decide that's a good enough reason not to buy our cupcakes, then they aren't the customers we want or need."

"Thank you, guys." Missy looked at each of her friends, their unwavering support shining like beacons in the darkness edging closer to her. Maybe like her drawing, the Berry Lake Cupcake Shop would rise from the ashes like the phoenix. "Cupcake Posse forever."

"Cupcake Posse forever," they repeated.

chapter eighteen

A S THE CUPCAKE Posse made plans for the cupcake shop reopening, Nell also spent her days healing. She was improving, but she still felt as if she had a boulder sitting in the pit of her stomach. She wanted it to go away.

Welles used the knee scooter to get around, which he preferred to the wheelchair. She didn't blame him for that. They had fun playing card games, watching TV, and visiting with whichever friend or family member was their caretaker for the day. Though the person was mainly there for him. She was fully mobile and just taking it easy to finish recovering.

Gage texted and called her every day from his business trip. The only problem? She still didn't feel engaged. Oh, the ring on her finger told her she was, and he said "I love you" enough and spoke about the future, but their conversations seemed… superficial.

She much preferred her conversations with Welles. They weren't solving any issues in Berry Lake or the world, but they communicated on a deeper level, even when joking around. No matter the topic, she learned something new about him. Gage, however, was always his typical self, minus the adrenaline rush. She'd asked him questions, but he always answered the way she expected. Maybe that wasn't a bad thing in that she knew him better than she'd realized, but a part of her wasn't so sure. Nell hoped things improved once he returned and she was fully healed.

Nell glanced at the clock. JoJo had an appointment and said the person taking her place would be there in a few minutes with dinner. That was thirty minutes ago.

It wasn't a problem. They had so much food, and Nell could easily heat it up, but she didn't know who was supposed to be coming over, and she hoped they were okay.

"You look too serious," Welles said from the couch. "If you're trying to decide between ordering French fries or onion rings from the Burger Barn tonight, I say order both. But be sure to get extra dipping sauce."

She laughed until her stomach hurt. "I wish I could do that, but I have no idea what's for dinner or who is taking over for JoJo."

"Maybe we can convince whoever it is to make a run to Burger Barn."

Nell found herself smiling more thanks to Welles. He always knew the right thing to say. "We can tag team them."

"You're on." His gaze darkened. "You only napped once today and not for long. You should take another."

"I was hoping to finally sleep through the night tonight, so I don't want to nap too much." Her nights consisted of tossing and turning, so she woke exhausted, but her naps rejuvenated her. "I have a week more off work, and I really need my sleep patterns to go back to normal before that."

He flashed her a charming, lopsided grin. "You know what you need, Nurse Nell?"

"What is that, Paramedic Welles?"

"You need me to spend the night here."

She couldn't tell if he was joking, but he had to be, right? "Why do I need you to do that?"

"Because you sleep fine whenever I'm around."

That was true. Without her naps when he was there, she would have been a zombie and not healing as well as she was. "I'm not sure why that is."

"You feel safe with me."

He wasn't wrong, but she shouldn't have needed him to feel safe. Nell bit her lip.

Wasn't that how she should have felt around Gage? But whenever he called before bedtime, he left her anxiety ridden.

"I appreciate the offer…"

"You can take a rain check." He winked. "The offer stands."

She laughed if only to relieve the tension in the air. That had never happened with her and Welles even though they'd been stuck together for days. "I'll keep that in mind."

A knock sounded and then the door opened. Gage walked in, carrying bags of takeout. "Sorry I'm late. I needed to stop off at home after my flight arrived."

"It's good to see you," Nell said.

Welles side-eyed Gage, which she thought was unlike him. "Yeah."

Gage glanced at Mr. Teddy, who sat next to Welles. "Hello, cat."

Mr. Teddy ignored him, which was typical, but she hoped they would get along better eventually given how much the cat seemed to love Welles.

"I missed my Nell." Gage went to the kitchen, placed the bags on the counter, and returned to the living room, making a beeline to Nell. "You look so much better."

He kissed her on the lips, and she waited for a spark—anything—to happen.

There used to be some chemistry. At least she thought so. Maybe she was still recovering. "Thanks. How was your trip?"

"Good." Gage glanced at Welles. "You don't look too much worse for the wear."

"Hanging in there." He pointed to his leg and lifted his arm. "I won't be doing much for a while. But I'm grateful Nell offered me a way to stay out of the rehabilitation center."

Gage's gaze bounced from Welles to Nell. "She always looks out for her friends."

"That's what friends do," she said.

His fingers laced with hers, and Gage raised her hand to his mouth and kissed it. "That ring looks so good on you."

"Thanks." Nell kept a smile on her face, but her mind was spinning. She was happy to see Gage—don't get her wrong— but she didn't feel excited or like she wanted wrap her arms around him or crawl into his lap. "It's very pretty."

"Wait until you see the wedding band." Mischief gleamed in his eyes. "You'll love it."

A chill ran along her spine, and goose bumps prickled her skin. The same sense of unease she'd felt on the climb hit like a runaway train. Her breathing sped up. Her pulse accelerated. "I…"

"Hey, I noticed you brought some bags in with you," Welles said a beat after her. "Did you bring us dinner?"

"I did." Gage continued holding her hand, oblivious to the reaction she was having. "Thai food. Are you hungry?"

"I don't know about Nell, but I am," Welles said. "Mind bringing it over for us?"

Gage let go of Nell's hand and kissed her cheek. "Be right back with your dinner."

All she could do was nod. She tried to slow her breathing.

"Hey," Welles whispered. "Inhale and hold your breath and then exhale."

As he repeated the words, she did as he instructed until her pulse settled. Nell waited until her breathing wasn't as ragged to speak. "I don't know what happened."

"Anxiety. Did you call that therapist?"

"I...I think so, but a lot was happening, and I might have forgot."

"Please do, Nell." His caring tone matched the look in his eyes. "You don't want to end up having panic attacks."

Nell didn't want that, especially if it interfered with her job and ability to care for patients. "I will."

Welles started to speak but then pressed his lips together as if he'd changed his mind.

"What?" she asked.

"Dinner is served." Gage carried out plates of food. "I put a little of everything on the plates. If you want more of anything, let me know."

"This looks great," Welles said.

"Yes, thanks." Nell stared at the chicken satay, the yellow curry, the shrimp pad Thai, and a cucumber salad. All her favorites, which she appreciated. It told her Gage had paid attention to what she liked. "This will hit the spot."

Beaming, Gage bowed. "Anything for my bride-to-be."

Welles stuffed a forkful of curry into his mouth. She had a feeling that was on purpose.

Unsure of what to say, Nell smiled at Gage. But her appetite had all but vanished. Why was she feeling so off around him?

Maybe because Mom had accepted his proposal, not her. Yes, that was probably the reason, and something they needed to discuss after Welles got settled in his bedroom for the night.

Two hours later, Welles lay in his own bed. He would have rather been with Nell, but Gage had kept making hints about being alone with her, so Welles had called it an early night. He still hated that he needed help, but he reminded himself it wouldn't be forever. "Thanks for helping me out."

Gage set a water bottle on the nightstand. "Least I can do. You seem to be doing better."

"I need this boot and cast off." Though that would take weeks not days. "I'm just glad Nell is doing so well. I only wish she could get more time off work."

"Maybe she doesn't have to go back." Gage placed the knee scooter next to the bed. He'd obviously gone over the checklist.

"That's what I want to talk to her about." Gage didn't have a subtle bone in his body.

Somehow Welles managed not to snort. "I thought there was something, but I'm not sure Nell is the stay-at-home-girlfriend type."

"She's my fiancée," Gage clarified. He picked up the baby monitor and fiddled with the power switch. "And she'll be busy with the wedding, so a little time off makes sense, especially with us moving out of the area."

Welles nearly bolted upright. He only allowed himself to push himself up onto his elbows. "Nell never mentioned anything about moving."

"It's a surprise."

One that likely wouldn't go over well. A part of Welles wanted to warn Gage that he shouldn't spring something like that on Nell. "Her family lives in Berry Lake."

"We can visit."

"Where would you move to?"

"Boston." Gage grinned as if he'd won the Powerball. "A fabulous job dropped in my lap. It's a once-in-a-lifetime opportunity. I'd be a fool not to take it."

Welles was torn. Nell had already lived in Boston with Andrew. She'd chosen to return to her small hometown because she wasn't a big-city woman, and Welles couldn't imagine her ever leaving her family and now the Cupcake Posse when she was buying a fifth of the business, but Gage didn't see that. Or maybe he chose not to see it.

Either way, not my circus.

"Good for you." What else was he going to say? "Is this in the same field you were working in before?"

"Adjacent, but at a much higher level. Telling them I was engaged to a RN gave me a leg up, too."

Welles didn't like the sound of that. He didn't trust the guy. "So the job offer came after the proposal?"

"Yes." Gage, however, smirked. "But it was perfect timing. I don't know if I'd have gotten the job if I wasn't getting married."

"That is lucky." And it sucked.

Welles didn't know what else to say. He didn't want Nell to move away. Sure, that would be the best for his heart and love life, but she was his friend. He knew she wouldn't be happy in Boston—or with Gage.

Not long term.

Gage flicked on the baby monitor and placed it on the night-stand. "Let me know if you need anything."

Welles's stomach dropped. He knew the answer, but he still had to ask. "You're staying the night at Nell's?"

Nell glanced at the baby monitor on the coffee table. As far as she knew, only one person had needed to go over there in the middle of the night. That was Juliet when Welles had dropped his pain medication. "Is Welles settled in for the night?"

Gage sat next to her on the couch, going to the side opposite where Mr. Teddy lay. The cat, however, kept giving him the evil eye. "The only thing missing is a teddy bear for Welles to hold while he falls asleep."

"He'd prefer a Sasquatch stuffy."

Gage rolled his eyes. "At least bears are real."

She'd listened to Gage and Welles debate the existence of Sasquatch too many times on their outings. "Well, in Berry Lake, people believe Bigfoot is real, too."

"You need to get out of this town."

"It's home." Her reply came fast. The place was far from perfect, but she enjoyed living there. The pros outweighed the cons.

He shrugged, but the last thing he appeared to be was indifferent. "But Berry Lake is a small town where everyone knows your business."

"My family and friends live here. And the cupcake shop is here, too. Or will be once we reopen."

"You could be a silent co-owner. That's a thing."

Nell didn't want it to be *her* thing. They were all looking forward to Logan retiring so Selena would live in Berry Lake, too, and then the Posse would finally be back together. "Why would I be a silent one when I live here?"

Gage ate a cookie that Jenny had dropped off yesterday.

The atmosphere thickened, and that feeling she'd had earlier returned, hitting Nell right in the solar plexus. She wanted to ask what was going on, but the words seemed to be lodged in her throat. She took a sip of water. It didn't help.

"Something happened when I was away," he said finally. "Nothing bad. Something amazing for *our* future."

Her heart thudded. "What?"

"I was offered a new job. Double the salary. A relocation package. Top-notch benefits."

Nell released the breath she'd been holding. She didn't know what she'd been expecting, but it wasn't that. "That's fantastic. Congratulations."

He nodded. "It's perfect, and I'll be making enough so you can stay home, if you like. I assume that's what you'd want to do when we have kids anyway. And the position is closer to my family."

Wait. What? She'd heard *stay home* and was focused on that, so she must've misunderstood the second part. "Doesn't your family live on the East Coast?"

"Yes."

"Is the job remote like your current one?"

"No, it's in Boston."

Boston. She shivered. She'd moved there with Andrew, and that was the last city she ever wanted to return to. "You want to leave the Pacific Northwest?"

"Working out here was only temporary. I didn't have a time-frame for when I'd go back, but the job offer has given me one. I'd be a fool to turn it down."

He might be right, for him. For her, the thought of leaving Berry Lake saddened her. Everyone she loved lived here. Moving away would be like uprooting her very soul.

"What are you thinking?" Gage asked.

"I left before. For someone. We weren't engaged, but I thought we'd marry someday. We landed in Boston eventually. And the relationship ended in heartbreak. Well, for me."

Gage held her hand with both of his. "This time will be different. We're not only engaged, but we'll also have a wedding date set as soon as you're healed. We'll make it work."

She didn't know what to say, so she bit her lip.

"The East Coast is my home," he continued. "But you're part of my life, too. I want you with me."

Her heart ached at the sincerity in his voice, but uncertainty clung to her like a second skin. "Berry Lake is *my* home. Everything I care about is here. I never thought I'd leave again."

Gage's expression softened. "I understand, babe. But we can make a home in Boston, too. One that will help our family's financial future. What matters most is that we're together, right?"

He seemed to have already made the decision for himself—and for her.

Was leaving Berry Lake truly worth it? And if she decided to stay, would she lose Gage?

The weight of those questions rested heavily on her chest, making it hard to breathe. Tears threatened to spill from her eyes.

Nell hadn't spoken up when he'd proposed, and she hadn't said yes. She couldn't do the same here. "I need some time to think about this."

Not a true answer, but at least she'd spoken up. That counted, right?

Gage's shoulders slumped, and Nell sensed the disappointment radiating off him. A sigh escaped his lips, and he looked away from her, rubbing the back of his neck.

"Of course. This is a big decision, but the company needs my decision. Is a week enough time?" Gage's voice was low, strained.

Mr. Teddy watched the exchange with narrowed eyes. As if sensing the tension, the cat emitted a low hiss in Gage's direction, adding insult to injury.

"A week is fine." Except as she said the words, she didn't think it was nearly long enough time to make such a huge decision.

"I hope you'll see how important this is to me," he said. "I want us to start our life together with a clean slate. And what better place than a new city in a new state."

"I can see that." Even if she didn't agree.

"This is important to me."

"I know." Nell's insides twisted. She couldn't make such a monumental decision without weighing each option. And doing so when she was healing physically and emotionally would be more difficult. But somehow, she would have to figure this out.

And fast.

chapter nineteen

THE POSSE SAT in Missy's living room. She'd made cupcakes—something she'd been doing daily with Sam's help—and Juliet had brewed three different flavors of tea. The atmosphere, however, was heavy, and Missy knew it was the unopened letter sitting on her coffee table—a letter from the State of Washington that contained either their cottage food permit or a rejection letter.

Missy had been so focused on Elias trying to get permission to go into the cupcake shop that she'd been shocked when the mail arrived with the letter. She'd called an emergency Posse gathering, and Sam went to have lunch with his parents.

Her impatience kept growing each second. She needed one thing to go right in her life. Well, other than Sam. She wanted that to be the cupcake shop for her friends and for Elise. But no one else seemed to be in a rush.

Were they nervous like her?

She didn't want to ask because that would only make her worry more.

"I love this lemon flavor. So light and fluffy, too." Bria finished one of the new cupcakes Missy had been experimenting with and wiped her mouth with a napkin. Her eyes were brighter today, but her smile seemed forced. It would take her time to get over Dalton. When this happened in high school, Bria had left Berry Lake and not returned until Elise's cancer diagnosis, but that was more than fifteen years ago. Bria wasn't that same shy and insecure girl. "I can't wait to see how the new menu does."

"Same." Nell had barely touched her cupcake, which wasn't like her at all. She fiddled with her engagement ring, twisting the band back and forth on her finger.

Maybe she wasn't feeling well.

"And I love all the new merch prototypes Selena came up with, including the logo." Nell nodded.

"They're great," Missy agreed.

Bria grinned. "Can you imagine seeing our logo on people's shirts and water bottles?"

"I love that we'll be expanding our customer base beyond Berry Lake." Juliet filled her teacup. "Birthday, anniversary, and special holiday-themed cupcake packs seem like the perfect way to do online sales."

Missy nodded, but her insides twisted. She couldn't wait any longer. "Yes, but none of that'll happen if we don't open the letter."

"We should play the Jeopardy theme," Selena joked, trying to lighten the mood.

"I can't believe you drove all the way back here for this." Nell sounded surprised, even though Selena usually made more than one trip a month. "I mean, I'm happy you're here."

Selena shrugged. "Well, the Volcanoes are on another road trip, so why do I want to be in that big house by myself when I can hang out with all of you?"

"We're much better company than your succulents," Bria said in a matter-of-fact tone.

Missy flexed her fingers. "So...are we ready to open it?"

"I guess we can't put it off any longer," Juliet said.

A heavy silence descended.

She swallowed around the cupcake-sized lump in her throat. "What's inside might change our plans, but..."

"Everything will be okay," Selena finished for her. "If we have to wait until the bakery is remodeled, so be it."

"Or..." Bria piped in. "We figure out what more we need to do to get a food permit."

Juliet nodded. "There's no reason to worry, Missy. Good or bad, we've got this."

"Cupcake Posse forever," Nell said.

"Cupcake Posse forever," they all repeated.

Missy wanted to believe they would be together forever, and the cupcake shop would reopen and be better than before, but she was so mindful of the monitor she wore on her leg. "It's hard not to think everything will fall apart. Things with Sam have been great. And you're all here..."

"Believe it'll all work out." Selena's kind tone seemed to dissipate the tension in the air. "So much is out of our control that assuming and believing it will turn out is all we can do."

Missy wished she could let go like that, but no matter how much she listened to Selena T's podcast, read the books, and did the exercises she'd been given, letting go was difficult. "I want to do that, but I feel like I need remedial abundance and manifestation training."

Her friends laughed.

Nell raised her hand. "Same."

"You guys are doing better than you know." Selena smiled at each of them. "Now, let's find out what's inside the envelope."

Juliet nodded. "Missy should open it."

Missy shook her head. It would be easier if someone else did. "No, that's okay."

Bria picked up the envelope and handed it to Missy. "You're the one who planned how this satellite cupcake shop would work. You interacted with the inspector. You have put your heart and soul into the cupcake shop since you were fifteen and ran it from the time Elise got her diagnosis. Open it."

Missy held on to the envelope, careful not to crinkle it. Her heart raced with a mix of dread and fear. It should have been anticipation and excitement, yet those emotions weren't even close to the other two. If she was convicted of arson, would it even matter what was inside?

For the rest of the Posse, yes. Just not her.

Think of them.

"Here we go." Missy slid her finger under the flap to open it and removed the folded papers. As she unfolded them, she forced herself to breathe. She glanced at the first page, and her jaw dropped.

Oh my goodness…

Juliet leaned forward. "What does it say?"

Tears stung the corners of Missy's eyes. She showed her friends the second page. "We got the permit. The Berry Lake Cupcake Shop's back in business."

Everyone cheered.

Missy stared at the permit. Hope overflowed in her heart. This had to be a good sign. Oh, what was she thinking? Missy didn't care if it wasn't. She would make the most of this for as long as she could. Sam would be so excited, too. Missy wiggled her toes.

"We have so much to do!" Juliet said.

Bria nodded. "We'll get it done."

"Whatever it takes," Selena agreed.

Nell looked at the permit, buried her face in her hands, and sobbed.

Missy glanced at the others, who seemed as confused as she was at Nell's reaction. Bria shrugged. Juliet's nose crinkled. Selena's eyes narrowed. Seconds later, they surrounded Nell.

"Hey." Selena had her arm around Nell. "What's going on?"

Nell raised her head slightly and wiped her face. "Gage got a job offer in Boston. He wants to move there."

Missy's stomach clenched. Boston was so far away, and that was where Nell had lived with Andrew when things fell apart. She thought Nell planned on staying in Berry Lake, but if she'd changed her mind, Missy wanted to be supportive. "What do you want to do?"

"Stay here. My entire life is here. Family. Job. You guys. The cupcake shop." She held out her left hand. The diamond sparkled brightly. "I thought getting engaged would make all my wishes come true, but now... I don't want to move to Boston. I barely know Gage, and he's given me a week to decide my future. At this point, I'm not even sure I want to marry him."

The words fell from her mouth like a mic drop.

Boom!

Nell's eyes widened. "Oh, my. I said that out loud, didn't I?"

Missy nodded. She thought Welles was the right man for Nell, not Gage, but that wasn't her decision to make. "You've been through a lot. And this is a lot to decide in a very short time."

"Missy's right." Juliet's voice was so quiet and calm. "It's natural to have doubts, but the question to ask yourself is: Do you love Gage?"

"I…" Nell took a breath. "I like him. But my mom's the one who said yes to his proposal, not me. I've been carried along since then like I'm caught in a riptide and I can't get myself out of it. I feel so stupid for not speaking up earlier."

"Hey." Selena leaned into Nell. "Like Missy said, you've been through a lot, and the proposal must have blindsided you."

Nell sniffled. "It did. Who am I kidding? It still does. But now that the cupcake shop is back in business, I don't want to be on the other side of the country, in a city that holds only bad memories. I want to be here, working with you all."

"You know what you want," Selena said. "You just have to discuss it with Gage. Maybe he won't take the job."

"He wants the job. He already told me that. If I don't move, he probably won't want to marry me. And my mother…" More tears fell from Nell's eyes. "She'll be so disappointed in me again."

"You can't get married and move away to keep from upsetting your mom," Missy said with as much kindness as she could muster when a part of her wanted to shake some sense into her friend. "I lost my folks when I married Rob, and I'd make the same decision again. You can't live your life trying to please other people. You'll end up miserable."

Nell half laughed. "I already am, not knowing what I should do."

Selena smoothed Nell's hair. "Then you have to figure it out."

"And if you decide you don't want to marry Gage," Bria said, "we're here to support you."

Juliet nodded. "We'll always be here for you if you decide to go to Boston, too."

"Thanks." Nell wiped her eyes again. "You're right. I need to figure things out. But first, I'm ready for another cupcake."

Missy passed her the plate. "And we need to decide when the bakery will be back in business."

"I suppose tomorrow's too soon," Bria teased.

"Nothing's impossible for the Cupcake Posse." Selena didn't miss a beat. "But we don't need to add that level of craziness to our lives."

They didn't, Missy agreed. But these women and their cupcake shop were just the right amount of crazy. Add in Sam and the cats and she couldn't ask for anything more. Everything was working out. She had to believe that would extend to the charges against her. And if not...

She'd cross that bridge when she came to it.

Sam sat at his parents' kitchen table. He hadn't been home for a few days, and Mom had made him lunch, but he would have much rather been with Missy. Her guest cottage felt more like home, even though he'd grown up in this house and had lived there since he'd returned from Seattle.

One more reason to make things official. He touched his pocket.

Mom placed the pan of sloppy joe sauce on a trivet. "How's Missy doing?"

"About the same," he admitted. "Elias keeps trying to get access to the cupcake shop, but it hasn't happened yet, and that worries Missy. She's been doing a lot of baking."

Dad, who was working from home today, put two of the sesame seed buns on his plate. "Thank her for the cupcakes you brought over. They look tasty."

"I will."

Missy had been struggling. So many things hadn't gone her way. The most recent had been her foster cats. She'd wanted the kittens and Mama cat to come back to her, but Sabine didn't want to move them again from their current foster. Sabine also thought Peach and Mario needed Missy's attention. But Sam thought Missy just wanted to go back to how things had been before her arrest.

"I'm worried about her," Sam admitted. "She needs something to get her mind off the arson charge."

Mom smiled. "She has you."

Heat rushed up Sam's neck. "I meant more than me. I was thinking…"

"Eat," Mom encouraged.

Sam filled his plate and added a handful of potato chips. He took a bite of his sloppy joe sandwich. "Tastes good, Mom."

"You always loved them when you were younger." She refilled his glass of iced tea. "Are you planning to stay at Missy's tonight?"

"If she wants me there. Her friends are there now."

Dad laughed. "So that's why you're here."

"Busted." Sam's heart rate picked up speed. "But there is something I want to discuss with you."

Mom leaned forward over the table. "Sounds serious."

Sam blew out a breath. He removed the ring box from his pocket, opened it, and placed it on the table. "I'm going to ask Missy to marry me."

Mom and Dad stared at the ring. Sam couldn't tell if they were shocked, but their silence made him think they weren't happy about his plan.

The only sounds in the kitchen were the hum of the refrigerator and Sam's heart beating. But he didn't care what they thought. Oh, he wanted their support, but he would propose without it.

The diamond solitaire wasn't anything fancy. But even after looking at the various rings, the design had made him think of Missy. The fact that it was one of the cheaper engagement rings at the jewelry store had been a bonus, given he was unemployed and living off his savings right now.

Mom smiled at him, but her gaze appeared wary. "That's a beautiful ring, honey. Any woman would be thrilled to marry you, but are you sure about this? You and Missy haven't been together that long."

"I'm sure. Dad said when it's right you know." Sam's gaze traveled back to the ring. "I know."

"I did say that." Dad leaned back in his chair. His jaw tightened. "You've had a crush on Missy for a long time, but it's a bit soon to propose."

Not soon enough in Sam's view, given he'd wanted her for more than half his life. "I want to make the most of our time together. Whether that's a few weeks, depending on what happens with the trial, or the next sixty years."

"Your mind is made up," Dad said without missing a beat.

"It is."

"We will always support you, Sam. I hope you know that." Mom's eyes gleamed. "But we want to make sure this is the right step for you."

"It's the most right step I'll ever take." The words rushed out of Sam's mouth like water from a broken fire hydrant. "Just because it's happening quick doesn't mean it's wrong for us. I only want what's best for Missy, and I know in my heart, that's me."

"Oh, honey." Mom rubbed her eyes. "You are the best thing for her."

"We just want to make sure she's the best thing for you," Dad added.

"I have no doubt about that." His heart overflowed with love for Missy. "She's not perfect, but she's perfect for me. I love her so much."

Mom and Dad exchanged a glance, and then Mom smiled. "So when are you going to propose?"

That evening, Missy didn't know what kind of surprise Sam had in mind. He'd sat her on the couch and tied a bandana over her eyes. She was still there, blindfolded, and unsure of what was going on. A purring Peach lay on her lap, but that was the only noise she heard. "Are we celebrating the cottage food permit?"

"You'll see," he said.

"Not unless you take off the blindfold," she joked.

"When the time is right…"

She wondered how long that would be. He'd returned after her friends had left like a man with a single purpose, straightening and cleaning even though the place was already spotless. Still, she appreciated his effort. Whatever the surprise ended up being, she would be very grateful.

The sound of rain came out of nowhere, pelting the roof and windows. "I'm assuming we're not going outside."

"Nope. We're staying inside. But that's not because of the rain."

That was the biggest clue he'd given her. Maybe he was cooking her dinner. He'd been a big help making cupcakes, and he'd made her breakfast, so she knew he could cook.

Though Missy didn't smell anything. She sniffed just to make sure.

"No peeking," he warned playfully.

"I'm not."

"Okay, it's time." He took her hands and pulled her to her feet. "I'm going to lead you. I won't let go, so you don't have to worry about bumping into anything."

Missy wasn't steady on her feet in the darkness, but she trusted Sam. She didn't seem to go far. "Now what?"

"Stand there for a minute. I'll be right back."

A click sounded, but she couldn't place the noise. Music played—a love song by one of her favorite artists. That was sweet of Sam to remember she enjoyed that one.

She smiled. Were they going to dance?

"Okay, everything is ready now," he said.

His arms brushed her shoulders. The blindfold loosened and fell off her face. She blinked, letting her eyes adjust.

The lights were dim, and every flat surface contained a lit candle. It was lovely and romantic.

She glanced around in awe. "Sam, this is beautiful, but I'm not sure the permit warrants this much effort."

Still, Missy would take it.

"This isn't for the permit. This is for you." Sam dropped onto one knee, and that was when she noticed they were standing in a heart made of rose petals. He pulled out a velvet ring box and opened it. A gorgeous diamond solitaire sparkled against the black.

Her heart slammed against her rib cage. She covered her mouth with one hand, unable to believe this was happening.

Sam took a deep breath and reached for her other hand, his touch calming her even though she struggled to breathe.

"This may seem out of the blue, but I'm not on my knee without knowing this We are one hundred percent right and belong together. I love you more than anything in this world, Missy, and I want to spend the rest of my life with you, to be with you through everything that comes our way. No matter what." His voice was soft yet determined. "Will you marry me and allow me the honor of being your husband?"

A flood of emotions washed over Missy—hope, love, and peace. Her love for Sam had grown steadily, filling the hollow ache left by Rob's death. She knew, without a doubt, that she wanted to be with Sam forever, but the fear of her current situation loomed large.

What-ifs swirled in her mind, making her want to tell him no because that was the best thing for him. Yet, as she stared into Sam's unwavering gaze, a spark of courage ignited within her.

Tears welled in her eyes. "Yes, Sam. I'll marry you. I love you, and I want to spend my life with you."

Sam placed the ring on her finger—a perfect fit. Just like the way they fit together.

With a huge grin, Sam stood. He pulled her into a tight embrace, his arms encircling her and creating a safe harbor. She would always feel safe, cherished, and loved by him.

Missy melted into his warmth, wanting to memorize the sense of security and belonging he gave her. Her pulse steadied, and her hope grew. Together, they could face and overcome anything.

He kissed her with such tenderness. Tears fell down her cheeks.

Sam wiped them away. "You're crying."

"Tears of joy and happiness." As she rested her head against his chest, her heart swelled with love and gratitude. "Thank you for believing in me and for wanting to spend your life with me."

"I'm the one who's grateful." His voice was thick with emotion. "You've been through so much. You're one of the strongest, kindest people I know."

Missy held on to him tightly and didn't want to let go. But she knew one thing—she wanted their forever to start now. "Can we have a short engagement?"

chapter twenty

NELL SAT IN the passenger seat of Gage's car. She was so excited about Missy's engagement to Sam, and all of them were meeting at Jenny's house to discuss wedding plans. Neither Missy nor Sam wanted a long engagement, which meant they'd asked Mom if she could pull together a wedding quickly. No date, however, had been mentioned.

Nell laughed. She could only imagine Mom's reaction to their request. Though at least it would stop her from doing more work on her and Gage's wedding.

Gage reached across the console between the front seats and held Nell's left hand. His was large and warm, and she waited for a tingle or something to strike. It didn't. But holding hands felt...nice. That counted for something, right?

Or maybe it didn't mean enough and she still had to figured things out. Except...

I'm not even sure I want to marry him.

That had been a constant refrain in her mind since she'd spoken the words aloud to her friends yesterday. A part of her wanted to chalk up her doubts to overwhelm. The other part wanted to take off the ring and give it back to him.

Gage pulled into Jenny and Dare's driveway. "Are you sure you don't want me to stay? I've got a hotspot on my phone, so I can work anywhere."

"Thanks, but do you really want to spend your morning talking about someone else's wedding plans with my mother?"

He cringed and then laughed. "Not really."

Nell figured as much. "I don't blame you."

"I suppose someone needs to be with Welles today."

She nodded. "I don't need the help now, but he still does."

"Guess I'll babysit the paramedic today," Gage teased.

"Don't let him hear you say that," she warned.

Welles was improving, but he didn't like not being able to do anything on his own. He didn't mind the knee scooter as much, but Nell got the feeling he would destroy the wheelchair once he had regained some of his strength. She would have to remind him that donating it to a charity would be a better use of the equipment, even if its destruction would be more satisfying to him.

He engaged the parking brake. "The one good thing about today is you can take notes."

"Notes?"

"For when we plan our wedding, though it sounds like your mom will have everything under control."

"Yes, but we'll have some say." At least Nell hoped so. If they got that far. "I'll get a ride back with someone."

"If not, just call and I'll pick you up." He brushed his lips over hers. "Have fun wedding planning."

Planning someone else's wedding would be more fun than working on her own.

Nell went to the front door and rang the bell.

Dare answered, holding Briley in his arms. "You're just in time. But prepare yourself. It's sheer wedding madness in here."

"Where are they?"

"The dining room." Dare shook his head. "I feel sorry for Sam being the only guy there."

"You could help him out."

"Not a chance." The former Army Ranger sounded horrified. "But he's more than welcome to join me and Briley upstairs."

"I'll tell Sam that if it looks like he needs to escape."

"Oh, he will. Trust me."

Nell made her way into the dining room. Excitement buzzed in the air. Jenny, Bria, Selena, Ava, Hope, Sam, Mrs. Cooper, and Missy sat around the table. Sam looked out of place, but the heart eyes he shot his bride-to-be more than made up for it. The guy was completely smitten.

Missy positively glowed, and the love in her eyes when she looked at Sam took Nell's breath away.

That's what love looks like.

It was nothing like what she and Gage had shared so far. Oh, some hot kisses and fun times, but nothing solid and lasting like she saw in Missy and Sam. The two hadn't been together that long. A far shorter time than she'd known Gage, but the differences were so stark Nell couldn't deny them.

Would that kind of love grow between her and Gage?

Mom and Juliet stood at the end with displays of wedding photos and sketches. Their eyes sparkled with the same enthusiasm they brought to every event they did, but this one was even more special because it was for one of their own.

Guilt coated Nell's throat. She imagined they had similar displays already for her wedding.

"Take a seat, Nell," Mom said in her no-nonsense event planner voice. "We've been waiting for you to get started."

Nell wasn't late—if anything she'd arrived a few minutes early—but she took the empty seat at the table. Charlene Culpepper set high standards for her three daughters.

Mom clapped her hands together. "These two lovebirds are getting married and want to have the wedding as soon as possible."

"We're sorry, but tomorrow is a little too soon," Juliet joked.

Everyone laughed, but Nell was surprised Missy and Sam wanted such a short engagement. She would have thought a longer one, under the circumstances, made more sense. But then again, love wasn't supposed to be logical…

Sam wrapped his arm protectively around Missy. "What about the day after tomorrow?"

More laughter sounded.

Mrs. Cooper shook her head. "My son has no idea what's involved in planning a wedding."

"We don't want anything fancy," Missy said. "Just a few friends. I can make the cupcakes."

"Not for your own wedding!" Mom's voice rose an octave higher. "You'll have other things to do as the bride."

"Missy doesn't need to bake, but she enjoys it," Sam said. "We appreciate everyone being here this morning, but we just want to get married as soon and as simply as possible. If Missy could go anywhere, we'd just elope."

"No!" everyone shouted.

"You need to have a wedding, Sam," Ava said, sounding very much like an older sister. Nell would know since she'd used the same tone with Evie and JoJo on many occasions.

"We can't elope now, but that's the kind of wedding we're thinking." Missy glanced at Sam. The affection flowing between them was palpable. "We also don't have much of a budget."

"Don't worry about that," Selena said.

Jenny nodded. "Neither of you have jobs right now, so you just let all of us take care of things for you."

Missy's gaze met Sam's once again, and then she shrugged. "Thank you."

At least the happy couple wouldn't fight having those who cared about them pay for the wedding. That was one hurdle they wouldn't have to overcome.

"Juliet and I looked over the calendar. We suggest having the wedding a week from Friday, in the evening. That's the same day as the next high school football playoff game, if the team continues to win, but it's the only day that isn't midweek until after Christmas."

"We'll take it," Sam said without missing a beat.

Missy laughed. "Guess we have a wedding date."

"Let's start with the venue." Mom picked up her tablet. "Jenny and Dare have offered to hold the wedding here. The backyard is big enough for a tent, but given the weather in November, I suggest having the ceremony and reception inside."

"That's not a problem," Jenny said. "We'll move the furniture into the garage. Whatever you need us to do, we'll do it."

"What about a guest list?" Juliet asked.

Missy glanced around. "Everyone who is here. The rest of Sam's family. Sabine, Max, JoJo, and Evie. Bentley. Welles and Buddy."

"We want family and friends there," Sam added. "Twenty-five, thirty at the most."

"Very doable inside the house." Charlene tapped on her tablet. "We'll make sure the day is one you'll remember."

"It'll be amazing," Jenny said to the happy couple.

Her enthusiasm was contagious. Nell wished she felt the same about her wedding. But maybe that should tell her something.

"I just want to make sure Missy and Sam are sure about this," Ava said cautiously. "You've both been through so much, and now you want to plan a wedding?"

The question hung in the air, heavy with tension.

Nell understood Ava's concern. She was Sam's older sister. But Nell had no doubt Sam and Missy belonged together.

"Of course, we're sure," Missy answered with conviction. "Everything is happening quickly, but I've never been more certain of anything in my life than I am about marrying Sam."

Sam kissed her cheek. "Ditto."

All her friends laughed.

"Thanks for your concern, sis." Sam's steady voice reinforced Missy's words. "But we know what we want, and we're ready to face this journey together."

Ava smiled. "Just wanted to make sure."

Nell didn't have to ask any questions. She could tell they were sure.

I wish I had that.

Maybe what Nell and Gage had would grow into that. Or maybe she would find it with someone else.

After spending the morning at Jenny and Dare's house, Nell rode in the passenger seat of Mom's car. "Nothing like planning a wedding in a day. I'm impressed with you and Juliet."

"She's been a huge help and is already growing the business." Mom smiled at Nell. "Just wait until you see what we've been putting together for your and Gage's wedding."

This was the opening Nell needed. "I appreciate all your work, Mom, but I'm not sure if I should marry Gage."

Mom shot Nell a sideward glance. "Why in the world would you say that? He's perfect for you."

"Maybe on paper, but I…" Nell paused, trying to keep her emotions in check. "I don't love him."

"You'll learn to love him."

Nell figured she might as well tell her the real problem. "He has a job offer that will require him to relocate to Boston. He wants me to go with him."

"Of course he does. Gage loves you."

He'd said the words, but somehow, they lacked the same emotion as she saw with Missy and Sam. "You'd be okay with me moving to the East Coast?"

Mom's expression softened. "I know how much Berry Lake means to you, sweetheart. But you're thirty-seven now, and you don't date much. This might be your last chance at marriage, and I know how badly you've always wanted a family."

Nell's throat tightened at her mother's words, the weight of her expectations adding to the pressure she already felt. She stared at her lap, tracing the geometric pattern on the colorful fleece throw with her fingertip as she fought the tears threatening to spill.

"Mom, I…" Nell's voice cracked with emotion. "I don't know if I can leave Berry Lake. Not even for Gage. It's my home. It's all I've ever known."

"Sometimes we must make sacrifices for the people we love, sweetheart." Mom touched Nell's arm closest to her. "You'll still be able to visit, and you've lived there once before and didn't hate it."

Until the life she'd dreamed about had imploded.

"Just don't make a rash decision," Mom added. "A man like Gage could have his pick of women, but he chose you. You should feel grateful he wants you."

The words hit like a left hook. Nell bit her lip, trying to stifle a sob. She knew Mom meant well, wanting her to be happy and settled with a family of her own. But the thought of leaving Berry Lake, the only place she'd ever truly felt at home, filled her with a sense of dread.

Especially when the only thing she'd ever wanted was to love and be loved. And Nell didn't feel the kind of love she'd seen with Missy and Sam or Jenny and Dare.

What am I going to do?

The next day, the scent of vanilla and cinnamon filled Nell's apartment thanks to Gage bringing breakfast for her and Welles, who hadn't arrived yet. That would give her time to talk to Gage about Boston and their engagement. She crossed her fingers, hoping it went well.

Gage leaned in, pressing a kiss to her cheek that left a lingering tingle. "Missed you."

"Breakfast smells delicious."

"I know you don't approve of Penelope Jones, but The Huckleberry Inn makes the best coffee cake."

That explained his sheepish expression. "It is delicious. Even Juliet would agree. Thanks for bringing a pan over."

"You're welcome." He carried two plates to the living room. "I have something else for you."

He'd walked in with the coffee cake and his laptop bag, so she didn't know what else he'd brought with him. "What's that?"

"I found some houses online you might like." He sounded excited and pulled out his phone. The screen displayed images of beautiful homes in the historic city, far away from her beloved small town in Washington. "Imagine raising a family in one of these."

Nell's fingers fidgeted with the edge of her shirt. Her stomach hurt, but the pain had nothing to do with her injury. "Are you sure you want to buy a place right away?"

"Positive. The rockfall accident made me reevaluate everything. Life's too short not to chase my dreams." His eyes met hers, searching for understanding. "*Our* dreams. You want a family."

It wasn't a question, and she did. She wanted a family of her own so much, but...

Nell felt a pang of empathy for Gage. If she loved him the way a wife loved a husband—or a future spouse—this would be a no-brainer decision, but her heart twisted at the thought of leaving her life behind. Her family, her friends, her job, and the cupcake shop anchored her to this town. She couldn't just pack up and leave, especially when she wasn't sure about her feelings for Gage.

Maybe someday, she would regret not grabbing hold of everything he was offering her, but he wasn't giving her the time to figure everything out. It wasn't like Missy and Sam, but seeing them yesterday made it clearer what she needed to do today.

"Gage…" She took a deep breath and another. "I understand why you want to take the job in Boston. I really do, but my life is here. I can't just move away to the other side of the country."

Her words hung heavy between them. But the more she thought about Missy and Sam, the more it clarified everything she'd been trying to make sense of—namely her engagement. And she knew without a doubt marrying Gage would be an even bigger mistake than leaving Berry Lake.

It wasn't what she truly wanted.

His gaze narrowed. "Where does this leave us?"

Swallowing hard, she eased the engagement ring off her finger and returned it to him. "I'm sorry."

Gage stared at the ring in his hand, his eyes wide with disbelief. "I love you."

Nell remembered what Selena had told her. "Sometimes, love isn't enough. I can't be the person you need me to be."

"Will you change your mind?" Desperation crept into his voice.

"No," Nell said, resolute. "This is for the best."

He opened his mouth and then closed it. "You're making a mistake. I could get you out of this small town and give you everything."

She didn't want to argue with him. "Thank you for everything. You pushed me out of my comfort zone on so many things." Nell kissed his cheek.

He cupped her face, gazing into her eyes as if he could change her mind, and then his shoulders slumped. "Goodbye, Nell. I hope you find what you're looking for."

Gage left her apartment. The door shut behind him.

She waited for the tears to come, but the overwhelming emotion flooding her wasn't sadness or regret—it was relief.

Guess I made the right decision.

A knock sounded.

Had Gage come back? She opened the door and found Welles on his knee scooter.

"Hey," he said. "I thought I saw Gage leaving. Did he forget something?"

"No."

As he studied her face, Welles's brows furrowed. "You look different." His gaze dropped to her left hand. "Your ring...."

Nell glanced down at her bare finger where the engagement ring had once sparkled. "I broke up with Gage."

Welles's eyes widened in surprise. "Why? What happened?"

"I didn't love him. Not like I should."

As she spoke, relief washed over Welles's features, visible in the slight lift of his shoulders and the lightening of his eyes. He leaned forward, holding on. "It's good you realized that. You deserve to be with someone you truly love."

"Thanks." Uncertainty gnawed at her. "My mom thinks Gage was my last shot at getting married."

"She's wrong. That guy is selfish and only thinks of himself. I'm glad you saw through him because I was trying to figure out how to tell you just how wrong he was for you." His voice was so gentle a lump in her throat burned. "And regardless, your happiness is what matters most."

"Thank you."

"You're welcome." Warmth radiated from his eyes. "But you know what this means..."

"What?"

"I can ask you out again."

She laughed, and doing so felt good. "Be careful. I might say yes the next time."

"That's what I'm counting on."

His gaze met hers, and something flowed between them—a connection that was both friendship and something more. She studied the curve of Welles's jaw, and her pulse sprinted. Her cheeks heated.

"But I'm not going to rush you."

"You're not?"

"Nope." He rode the scooter to the couch and sat there. "Not after everything that's happened."

"Thank you." The words felt like both a relief and a disappointment, leaving her heart aching for something she couldn't quite grasp. "I appreciate that."

He smiled, but Nell couldn't help but notice the way it didn't quite reach his eyes. "But when the time's right, watch out, Nurse Nell."

That made her laugh again. "Thanks for the warning, Paramedic Welles."

Nell just wondered how long it would take for the timing to be right

chapter twenty-one

ISSY'S WEDDING DAY arrived so fast she could hardly believe it, but somehow all the plans came together. Natural light filtered through the curtains, casting a warm glow on Missy's wedding gown adorned with intricate floral embroidery. For something "off the rack" as Charlene called it, the dress was something out of a movie and fit like a dream. Missy couldn't believe she was wearing it now.

Now that she finally had a minute to herself while everyone did last-minute stuff, Missy took one breath then another to calm her nerves. No cold feet, but she felt as if they'd stomped on the accelerator, and she needed a moment to lift her foot. She stared at her reflection in the free-standing mirror Dare had carried into their guest room that Jenny had turned into the "bridal room."

The elegant A-line gown with an illusion neckline and long sleeves had been a gift from Sheridan and Michael, a thank-you for Missy giving Sheridan a job when she'd found herself jobless last year. The dress was divine and belonged on the cover of a glossy bridal magazine, but it fit Missy perfectly. She not only looked like a bride, but also felt like one. Her smile reached all the way to her bridal-pink-painted toes.

Love and second chances.

She would focus on those two things today.

Like her first wedding to Rob, this one would be as intimate because few in town supported her. She had no doubt that the wedding Charlene—this time with help from Juliet—planned would be as lovely. Missy couldn't ask for a better location than Jenny and Dare's house.

A knock sounded on the door. "Can we come in?"

Missy recognized Nell's voice. She turned to face the doorway so her friends would see her in the dress. "Of course."

The door opened, and five gasps immediately followed. Jenny stood behind her four friends.

Nell's eyes widened. "You're absolutely stunning."

"A radiant bride," Bria said.

"I've never seen you look so lovely." Jenny sniffled. "I'm so happy for you, Missy."

Selena nodded. "That dress is divine."

Juliet placed her hand over her heart. "You look like a real-life princess."

"Thank you." Missy motioned to her dress. "At first, the dress seemed a little much, but I love it."

"It's perfect," the five said in unison.

"We have some things for you." Bria, dressed in a lovely blue dress, handed her a vintage handkerchief. "Something old. I found this in Aunt Elise's room. I know she would want you to have this on your wedding day."

Missy clutched the cloth. "This is lovely. I'll wrap this around my bouquet handle in case I need it during the ceremony, and that way Elise is with me at the altar."

Bria's eyes gleamed. "She's always with you, Missy."

Not trusting her voice, Missy nodded. Elise's spirit—and Rob's, too—would be with her and Sam today. "Thank you."

Selena stepped forward, looking like a model in a green dress, and held out a black velvet-covered jewelry box. "Something new."

Missy took it and opened the lid to find a pair of pearl earrings with a diamond stud on each. "Oh, they're beautiful."

"Nell made me sanitize them," Selena teased. "So you can put them in as is."

Nell shrugged, but she always looked out for her friends.

"I'll do it right now." She removed the fake pearls she'd ordered online—those would have been fine, but these were better—and put in the new ones. "They're so perfect with the dress. Thank you."

"You deserve them," Selena said sincerely.

"Now for something blue." Nell handed her two lace-trimmed blue garters. "I got an extra so Sam can throw one and you can keep the other."

Missy clutched the two to her chest. None of the Cupcake Posse had been at her wedding to Rob since they'd all lived out of state at the time. Missy's family had disowned her, and she'd only been eighteen. Jenny, Charlene, and Elise had done their best, but no one had done the time-honored bridal traditions with Missy. She hadn't minded. All she'd wanted was to say "I do" that day. She'd been so young and starry-eyed the first time, but this time she wanted to savor each part of her and Sam's wedding day.

Juliet held out her hand for the garters. "Let's put these on you."

Missy gave them to her, lifted her dress, and stuck out her left foot. Juliet put the garters over her foot. "There you go."

Missy brought them up onto her thigh. "You guys. I can't thank you enough."

"We're not done yet." Juliet took the bracelet off her wrist. "Hold out your arm."

Missy did.

"Something borrowed." Juliet clasped a pearl bracelet around Missy's wrist. "These belonged to my grandmother, and though we all know she's not the same person she used to be, she wore them on her wedding day. Ezra didn't want me to wear anything he hadn't bought me, so you're the next bride to wear it."

"Thanks." None of them associated with Penelope now, but the woman had treated her, Jenny, and Elise to a bridal tea before Missy married Rob. That had meant the world to Missy.

Now the jewelry was likely one of the few things Juliet had of her grandmother's, which made wearing the pearls even more special. "I'll be sure to give them back after the wedding."

Not that they were going anywhere but the cottage for their honeymoon. But that was as good as it would get until...

Nope. She wouldn't think about anything except her wedding today.

"I have one more thing for you." Jenny came forward, wearing a lovely burnt-orange dress. The hem flowed around her legs.

Missy and Sam had decided on an autumn-themed wedding, and her matron of honor had found the perfect dress to go with the color palette.

Jenny held out a coin. "A sixpence for your shoe. Or in this case, a penny."

Missy accepted the coin. This was all the luck she and Sam would need.

No matter what happened, Jenny would always be Missy's sister of the heart. Jenny and Dare had already said Missy and Sam could live in the guesthouse as long as they wanted. "Thanks."

She held on to Selena while she put the penny into her shoe, a white lace ballet flat, and then straightened. She blinked and fanned her empty hand in front of her face. "I don't want to cry and mess up my makeup, but thank you. I can't thank you enough for everything you've all done for me."

Juliet touched her arm. "I'd say for us to do a group hug, but I don't want us to mess up anyone's dress or makeup."

"No, we're not going to do that." Jenny shook her head as if to emphasize the point. "It was hard enough to get Missy to sit still this morning."

"Truth," Missy admitted.

"Totally worth it though." Selena studied her. "I'm so proud of you for following your heart with Sam."

A lump formed in Missy's throat. She'd never expected to be a bride again. Marriage was something that would happen to Bria and Nell and then Juliet, not Missy. "That means so much."

Juliet gave Missy a squeeze. "I need to see if Charlene needs any help. I'll see you downstairs."

"We should go to our seats," Bria, ever practical, said.

Nell blew Missy a kiss. "We'll see you soon."

"In a short time, you'll be Sam's wife." Selena grinned.

Missy inhaled sharply, managing a slight nod. Her friends left.

"Are you okay?" Jenny asked.

"A little overwhelmed."

"You've been through so much these past weeks, but I believe things are turning around for you now."

Missy wanted that more than anything. "I hope so."

Jenny hugged her tightly and then stepped back to help put on Missy's veil. "You're so beautiful."

Missy watched as the veil made her feel even more like a bride. "I can't believe today's my wedding day."

"Rob would have wanted this for you, Missy." Jenny brushed away a tear, her smile bittersweet but genuine. "He'd be so happy you found love again, and he always thought the world of Sam."

Missy's heart filled with so much gratitude she thought it might burst. "Thank you. For everything."

"That's what sisters are for. And no matter what your last name is, you'll always be my sister." Jenny winked. "Now let's get you married!"

Missy took a deep breath and followed Jenny out the door. Two bouquets, one larger than the other, sat on a table in the landing. The flowers took Missy's breath away. Charlene and Juliet had made her go through what flowers she liked, so Missy knew some of the names: alstroemeria, eryngium, eucalyptus, carnations, hypericum, ranunculus, roses, solidago, spray roses, stock, and waxflower. But she'd had no idea all of them together would look that good.

"Sam's a lucky man, Missy," Bentley said, looking sharply dressed in a tuxedo with a burnt-orange bowtie and cummerbund. He held on to Briley.

"Thanks." She still wasn't sure why Bentley had her niece. "You and Briley…"

With his free hand, he showed her the black pouch hanging off his shoulder full of orange petals. "We're your flower girl and boy."

"This was Dare and Sam's idea," Jenny said amused. "You have to admit they look good together."

Missy laughed. "Yes, and this is a wonderful surprise. Thanks, Bentley."

"Least I can do for you, boss." He winked. "Sam, Josh, and Dare took me to get this tux. Totally slay, don't you think?"

She nodded, imagining the three guys trying on tuxedos. Sam and Dare weren't the fancy or high-fashion types, so she hoped they hadn't caused too much trouble for Josh. "You look amazing."

Music played.

Bentley straightened. "That's our cue. See you down there."

He danced down the stairs with Briley in his arms. The little girl grinned, seeming to love every minute. When he reached the first floor, the dancing continued, as if he'd choreographed a routine, and the petals flew. As Briley giggled, guests oohed and aahed.

The music changed to another song.

"My turn." Jenny's gaze met hers. "You good?"

"Extremely." Getting married again was something Missy never could have imagined happening a month ago, but she had no doubt this was what she wanted—no, needed. "I can't wait to be Mrs. Sam Cooper."

"Okay, then." Jenny reached out and squeezed her hand. "Let's do this."

As Jenny headed to the first floor, Missy knew her cue to meet Dare at the bottom of the stairs, and he would walk her down the aisle.

The music changed again.

A thrill shot through her, but no nerves appeared. This felt as right as the first time had, though she was older and wiser.

Flowers, greenery, and white fairy lights decorated the banister. Charlene and Juliet had gone overboard to make this a dream wedding. As Missy descended the stairs, her gown cascaded behind her, each step bringing her closer to her new beginning with Sam.

She reached the bottom, only it wasn't Dare who joined her. Her lips parted. "Sam?"

Tears welled in his eyes. He wiped them, took her hand, and kissed it. As his gaze locked onto hers, a tender smile graced his lips. His eyes shimmered with love and anticipation, mirroring Missy's same emotions.

He took a breath. "You're stunning." Sam wore a tuxedo, only his bowtie was white. He looked more like a model than her future husband.

"You're breathtaking."

"I'll take that," he joked. "Dare and I were talking, and well, here I am. Is that okay?"

"I can't think of anyone better to walk me down the aisle."

He squeezed her hand. "Let's start our forever."

Sam led her toward the living room. White chairs were meticulously arranged, and the seated guests stared. Missy glimpsed Welles sitting next to his father. Her heart swelled with joy. Without Welles, she never would have survived the fire or been there to get married.

The Cupcake Posse was all there. Sheridan and Michael, too. Sabine, Max, Charlene, Elias, his dad, and grandparents. All of them sat on the left side. Sam's family filled up the two front row seats on the right side. Behind them was Mary from the sheriff's office.

An intimate wedding with everyone who loved and supported her in attendance. That was all she and Sam needed. He squeezed her hand as if he felt the same.

They reached the aisle between the two rows of chairs. Orange petals lay on the aisle, courtesy of Bentley and Briley.

Missy's smile widened. "Magical."

"It is," Sam said softly. "And so are you."

In front of the fireplace stood an elegant arch. Orange and cream blooms and twining greenery created a picturesque backdrop for the exchange of vows. The officiant, a nice woman Charlene had used before, stood in the center. Josh, the best man, stood on the right side, offering a reassuring nod in her direction. Jenny stood on the left, smiling big. Bentley and Briley sat next to Dare in the front row.

The officiant greeted them. "I know you're both ready, so let's not waste any more time."

As she did a reading, Missy listened, wanting to memorize every moment about today, but she was most aware of the man standing next to her.

"The bride and groom have written their own vows," the officiant said to murmurs from the guests.

"Missy." Sam's voice, full of emotion, cracked. "From the moment we met when we were younger, I knew you were special. I had the biggest crush on you back then, but that was nothing compared to how I feel about the woman you've become. You're strong, kind, and have faced challenges that would break most people." He paused, swallowing hard, before continuing. "But you didn't break. You fought. And now here we are, starting our lives together. I promise to be your rock, your support, and your partner in all things. I will love you for who you are and who you will become."

As tears slid down Missy's cheek, her chest tightened with emotion while she listened to Sam's heartfelt words. She dabbed at her eyes with Elise's handkerchief.

Now, it was her turn to speak. She drew in a shaky breath, trying to steady her voice. "Sam, you've shown me that love can heal even the deepest wounds. My heart had been closed off for nine long years. I thought that would last forever, but you've proven me wrong. You've shown me that it's possible to love again, and for that, I'm eternally grateful."

Sam wiped his eyes. Jenny sniffled.

"You've been my rock and support and my everything. You left your job for me. You've continued to put me first and love me when most people would have walked away. Your unwavering faith in me has given me hope when I thought there was none left. I promise to stand by you through thick and thin, to be your best friend, and to love you unconditionally." She took a breath. "Thank you for being you. I couldn't ask for more. I love you. So, so much. Together, we'll build a life filled with laughter, love, and endless possibilities."

"Now it's time for the ring exchange," the officiant said with a smile.

As she looked at the symbols of eternal commitment, Missy couldn't contain the joy bubbling up inside her. Her fingers trembled slightly as she slid the ring onto Sam's finger, the weight of the moment settling in her soul. She stared at the matching silver and gold bands on her finger, and her heart sighed.

"By the power vested in me by the state of Washington," the officiant said, her voice warm and steady, "I now pronounce you husband and wife."

Tears cascaded from Missy's eyes like a waterfall of joy. She hadn't imagined she could ever feel this level of happiness again, yet as she stood with Sam, hand in hand with the man she loved, a sense of peace settled over her. For the first time in nine years, Missy felt whole, as if the shattered fragments of her heart had finally found their way back together. With Sam by her side, the future held so much promise.

"You may kiss the bride," the officiant said.

Sam's eyes twinkled with a mix of happiness and mischief as he gently cupped Missy's face in his hands, pulling her in for a tender, loving kiss. Their lips met, sealing the promises they'd made to one another. Missy felt gratitude course through her veins. It was a second chance at love she'd never thought possible, and she would cherish it and Sam.

The guests erupted in applause and cheers.

After they broke apart, Missy held Sam's hand, gazing into his eyes, and he gave her a knowing smile, understanding her unspoken thoughts.

We're married!

"Ready to start our forever, Mrs. Cooper?" Sam whispered.

Missy doubted her feet were touching the ground or would be for a very long time. "More than ready, Mr. Cooper."

chapter twenty-two

FOR THE FIRST time since she walked away from Dalton, Bria felt at peace. The emotion was unexpected, but welcome. She stood at the edge of the makeshift dance floor watching Sam and Missy dance for the first time as husband and wife. Their love seemed to spread out to each wedding guest, and maybe that was why Bria felt so content. She never thought she'd feel this way at the wedding when her heart hurt so badly getting ready earlier.

The power of love?

She was sure that was what Selena would say.

Not that Bria would have missed Missy's wedding. Bria had skipped her friend's first one for selfish reasons—she hadn't wanted to return to Berry Lake and bump into Dalton. But she'd been younger then. A different person, really. No way would she have allowed him—rather, her feelings because of him—to keep her away again.

That would have been not only selfish but also stupid.

Sam spun Missy. Her bright smile could light up all of Berry Lake. Despite the charges against her, Missy was making the most of her life and love, and she deserved today and more days like this one.

Seeing the newlyweds so happy filled Bria with joy. That was so much better than the sadness and resignation that had become her new normal.

Selena walked up and handed Bria a cupcake. "These are to die for."

"Of course they are." No one had mentioned Missy baking them, but they had her signature frosting written all over them. "What would a Cupcake Posse wedding be without delicious cupcakes?"

"Charlene and Juliet did an amazing job pulling the wedding together in such a short time." Selena stared at the beaming newlyweds. "I only wish Logan could be here."

"Game tonight?" She took a bite of the cupcake—yummy.

Selena nodded. "He's looking forward to getting to know everyone after the season ends."

Bria knew how much Selena looked forward to his retirement. All of them couldn't wait for it to happen so she didn't have to drive all the way from Seattle to see them. "I can't wait for when you guys move here permanently."

"Me, too. I offered the contractor a bonus if they finish ahead of schedule." Selena's gaze narrowed. "You seem to be handling today well."

"Better than I thought, but it's easy to get wrapped up in a storybook love."

"Especially this one, but that doesn't take away what happened with you."

"No, but…" Bria's smile spread, and not the forced one that she'd relied on for more than a week now. This one was one-hundred percent natural. "But I'm doing better than I expected, and that feels really good. Like maybe I can put him behind me once and for all."

"You will, and I'm so glad you feel that way." Selena looked around at the guests surrounding the dance floor. "Love's overflowing here."

Sam spun Missy again. The two laughed.

"It is. And seeing how in love our bride and groom are reminds me that love heals. I've only been thinking about how much it hurts."

"Given what you went through, that's a normal way to think, but love can do so many things."

Sam cupped Missy's face and stared into her eyes. Bria couldn't help but sigh.

"I'm happy they found each other." Bria couldn't take her eyes off them. "I remember Missy and Rob when they were in high school. I left town before we were adults so I never saw them as adults, so I remember them being very much in a puppy-love stage. But now seeing Sam and Missy…relationship goals."

"I'm so happy for her." Selena looked at Bria. "But we're all worried about you."

"I'm doing better. It just takes time. I'm sure Juliet and Nell would agree." The three of them were single. "But I'm better off without Dalton."

"You are, but that realization still sucks."

Bria laughed. "It really does."

"We tend to believe once we find that special love everything will work out somehow, but sometimes love isn't enough."

Bria hoped love would be enough for Missy and Sam. The two looked so happy together, but... "It wasn't enough in our case, though I wonder if he really loved me."

"You might never know, but all you can control is you and your feelings."

Bria nodded. "I wish I could just flip a switch and turn all my feelings for him off."

"Give it time," Selena said. "And remember. He came into your life for a reason. He just wasn't meant to stay there permanently."

As the song ended, Sam kissed Missy. Everyone applauded and whistled.

Longing built inside of Bria. Even back in high school, she thought she would marry Dalton someday. She'd believed the same thing when they reunited. "I would like to fall in love again someday."

"Great." Selena motioned to Missy and Sam. "You can end up like them."

The way the couple stared into each other's eyes with pure devotion tugged on Bria's heartstrings. She had imagined it would be Dalton. "In my dreams."

"That you can make your reality." Selena smiled at her. "Your heart needs to heal but don't let that stop you from putting your desire out into the universe. It'll happen when the time is right."

Bria half laughed. She felt like she was a guest on Selena T's podcast. "You make it sound so easy. I mean, I know manifesting is supposed to be all about the ease and believing, but maybe I'm not there yet."

Another song played. Jenny and Dare, Hope and Josh, Sabine and Max, and Mr. and Mrs. Cooper joined the bride and groom on the dance floor.

"And that's okay. You'll get there." Selena's tone was patient and kind. "It does become easy when you open yourself up to receiving and stop focusing on how it'll happen."

Bria wanted to believe that was possible even if the logical CPA in her struggled with some of the more woo-woo things that came naturally to Selena. "Is that what Missy did?"

"No, but I wouldn't be surprised if Sam did. Look at them dance. It's like they've been together for years." A soft expression formed on Selena's face. "In Sam's mind, they have been. He's wanted Missy since his freshman year of high school, even when the odds were stacked against him, and he had to wait a long time. But he never gave up on what he wanted, and now they're married."

Things had happened fast for them when Sam returned to Berry Lake. But Bria also knew the upcoming trial played a role, too. "Is wanting love enough?"

"Love takes many forms. Do you mean romantic love?"

"Yes." Bria didn't hesitate to answer. She wanted the same love pouring off Missy and Sam.

"You know what you want so now imagine how that love feels. Don't think of the emotions in words but try to feel the emotions in your body. This might take you some time to do, but don't give up. Once you get those feelings, remember them, and evoke those feelings, whether it's a toe-curling kiss or tingles or flutters in your stomach, every day."

"Sounds like a lot of work," she joked, even though a part of her was serious.

"It gets easier. And the payoff is huge." Selena smiled at her. "I have some resources I'll send you."

If only Bria had everything together like Selena did. Now that was a life goal.

Bria hugged her. "Nothing like having Selena T as one of your besties. Thanks."

"You don't have to thank me. That's what friends are for."

Selena was correct, and Bria had the four best friends ever. She didn't know what she would do without the Cupcake Posse. She hoped she would never find out.

Dalton parked in front of Mom's house and waited for Ian to get his bag. It was dark outside. The temperature had dropped since the football game ended, but it still hadn't rained despite the forecast. His brother's shoulders slumped, and he limped—the result of a sack in the third quarter.

"Did the trainer have you ice after the game?" Dalton asked.

"Yeah. Doc looked it over. Just a bruise." Ian kicked a rock as if to show his leg still worked. "I can't believe we lost. We're so much better than that team. We should be the ones playing for the state championship."

Dalton understood his brother's frustration, but that was the thing about football. Sometimes the better team didn't win. That was the case today. "You did all you could. Your stats were the best all season, but the defense couldn't stop them."

Ian opened the front door and tossed his bag onto the floor. The loud thud echoed through the entryway. "Still should have won."

"Yes, so sulk tonight. Then tomorrow put the loss behind you." Dalton remembered from his playing days. "Next fall, you'll be playing at college. This playoff game will be a distant memory."

Ian shrugged, not appearing convinced.

Someone laughed. It sounded like Owen.

Dalton went into the great room area, and Ian followed him. Owen sat on the couch alone, holding a glass half full of a clear liquid. The TV was on with the sound low. The coffee table looked like a bar with bottles of wine, tequila, and vodka along with glasses of different sizes. More glasses than one person needed.

Owen's gaze was glassy. His face was flushed. "Too bad about the game, baby bro. Have a drink. It'll help."

Ian stared at Owen with disgust. "You sat here drinking all evening instead of coming to my game?"

Owen poured himself a shot and drank it. "Mom, Sal, and I watched the game on TV. We took a drink whenever you made a good play, which has made for a fun night. You looked good, but the defense sucked. At least alcohol eased the pain of losing."

Ian glanced over to the kitchen. "Where's Mom?"

"She had too much to drink so Sal put her to bed. He was pretty wasted so he must have joined her. Though he took a bottle with him so maybe he's drinking upstairs." Owen lined up shot glasses and filled them with tequila. "Who wants one?"

Dalton needed something to take the edge off. "Me."

Ian shook his head. "This family…"

Dalton took the glass offered and drank it. He guessed they weren't using salt and a lime with the tequila shots. "That hits the spot."

Owen took a shot himself. He swayed and nearly fell off the couch as he put the glass down to refill it. "Plenty more."

"I'll take another." Getting drunk sounded like the perfect way to spend another evening. He'd been working remotely this week, and managing even with a hangover each day, but tomorrow was Saturday so he wouldn't have to worry about that.

Owen refilled two shot glasses. "Bottoms up, bro."

Dalton drank and then gave his glass to Owen for a refill. He needed something to help him forget about Bria, but then he remembered Ian. Dalton didn't want to desert his brother when he was down after having his senior season end with the playoff loss. "Are you doing anything tonight with your friends?"

Ian shrugged. "Some people are having a party later."

That didn't sound like he wanted to go. "What about hanging out with Bentley?"

Ian shook his head. "He's at Missy Hanford's wedding, so he couldn't be at the game. Not that he missed much."

Dalton flinched. "Missy's getting married?"

"To Sam Cooper, and they're already married," Ian said. "Bentley sent me some pics. The reception is happening right now."

"Hope Missy enjoys the honeymoon." Owen poured Dalton a shot and drank another himself. "Bet Sam divorces her when she's sent to jail."

"Innocent until proven guilty," Ian countered.

Dalton felt nothing from the shots yet. He couldn't wait for the alcohol to hit him. He never drank enough to black out, but the buzz helped him forget how bad he felt. He drank another one, held out his glass for a refill, and Owen managed to pour without spilling too much.

Owen drank straight from the bottle. "Or not."

Ian rolled his eyes. "You're wasted. Missy is innocent."

"Oh, Missy's innocent," Owen's words slurred. "But she's still going to jail."

Owen was drunk, but he sounded so certain. That bothered Dalton. He set his full glass on the table. "That's not how the court system works."

"It will, and it's all thanks to our little brother's geeky friend. To Bentley." Owen finished off what remained in the tequila bottle.

"What does Bentley have to do with this?" Ian asked.

Owen sank lower on the couch. "You tell me."

Ian grabbed the bottle of vodka and filled Owen's shot glass. "Looks like you need another drink."

"I would agree with that." Owen drank.

Ian refilled Owen's glass again. "So Bentley…"

"Right." Owen swayed. "Mom made sure we could use his keys, and she'll make sure Missy goes to jail."

What? Dalton glanced at Ian, who'd gone ramrod straight. Their gazes met.

"Drink up," Ian encouraged Owen.

"I will." He downed the shot. "I'm not nearly drunk enough. Need to black out."

Dalton wished he hadn't drunk those shots. "So, Owen, when you said Mom. You mean our mom?"

"Yeah. Who else?" Owen motioned to his empty glass. "More."

Ian poured another shot. "Here you go, but how did Mom get Bentley's keys?"

Owen drank. "Remember that kegger she had for you and your friends?"

Ian swore under his breath. "Bentley's keys were missing from the bowl when it was time for him to go home."

Dalton had no idea what kegger they were talking about.

"Who needs a glass?" Owen snagged the vodka out of Ian's hand and drank from the bottle.

"Did Mom take Bentley's keys out of the bowl?" Ian asked, sounding like he couldn't care about the answer, but a vein twitched at his jaw.

"No idea, but she kept refilling Bentley's cup, so he couldn't drive home."

Dalton's stomach knotted. "He's just a kid."

Ian's jaw clenched, the muscles in his neck standing out like cords. "Bentley had never been drunk until that night. I drove him home since I wasn't drinking."

Dalton was proud of Ian. "Good thing you stuck to your football contract."

"I wasn't going to screw up the season for a beer." Ian sounded disgusted. "I found Bentley's keys in the bowl the next morning and returned them to him at school."

Owen cackled. "Mom always gets what she wants."

Dalton couldn't believe what he was hearing. He picked up his glass and drank. "What does Mom want?"

"For Brian Landon to pay." Owen took another swig. "She hates them."

Dalton froze. "Hates Brian."

"She hates all the Landons, especially your ex. That's why she got rid of her. Bria looks just like Molly, who Dad spent all our money. Taking care of her, so nothing was left when he died."

Dalton's heart pounded, each beat echoing in his ears. But was his drunk brother telling the truth? Or were these just lies?

Owen drank more. "Mom wanted Brian to be charged, but that case fell apart. Now Missy will be convicted. Mom's made sure it will happen, so we'll all be safe."

Safe? That made it sound like someone in the family was guilty. Unless Dalton misunderstood. "What do you mean we'll all be safe?"

Owen burped. "I'm going to be sick."

He stood, stumbled his way to the patio door, and went outside.

"You heard him. Missy is innocent." Ian's voice sped up with each word. "We have to do something. Tell someone what's going on."

"He's drunk," Dalton said. "He doesn't know what he's saying."

"Those shots must be hitting you." Ian shook his head. "Drunk words are sober thoughts. At least that's what they say on Reddit. And don't you think it's odd that, until the fire happened, Owen and Sal didn't drink that much? Mom, either. Since then, it's a race to see who destroys their liver first. And now they're all chummy with every first responder in town."

It was sketchy, but something else bothered Dalton. "Did Mom tell you what happened with the Landons?"

A sheepish expression crossed Ian's face. "Yeah. Mom admitted Dad used his money to help Bria's mom, but she said you knew."

A knot formed in the pit of Dalton's stomach. He scrubbed his face. Mom hadn't changed. Bria had been right. And now... "I didn't know. Mom lied to me."

"Sorry, dude, but you're the one who believed her." Ian held out his hands. "Let me have your keys."

"Where are you going?"

"Missy didn't set that fire, man." Ian's brows furrowed. "She's being framed for arson, and I can't stand by and let her take the fall, especially when Mom and whoever did this used me and my friend."

Dalton hesitated, weighing the consequences. "You realize if what Owen said is true it could implicate Mom, Sal, and Owen."

"I don't care. It's the right thing to do. And I don't remember much about Dad, but I do remember he told us to always do the right thing."

Dalton's heart clenched. He could almost hear Dad saying that. "You remember one of the most important parts."

"Keys, now."

It wasn't a question. Dalton handed them over. "Where are you going?"

"To the wedding. Everyone who needs to know what's going on will be there."

Bria would be there. "I'm going with you."

Ian clutched the keys. "I just watched you drink like three shots in five minutes. I'm driving. I just hope this will help Missy's case."

Dalton followed his brother, who rushed toward the front door like he was on a mission. He hoped the same thing about Missy, but he also hoped Bria would forgive him one more time and give him yet another chance.

chapter twenty-three

STRANDS OF TWINKLING fairy lights lit up the ceiling and were wrapped around the great room's wooden support beams. Garlands of flowers and greenery hung everywhere, providing visual and aromatic appeal. Sam couldn't believe how Jenny and Dare's house had been transformed into his and Missy's ideal wedding venue in less than a week.

As Sam stood next to Missy by the dessert display, laughter rang out. The tantalizing scent of cupcakes filled the air. Wedding guests danced to music the DJ played. And warmth emanated from his bride, who hadn't stopped smiling since he'd greeted her at the bottom of the stairs.

Today was the most perfect wedding day, and Sam was so grateful to be married to the woman he'd dreamed about since he was fourteen.

Missy was turned slightly away from him while she spoke to Selena, Bria, Nell, and Juliet. The Cupcake Posse along with Jenny, Dare, and Briley were a package deal so to speak. Add in

Peach and Mario and Sam had more than doubled the size of his family. And he couldn't be happier.

Missy was his now. And he was hers.

Nothing else mattered.

He would move into the cottage after their honeymoon at home. But as soon as the monitor was off her, he would take her on a real vacation, wherever she wanted to go.

Josh came up to him with a big smile on his face. "I can't believe my little bro is a married man."

Sam held out his left hand to show off his ring. He loved seeing the wedding band on his finger. "Best day ever."

It had been. The past few hours seemed like a dream, and Sam never wanted to wake up. He reached behind himself and grabbed hold of Missy's hand. As she laced her fingers with his, she continued talking to her friends.

"Happy for you, Sam." Josh clapped Sam's back. "Nothing like spending the rest of your life with the woman you love."

"Speaking of which, Hope is positively glowing today."

"She's always been a fan of yours and is thrilled for you and Missy." Josh was back to being the older brother Sam had worshiped growing up. Sam was grateful Josh had stayed sober after being such a hot mess for so many years. "And wait until you see the wedding gift she painted for you. I'm biased, but it's spectacular."

"Can't wait to see it, but she didn't need to go to so much trouble."

"You're family, and that's what Hope does. It was only her and Von. Now she has you, Ava, Marley, and Missy as in-laws."

"Ava will be next. I've heard she's got her eye on catching the bouquet."

Josh laughed. "That I want to see."

Sam eyed the small wedding cake that he and Missy had fed forkfuls to each other earlier. The cake had been tasty, but he wanted another one of the cupcakes with "Mr. & Mrs." picks stuck in the frosting. The red velvet flavor melted in his mouth. "Don't forget to grab a cupcake."

Josh held up his hands as if to ward Sam off. "Dude, I've had three already. They're delicious."

Missy glanced their way. "Thank you."

Sam raised their linked hands and kissed the back of his wife's. Man, he loved calling her that. "Can you believe she baked her own wedding cupcakes?"

"Impressive," Josh said. "No wonder they taste so good."

"Sam helped me make them." She rose onto her tiptoes and kissed Sam's cheek.

"I told her it wasn't necessary," Sam explained.

She shook her head. "Everyone else was doing stuff for our wedding. I wanted to do something, too."

"Well, they are the best." The same as Missy's kisses. Speaking of which, Sam brushed his lips against hers. He couldn't get enough of her. "I hope today is everything you hoped for."

"I couldn't ask for anything more," Missy said. "Truly."

"Aw." Josh shook his head, but amusement lit his eyes. "Hope told me how cute you were together, but I had no idea it was this bad."

"Just ignore him," Sam teased. "Want to dance, Mrs. Cooper?"

A wide smile spread across her face. "Please, Mr. Cooper."

He led her onto the make-shift dance floor. As a romantic song played, Sam held her in his arms, their bodies moving gracefully to the music. He found himself lost in Missy's eyes—eyes that held the promise of love, laughter, and a lifetime of togetherness. "I love you."

"I love you."

One song ended and another started. Sam would have gladly held her like this the rest of the night.

But as another song played, he noticed Bentley and Elias motioning to him. That was odd.

"Hey, sweetheart," Sam whispered in her ear. "Bentley and Elias look like they want to talk to us."

"Oh, okay. I wonder what about."

"Probably the wedding."

Worry flickered across her face. "I hope it's nothing else."

He squeezed her hand. "Today is our day. Nothing will spoil it."

Missy nodded, biting her lip.

Sam wished he could kiss away her concern, but the sooner they found out what the two wanted, the better for Missy. He led her over to Elias and Bentley, not letting go of her hand. "Hi. What's going on?"

Bentley shifted his weight between his feet. He wouldn't look Missy or Sam in the eyes, but he glanced at Elias.

"Would you mind stepping outside for a few minutes?" Elias asked. "It's important."

That didn't sound like them giving their best wishes. Sam gave Missy's hand another squeeze. He remembered the schedule that Charlene and Juliet had made for the reception. "Will it take long? We have the garter and bouquet toss coming up."

Elias wasn't smiling. "It won't take long."

"Okay." Sam led Missy to the front door.

She stepped outside and stopped abruptly. "Dalton? Ian? What are you doing here?"

Sam had the same questions, but he didn't say anything. Dalton was persona non grata around after what he had done to Bria. He had some nerve showing up here.

Bentley stood next to Missy. He kept looking at Ian, who hunched his shoulders as if ready to bolt. Dalton's eyes were bloodshot. He had dark circles under his eyes, and his complexion was pale. Sam didn't consider Dalton a friend or acquaintance, but he'd never seen the guy look so bad. Strange, given he was the one to blame for what had happened with Bria.

But Sam's hinky meter blared a warning. He wanted to know why the Dwyers were there. "Elias…"

Elias cleared his throat. "Ian and Dalton came over because they have some information about the cupcake shop fire."

Missy inhaled sharply. She clutched Sam's hand. "What?"

The one word spoke volumes, but Sam understood her fears. She didn't want to return to jail, and he wanted her cleared of the charges so every day going forward could be like their wedding day.

Dalton nudged Ian, who sighed heavily.

"I'm so sorry, Missy," Ian said. "The night of the fire, my mom told me to throw a party. It was a school night, but she was all for it, so I figured why not. The only requirement was everyone had to put their keys in a bowl since she provided a keg of beer."

"I don't understand." Missy looked at Ian. "What does your party have to do with the fire?"

"I was there, Missy." Bentley's eyes gleamed. "I put my keys in the bowl. The cupcake shop key was on my key ring. I'm so sorry."

"But you said you had your keys in your possession when you were questioned," she said, the words rushing out of her mouth.

Sam didn't know where this was going, but he was still working in Seattle during the early days of the investigation.

"They were in my possession on Friday. But Thursday night, I drank too much and Ian drove me home. I was in bad shape the next day, but my folks made me go to school to teach me a lesson. Ian returned my keys that morning." Bentley's voice cracked. He sniffled. "I rarely drink, and I'm pretty much a lightweight. I just wanted to fit in. I didn't even think about my keys being in the bowl until today when Ian mentioned it. I can't believe someone used my keys to get into the cupcake shop and almost killed you…"

"Hey." Missy placed a hand on Bentley's shoulder. "It's okay. You didn't know."

"I would say take fingerprints off the key, but the sheriff took it off my key ring when he questioned me."

Sam didn't need to be a former deputy or police officer to put the puzzle pieces together. Dooley was on the take, and when Brian Landon had provided an alibi, they went to the next name on the list. "Someone at the Dwyers' house that night had access to Bentley's keys."

She shook her head. "I appreciate you guys coming over here to try to help. But I can't imagine a teenager, even a drunk one, setting fire to the cupcake shop."

Dalton nodded. "It most likely wasn't a high school kid."

His voice didn't waver, but that only led Sam to ask the next obvious question. "Then who?"

Dalton and Ian shared a glance.

"Please tell us," Missy urged.

Bentley nodded. "She deserves to know."

"We don't have any proof, but based on what Owen implied about the keys when he was drinking, I think it's someone in my family. Possibly him or Sal," Ian said finally. "They've been drinking a lot since the fire."

"If my family is involved, it explains why my mom suddenly is supporting first responders and inviting them over for dinner," Dalton added.

Elias nodded. "Deena and Sal have enough money to pay people off like Reggie Lemond and Royal Dooley. Neither have acted the way I'd expect with an investigation like this one."

"Why would they do that?" Missy's voice was whisper soft, and Sam pulled her close against him. "It doesn't make sense."

Dalton shrugged. "My boss wants to buy commercial real estate and turn Berry Lake into a destination resort. If property values rise, that would help Sal's art shop."

Money was a powerful motivator, but Missy was right; it made no sense. But neither did the DA trying to use her old journals to prosecute her. *Except...*

"We can't take this information to the sheriff." Saying that went against years of Sam's training, but Missy's future—and his—was at stake. "If Dooley's being paid off..."

"They'll never investigate properly," Elias said.

"So what happens now?" Dalton asked.

Elias looked at each one of them. "Don't mention this to anyone. Not to each other. Not even to yourselves."

"What if we get a confession?" Ian asked. "Sal and Owen are drunk every night. Maybe they'll say something more incriminating."

"You could tape them," Bentley suggested.

"You'd need their permission," Elias said. "But we need some kind of proof. Does your family have security cameras?"

"All over the place," Ian said. "But I don't know how long they keep the recordings."

Sam's gaze met Elias's, and he knew the attorney was thinking the same thing as him—subpoena. That could show when people left the Dwyer household that Thursday night and if anyone returned.

"I'll take care of it," Elias said. "But I need all of you to promise not to say a word and act like nothing is wrong."

"Anything to help," Ian said, and Bentley nodded.

"I'm sorry, Missy." Dalton stared at the door. "Is Bria—"

"This isn't the time or place," Sam interrupted.

As Dalton took a step forward, Sam got a whiff of alcohol in his face. It brought back the darker days when Josh's drinking had been out of control. No one inside needed to deal with Dalton Dwyer right now.

Dalton's lips twitched. "I just want to see how she's doing and apologize."

Bentley and Elias stepped in front of the door as if to block Dalton's access.

Sam stepped in front of Missy. He didn't want her near the guy. "You've been drinking."

"I had a couple of shots. Three. That's all. I'm not drunk." Dalton's eyes gleamed. "Please. I have to speak to her."

"No!" Missy's voice was harsh, a way she'd never sounded before. "You broke Bria's heart one too many times. Leave her alone."

Dalton's face fell. Ian led him off the front porch.

"I knew something wasn't right with the investigation." Elias brushed his hand through his hair. "Now I know how to proceed."

Sam only hoped they could easily prove Missy was being framed, but given Deena and Sal's money, he had no doubt this would tear the town and the sheriff's department apart. But he knew one person who might be willing to help from the inside—Mary.

chapter twenty-four

A S NELL STARED out the window, the wedding guests laughed, danced, and chatted behind her. The fairy lights twinkled in the backyard. They matched the ones strung in the house, giving the place an enchanted, fairy-tale feel, which the newlyweds deserved. It was so easy to get caught up in the happily-ever-after vibe in the air. If there'd been a wishing well present, Nell would have wished for whatever she deserved, too. Unfortunately, she had no idea what that might be.

Holding out her left hand, Nell focused on her bare ring finger. She hadn't worn the engagement ring for long, and to be honest, it had never felt right, but...

At least I know what it's like to be engaged.

That was one step closer to marriage. She nearly snorted. Her brief engagement could be as close as she'd ever get to a wedding. She had to face facts. Mom might have been right that Gage was Nell's last shot at having a family of her own.

But she couldn't live with herself if she married a man she wasn't in love with. Saying "I do" for the sake of being married was wrong. She wanted to make a commitment out of love.

Nell needed to be content whether she was married or single. No matter what happened, she had friends and family who loved her. That would be enough. It had to be.

Mom left the DJ and walked over to Nell. "Do you need to go home?"

"Not yet," she said honestly. Though a part of her wished she didn't get so tired standing for more than a few minutes. "I was looking at the decorations outside. I hadn't noticed them until it got dark. You and Juliet did a fabulous job putting on the wedding with very little notice."

"Thank you, but it is my business." Mom sighed. "I only wish I could use my skills on your wedding."

The disappointment in Mom's voice cut deep, but a part of Nell was beyond the point of caring. "I know, but I made the right choice for me and for Gage."

He wouldn't have been happy with her long term. One day, he would realize that.

"So you keep saying." Which meant Mom didn't see it herself. "At least I still have Evie and JoJo."

Except Mom still had Nell, too. But a daughter who gave back an engagement ring wasn't as important as two younger daughters who still had marriage potential.

Sucks to be me.

Not really though.

No matter what Nell did, if it didn't match what Mom wanted, Charlene Culpepper would never be satisfied.

Nell's thought echoed in her head, the words sharpening with stark clarity.

She took a step back.

If she hadn't cared so much about what Mom did or thought, Nell never would have let things get as far as they had with Gage. But she'd pretended to be more serious than they were and hadn't spoken up right away about the engagement because of Mom.

No more.

A weight lifted from Nell's shoulders. No way would she pass her baton to her younger sisters. They deserved better. "Just remember, Evie and JoJo need to live their own lives, even if you don't agree with their choices."

"Well, let's hope they don't follow in your footsteps and decide to be spinsters."

Talk about a low blow. But Mom's words didn't hurt as much as they once would have. Nell took that as a good sign—progress.

Mom glanced at the dessert table. "I need to check a few things. Be sure to sit or you'll wear yourself out."

Nell didn't get her. Mom acted like she cared but then would say the worst things. Nell, however, felt an odd sense of detachment. She loved her, but she didn't need to let Mom bring her down. She would no longer allow herself to be pulled into the craziness. If Mom wanted to meddle or play matchmaker or make wedding plans, Nell wouldn't be a part of it.

"Can I have your attention, please?" the DJ asked. "I need all the single ladies to come out onto the dance floor."

Nell stayed where she was. She'd had her chance and turned it down. No sense getting in the way out there.

Bria came over with a determined look on her face. "Come on. We're both going out there."

Nell shook her head.

Bria nodded.

"Seriously?" Nell asked.

"Yes." Bria grabbed Nell's hand and led her onto the dance floor toward the other women gathered there. "Juliet said she can't because she isn't divorced yet."

Nell shook her head. "Semantics."

"But you know Juliet."

"True." And it was part of why she was such a sweetheart. Legally, she was still married, so she would act accordingly.

Missy would want all the single Posse members to participate. Some brides and grooms no longer did the bouquet or garter toss at their receptions. But Mom loved all the traditions—new and old—and would want this one included if only to give her eldest daughter a chance—albeit a long shot—at marriage. Logical or not, that was how Mom's mind worked.

Nell, however, knew catching the bouquet meant nothing. Still, she didn't want to be a spoilsport. "Let's get out there."

Bria smiled, though it didn't reach her eyes. She seemed to be having fun at the wedding, but she didn't appear to be herself. Heartbreak took a while to get over. "Thank you."

Nell nudged her. "Hey, the Posse sticks together."

"Yes, we do." Affection filled Bria's voice. "No matter what. Now, let's get out there before Selena gets on the microphone and calls us out."

"She would so do that."

"I know, right?"

They both laughed.

As Nell followed Bria onto the dance floor, Selena and Juliet gave them a thumbs-up. Welles twirled the blue bridal garter on his index finger. His deep-blue suit complemented his hair and strong features. Nell had missed the garter toss completely, but the only single men in attendance were Welles, Bentley, Elias, and Buddy, so the odds had been pretty good for him to catch it.

Welles was using his knee scooter, but that didn't detract from how handsome he looked in his suit.

Missed my chance.

Though not really, she realized.

Given he hadn't asked her out or made a move since their talk, he must've changed his mind or not been serious about liking her. It only proved how bad her luck was when it came to men, but she didn't blame him. Welles Riggs was the kind of guy who would never want to hurt anyone. That was why he'd said it wasn't the right time.

It would never be time.

He was staying at her house during the day, and him saying that had made things less awkward between them. But…

I wish my luck with men would change.

Not with men, she realized. Nell wanted Welles. He was the one who made her feel safe and attractive and accepted for who she was, sweet tooth and all.

Ava, Sam's older sister, playfully jockeyed for position in the middle with Evie and JoJo. Dare said Briley was too young and wouldn't be dating until she turned thirty. When someone yelled for Sheridan DeMarco to join them, she showed off her Titanic-sized engagement ring and pointed to her fiancé, Michael. Their Christmas-themed wedding would be held next month.

Bria went onto the right side. Nell stood off to the left side. Her gaze locked on the cascade of flowers on the throwaway bouquet that was a smaller replica of Missy's bridal bouquet.

"It's all mine, ladies," Ava teased.

Evie stepped in front of Ava. "Not if I get it first."

"Don't forget I played volleyball and basketball and can jump," JoJo joked.

Nell laughed. She hoped Ava, who was a schoolteacher and the same age as Selena and Nell, caught the bouquet. The Coopers had been so welcoming to Missy, accepting her as one of them from the day she'd been arrested. Their family life hadn't always been easy with Josh's alcoholism, but things had improved with his sobriety, marriage, and now impending parenthood—everyone had noticed Hope not drinking and they confirmed the pregnancy, much to the delight of everyone there. Surprisingly enough, the only person who seemed to know besides the parents was Missy. Nell wasn't sure how that had happened.

"All right, single ladies," Missy called out playfully, holding the bouquet high above her head. "Get ready!"

Nell's palms sweated, and she took a deep breath. She didn't care about catching the bouquet, but she yearned for a similar type of love story Missy and Sam had found—minus the arrest and upcoming arson case. That had nothing to do with Mom's desires and everything to do with Nell's wish for a family of her own.

"I'll do a countdown," the DJ said. "Three, two, one..."

Ava, Evie, and JoJo readied themselves. Bria laughed. Nell shook her head.

"Here it comes!" Missy shouted, launching the flowers over her shoulder into the air.

As if in slow motion, the bouquet spun gracefully through the air. A collective gasp echoed through the crowd. Ava held up her arms. Every woman vied for their chance at love.

The flowers soared toward Nell like a homing missile. Instinctively, she reached out, her hands trembling, and the bouquet hit her palms. Her fingers brushed against the smooth satin ribbons and wrapped around the flower stems. A light floral scent enveloped her, tickling her nose. She stared at the flowers, hardly daring to breathe. It was as if she'd been dreaming, but the bouquet lay nestled in her hands.

"Oh my goodness. You caught the bouquet!" Bria squealed, giving Nell a hug. "That means you're next!"

Not really, but this was unexpected. "Thanks."

Welles put the blue garter on the arm that wasn't in a cast. His gaze met hers as if in a challenge. She didn't know what was going on, but her fingers tightened around the stems as her pulse quickened.

"We need photos," Juliet announced with the photographer at her heels. "First, Welles and Sam. Next, Missy and Nell. We'll do all four of you. Then finally, Welles and Nell."

The photos went quickly since the photographer and Juliet knew exactly what poses they wanted.

"Thank you," Juliet said before running off to check on something.

"Congratulations." Welles grinned at her, his blue eyes glinting with humor and something more. Something that made her heart bump.

Stop being foolish. He's just being polite and flirty. Two things Welles was known for. She clutched the bouquet with both hands.

"Looks like you're the next Culpepper to tie the knot."

Her cheeks heated. She tucked a loose tendril of hair behind one ear. "Only if you believe in silly traditions."

"You're all about those things, and they aren't silly."

Not trusting her voice, she shrugged.

He quirked an eyebrow. "You know I'm right."

"Maybe."

His gaze searched hers. "Having fun tonight?"

Nell nodded. "Missy is a beautiful bride. She and Sam will be very happy together."

"They will be."

A romantic ballad played.

"May I have this dance?" he asked, his voice warm and inviting.

His tender gaze ignited a flicker of hope within her. "You think you can manage a dance using a knee scooter, Paramedic Welles?"

"Indulge me, please?" A wry grin formed on his lips. He was devilishly charming. "I have skills you've never even imagined, Nurse Nell."

Her stomach filled with butterflies. "Show me what you've got."

Positioning her so one of her legs was between his and the other on the side of his good leg, he placed one hand at the small of her back, the other clasping hers, and she relaxed into his embrace. Her pulse kicked up a notch.

"We'll only be able to sway back and forth," he said.

She was surprised how well they fit together, his taller frame sheltering hers the way it had on the mountain. Only this time his warmth and scent were as familiar as coming home. "This is better than I thought it would be."

"You don't give me enough credit." There was a hint of playfulness in his tone.

Warmth flooded her cheeks. "I'm trying. How does your leg feel?"

"Dancing with you is worth a little discomfort."

She didn't know what to say to that. Instead of speaking, she enjoyed the moment.

"I like holding you like this," he whispered into her ear, his breath caressing her neck.

"Me, too."

"It's time."

Nell peered up at him through her lashes. "Time to go home?"

"No. I told you I'd let you know when it's time for us. I needed to make sure you were over Gage."

"I am." Her strong tone left no doubt to that.

His eyes sparkled with an intensity that sent shivers down her spine. "I was hoping you were. Ready to be more than friends and finally go out with me?"

Joy rose inside her, as light and effervescent as the song playing. "I am."

"That calls for a celebration. May I kiss you?"

She nodded with anticipation. "Please."

Welles lowered his mouth to hers, a slow and sweet kiss. Murmurs and laughter faded around them, and time seemed to stop. She pressed harder against him, wanting to remember every minute of this first kiss, one sealing the promise of a new beginning and the possibilities of a future together.

He tasted sweet like chocolate from the cupcakes, and it was her new favorite flavor. Had the love she craved been right in front of her all along?

As Nell's heart raced, Welles ended the kiss. "Exactly as I expected, Nurse Nell."

She tried to control her breathing. "What did you expect?"

"That we'd have a spark." He gently cupped her face with his strong, calloused hand. "We have enough of a spark to set off an explosion. A perfect fit, don't you think?"

"I'd agree with that assessment, Paramedic Welles." She wondered if anyone else could hear the heartbeat that thundered in her ears. "So what do you want to do about it?"

"This." He leaned in and kissed her again.

A chorus of cheers and applause erupted from the guests, pulling them back to reality. So many eyes were on them. Nell's face heated more. Mom stood nearby, her mouth agape in shock, while Buddy, Max, and Sabine clapped enthusiastically, grinning from ear to ear. Selena, Bria, and Juliet smiled and cheered.

"Whoa!" Sam exclaimed with a chuckle, nudging Missy playfully. "Didn't see that one coming."

Missy's eyes, shining with happiness, met Nell's. She smiled. "I did."

Nell looked at Welles. "Thank you for not giving up on me."

"Never." He placed his forehead against hers. "In case you haven't figured it out, I would have waited for you forever. You're stuck with me."

Nell smiled, a sense of joy washing through her. "I can live with that."

chapter twenty-five

A T THE ARENA, Selena settled into her seat. She had missed last night's game while she was in Berry Lake, but Logan understood she'd needed to be with her friends, even though he was leaving on another road trip after this game.

She pulled her knit cap lower over her ears. The chill of the rink seeped through her layers of clothing. Not unusual in there, but the chilly temperature reminded her November would soon give way to December. She would love to spend Christmas in Berry Lake where it snowed, but that wouldn't happen this year. Logan had a couple of days off around the twenty-fifth, but he preferred to stay home. She didn't blame him. Next year they would have a white Christmas.

Roxy sat beside her, cooing softly at Murphy. They both wore versions of Grable's jersey. Selena had on team colors, but she would save Logan's jersey for the playoffs if they made it. That was what they'd done on his old team, and hockey players were so superstitious that Logan wanted her to do the same thing every season. Only time would tell if the team made it that far, but fans were hopeful even though it was early in the season.

"That older guy is back in the owner's box," Roxy said. "Logan's agent."

Ted. Selena's muscles tensed. Every time she saw the man, her discomfort worsened. She couldn't wait until he was out of their lives for good.

Spring wasn't that far away, and she'd be fine if the Volcanoes made playoffs. A post-season run would be a great way to close out Logan's final season and career.

But was Ted there for a reason? As in Logan was announcing his retirement?

Tingles shot to the tips of her toes. That would be the perfect end to a magical weekend with Missy and Sam's wedding.

"I didn't know he was in town." Selena's gaze slid to the owner's box, where Ted stood in his expensive wool coat, surveying the crowd with a smug smile on his ruddy face.

Her stomach knotted, nerves churning inside her. That didn't look like the expression of someone who was about to lose his cash cow. Logan hadn't mentioned Ted would be back in Seattle, and Ted never did anything without a motive. Maybe one of those endorsement deals had come through…

"Attention, Volcano fans!" The announcer's voice boomed through the stadium, snapping Selena back to reality. "We have some exciting news about our very own Logan Tremblay."

"Oh!" Roxy squealed. "Do you know what it is?"

Selena's heart thudded. "No."

But she hoped it was his retirement announcement. She swallowed.

"The Volcanoes are thrilled to announce that Logan has just signed a contract extension for next season." The announcer's voice rose with each word as if he were calling the final game in the cup and not a pre-game announcement. "And hold on to your seats. Our captain is going to be one of the Volcanoes' future coaches!"

The words hit Selena like a punch to the gut. She took a step back, hitting the seat. Her breath caught in her throat, ice flooding her veins.

Not only a contract, but becoming a coach, too?

Images of what the future would look like swirled in her brain. But she knew one thing. Logan becoming a coach would mean he'd be staying in Seattle. Oh, he might be assigned to one of the lower teams, but Berry Lake would only be a vacation option. Coaches worked year-round, not only during the season.

She forced herself to breathe.

Logan skated to center ice, waving at fans. The rest of the team crowded around, slapping him on the back and hugging him. His gaze searched the seats until he found Selena. Even from this distance, she recognized the question in his eyes.

Selena didn't smile. She couldn't.

Why hadn't he discussed this with her?

This decision of his made zero sense.

They'd agreed. Not once, but multiple times. Logan had promised this season was different. That he *would* be retiring, and they'd move to Berry Lake once their house was finished.

And now…

Ted positively gloated. Someone handed him a flute of champagne and he raised the glass in a toast.

Anger bubbled inside her. Frustration quickly followed. This shouldn't have been happening. Logan had always kept her in the loop.

The entire arena celebrated the new contract with cheers and applause, but this was her life—her marriage. The fact that Logan hadn't mentioned a new contract and a new job with the team cut deep. She'd never imagined him hurting her this way, but he had and treated her and their marriage with total disregard.

She clenched her fists tightly, nails digging into her palms. How could he not have told her? Had he thought she wouldn't care? Or worse, had he not wanted her to know?

"Isn't that great?" Roxy gushed beside her, bouncing her baby in her lap. "Logan's still got the goods, but he'll be an amazing coach when the time comes."

"Sure," Selena responded tersely. This wasn't the life she wanted or how a husband who loved his wife would treat her. And at that moment, she knew this was the end.

Selena's heart raced, the anger and betrayal surging through her veins.

Those long nights spent alone, waiting for him to return from road trips, would never go away. Not if he went into coaching. The missed holidays and family gatherings, the countless conversations about retirement put on hold as the lure of one more season pulled him back in with the future of a life full of hockey.

How could Logan not even discuss it with her? Was their marriage so fragile that he hadn't trusted her enough to discuss him changing his mind?

She understood his passion for the game, but it had slowly consumed them both, leaving little room for anything else. The idea of this lifestyle continuing suffocated her. He—and she—would be indefinitely tethered to the world of professional hockey for years more.

No, thanks.

She'd told her clients and listeners to "follow their heart." It was time she did the same.

Pulling out her phone, she forced herself to take a deep breath before typing out a message.

> **SELENA:** *Logan just signed a contract extension without telling me.*
> **TAMIKA:** *Form's already drawn up and ready to go.*
> **SELENA:** *How did you know?*
> **TAMIKA:** *Because I know you.*
> **SELENA:** *Thank you!*
> **TAMIKA:** *I've got you, Queen.*
> **SELENA:** *I know you do.*
> **TAMIKA:** *Do you need a place to stay tonight?*
> **SELENA:** *No, the team is leaving after the game.*
> **TAMIKA:** *Call if you need me later. I'll talk to you tomorrow.*
> **SELENA:** *Love you.*
> **TAMIKA:** *I love you.*

Selena's fingers trembled as she clutched the phone. She took her seat, feeling as if her heart had been ripped out of her chest and everything she'd worked so hard for over the years had blown up in her face.

"Everything okay?" Roxy asked, her eyes full of concern.

"Fine." Selena tucked her phone away and plastered on a smile. "Just some work stuff."

"Well, whatever it is, I know Selena T has it under control," Roxy said.

She wasn't wrong, only this wasn't where Selena had ever thought she would be. "I do. Thanks."

The rest of the game passed in a blur, the cheers and excitement around Selena a distant hum as thoughts over what Logan had done consumed her. She'd believed they were as much a team as the Volcanoes were. He'd been Selena T's biggest fan. She'd spent years supporting him, putting her own dreams on hold for his career, and now it seemed as if he were throwing it all away without a second thought.

But she deserved better.

She'd told her friends and clients that for years. Now it was her turn.

When the final whistle blew, Selena stood and made her way with Roxy and Murphy through the crowd toward the family room to wait with the other wives and girlfriends. Then they would say goodbye to their guys before the team boarded the bus that would take them to the airport for their flight.

This is the last time.

She knew that with heart-pounding certainty. Never again would enter the arena or be considered a WAG.

Come on, Selena T. Hold it together.

She glanced around the room at the other women. She was one of the oldest there. Some were very young. Many had kids and babies with them.

Once again, Roxy and Murphy stayed off to the side and no one interacted with them. Selena didn't want the young woman to feel like an outcast. She made her way toward her. "If you need anything, you've got my number."

Roxy shifted Murphy in her arms. "And you know I'll use it."

Selena had enjoyed getting to know the young mother and would miss sitting next to her at the games and holding little Murphy.

"Selena!" Logan called out.

"Take care, Roxy." Selena kissed Murphy's head. "Be a good boy for your mommy."

Selena turned. A huge smile brightened Logan's face.

Pain sliced through her heart. Somehow seeing how happy he was hurt more.

He jogged over to her and pulled her into a tight hug. "What did you think of the game?"

"Congrats on the win." She stepped back and met his gaze. "Let's go outside to the bus."

Selena didn't want to air their business in front of others. She walked so fast that Logan had to jog to catch up to her. She stepped outside.

"Hey." He stopped her before they reached the door. "What's the hurry?"

She couldn't believe he was being this dense. At least no one was around them there. "Why didn't you tell me about the contract extension?"

He blinked, confusion flickering across his face. "I...I wanted to surprise you. I thought you'd be happy."

"Happy?" She bit her lip, holding back the tears blurring her vision. Her control slipped a notch. "You made a decision that affects both our lives without even talking to me about it. How can you expect me to be happy about that?"

"I'm sorry." He reached for her hand. "I didn't mean to hurt you."

She choked back a sob. "Let's say goodbye before your bus leaves."

As they walked toward the bus in silence, Selena couldn't help but think of all the times she'd stood by his side, cheering him on and supporting his every move. Now she felt betrayed, and a part of her seemed to know this would be the end or she would have never mentioned her concerns to Tamika, but like some of her clients, she'd clung to the hope things would turn out differently.

But as she would tell them, they needed to choose themselves, even if it hurt.

I choose me.

Easier said than done. Because, man, did this really hurt.

As the bus idled, they stood off to the side as other couples said goodbye.

Selena glanced at Logan. His jaw jutted forward as he struggled to find a way to make them both happy, but this life would never be enough for either of them. That was clear now.

She took a deep breath, mustering up her courage for what came next.

"You can have the Seattle house. I'll take the Berry Lake place." She sounded calm, but she was about to crumble. "Tamika will be in touch with Ted about the details. I'm sure Ted will find an attorney for you."

"Wait. Why do I need an attorney?"

"Divorce."

"You want a divorce?" He sounded stunned.

"I can't keep doing this, Logan. You agreed this was your last season." Somehow her voice only wavered a little. "Ted probably already has an attorney lined up since he's wanted me out of your life for years now."

"Selena, that's not true," Logan protested, his eyebrows furrowing in confusion and hurt. "Ted said you'd be okay with the new contract."

Selena's chest tightened. "Ted was wrong." But this explained Ted's smugness earlier in the evening. The agent had manipulated the situation, but Logan had once again let him. She swallowed hard against the lump in her throat. "Just watch your back. Ted only cares about the money you bring him. Nothing else."

"Selena, I don't want a divorce."

"I see no other option. The divorce shouldn't be too complicated since we have a prenup." Her heart clenched at the thought of the document they'd signed years ago, when her personal development business was just taking off, full of hope and the belief that they'd never need it. "Things will be cut and dry. Unless you want alimony."

He flinched. It was a fair point to bring up, given she made significantly more money than him. "Are you sure?"

The anguish in his voice stabbed at her heart. "Yes. We agreed you would retire this year. Then you changed your mind without even discussing what you were thinking with me and decided on your own, even though I've communicated my feelings about our lives being centered around hockey."

"You said you'd never give me an ultimatum."

"I haven't." As tears threatened to fall, she raised her chin. "You made your choice to continue playing. Now I'm making mine. It's what's best for both of us."

"It's only a year."

"It's been only a year for years now." Selena's voice remained steady even if she trembled inside. "And don't forget you'll be coaching after that."

"We can work this out." His desperate voice matched the expression on his face.

She couldn't let herself care. "Maybe, but I don't want to. I know how much hockey means to you. But another year of playing and then having you coach after you hang up your skates… That's not the life we agreed on. It's not the life I want." She searched for any sign he understood her need for more. "You told me you were ready."

He cupped her cheek with his large, rough hand. "I want you."

As she savored the warmth of his touch, Selena studied the earnestness in his eyes. He meant each word. He wanted her, truly and deeply, but his love for hockey held a stronger sway over him. "Yes, but you want hockey more."

Logan's hand dropped away, his expression a mix of pain and resignation. "Selena, I…"

He didn't deny it, which reaffirmed her decision.

"That's okay." Her voice sounded hoarse. "We all have our passions and dreams, and yours just happen to lie elsewhere."

He didn't say anything.

"You deserve someone who can share your love for hockey, who won't feel left behind or resentful of the life you've chosen." Her words hung heavy in the air between them, the finality of it all settling in. "I just can't any longer."

He reached out, his fingers brushing against hers before holding her hand. Tears filled his eyes. "I love you."

Her breath hitched. Tears prickled the corners of her eyes. Their love was real, but they wanted different things from life. "I love you, too. But sometimes love isn't enough."

A dam broke within her, flooding her chest with emotions she had been trying to keep at bay. She glanced at their entwined hands, memorizing the feeling of his skin against hers—the warmth and rough texture from years spent gripping a hockey stick.

"Goodbye, Logan." Her voice was barely audible over the distant hum of the bus's engine.

"Selena, please. Reconsider." His words were thick with unshed tears.

"I…can't."

Logan started to speak and then pressed his lips together.

She waited in case he wanted to say something, but he just stared at her. The fact that he didn't fight her on this told her divorce was the right option.

Not wanting to break down in front of everyone, she turned her back on the man she loved and had believed would be hers forever and hurried to her car. With each step, her heart shattered into a million pieces.

Had Ted anticipated this outcome? He'd wanted her out of Logan's life ever since she'd entered it, and now she would be. But no matter how much her heart hurt right now, she was making the right decision. Of that she was certain.

Sometimes love just wasn't enough.

And in this case, it wasn't.

Thank you for reading **Weddings & Wishes**. If you want to know what happens next to Selena, Bria, Juliet, Missy, Nell, and the Berry Lake Cupcake Shop, read **Babies & Biscuits**, the fifth and final book in the series.

Missy Hanford first appeared in the book *Jenny*. Sam Cooper made his first appearance in ***Sweet Beginnings***. Sheridan DeMarco, Sal DeMarco and Sabine Culpepper's daughter, story is told in ***Sweet Yuletide***. To learn more about those books, check out my Beach Brides/Indigo Bay miniseries which contains prequels to the Berry Lake Cupcake Posse series.

If you'd like to get to know Elias Carpenter better, you can read about him in The Last Cottage on Pinewood Lane. This is a standalone Christmas romance set in Berry Lake.

Join my newsletter to receive a FREE story and hear about new releases, sales, freebies, and giveaways. Visit

https://www.subscribepage.com/w9w0yl

I appreciate your help spreading the word about my work. Tell a friend who loves friendship women's fiction about this book and leave a review on your favorite book site. Reviews help readers find books!

Thanks so much!

about the author

USA Today bestselling author Melissa McClone has written over fifty sweet contemporary romance and women's fiction novels. She lives in the Pacific Northwest with her husband. She has three young adult children, a spoiled Norwegian Elkhound, and cats who think they rule the house. They do!

If you'd like to find Melissa online:
melissamcclone.com
facebook.com/melissamcclonebooks
facebook.com/groups/McCloneTroopers
patreon.com/melissamcclone

other books by melissa mcclone

The Beach Brides/Indigo Bay Miniseries
Prequels to the Berry Lake Cupcake Posse series…
Jenny (Jenny and Dare)
Sweet Holiday Wishes (Lizzy and Mitch)
Sweet Beginnings (Hope and Josh)
Sweet Do-Over (Marley and Von)
Sweet Yuletide (Sheridan and Michael)
Indigo Bay Sweet Romance Collection (Box Set of all five books)

The Berry Lake Cupcake Posse Series
Can five friends save their small town's beloved bakery?
Cupcakes & Crumbs
Tiaras & Teacups
Kittens & Kisses
Weddings & Wishes
The Last Cottage on Pinewood Lane

Silver Falls Series
The Andrews siblings find love in a small
town in Washington state.
The Christmas Window
A Slice of Summer
A Cup of Autumn

Her Royal Duty
Royal romances with charming princes and dreamy castles...
The Reluctant Princess
The Not-So-Proper Princess
The Proper Princess

Quinn Valley Ranch
Two books featuring siblings in a multi-author series...
Carter's Cowgirl
Summer Serenade
Quinn Valley Ranch Two Book Set

A Keeper at Heart Series
These men know what they want, and love isn't on their list.
But what happens when each meets a keeper?
The Groom
The Soccer Star
The Boss
The Husband
The Date
The Tycoon

For the complete list of books, go to
melissamcclone.com/books

Made in the USA
Middletown, DE
15 July 2024

57350063R00191